ROBERT B. PARKER'S
THE DEVIL WINS

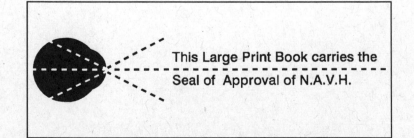

This Large Print Book carries the
Seal of Approval of N.A.V.H.

A JESSE STONE NOVEL

ROBERT B. PARKER'S
THE DEVIL WINS

REED FARREL COLEMAN

THORNDIKE PRESS
A part of Gale, Cengage Learning

GALE
CENGAGE Learning·

Farmington Hills, Mich • San Francisco • New York • Waterville, Maine
Meriden, Conn • Mason, Ohio • Chicago

Copyright © 2015 by The Estate of Robert B. Parker.
Thorndike Press, a part of Gale, Cengage Learning.

LIBRARY OF CONGRESS CATALOGING-IN-PUBLICATION DATA

Coleman, Reed Farrel, 1956-
    Robert B. Parker's the Devil wins : a Jesse Stone novel / Reed Farrel Coleman. — Large print edition.
        pages cm. — (A Jesse Stone novel) (Thorndike Press large print core)
    ISBN 978-1-4104-8027-9 (hardback) — ISBN 1-4104-8027-5 (hardcover)
    1. Stone, Jesse (Fictitious character)—Fiction. 2. Police chiefs—Fiction. 3. Large type books. I. Title. II. Title: Devil wins.
    PS3553.O47445R64 2015b
    813'.54—dc23   2015027850

Published in 2015 by arrangement with G. P. Putnam's Sons, an imprint of Penguin Publishing Group, a division of Penguin Random House LLC

Printed in the United States of America
1 2 3 4 5 6 7 19 18 17 16 15

To Mel Farman and Jim Kennedy,
for taking me in as one of their own

1

Jesse Stone no longer felt adrift. No longer a man caught between two coasts, he had finally left his days as an L.A. homicide detective behind him. If not his private shame at how his life there had gone to hell. He was chief of police in Paradise, Mass. This was his town now. Yet there were still some things about the East Coast and the Atlantic he had never gotten used to and wasn't sure he ever would. Nor'easters, for one. He found their brooding, slate-gray clouds and roiling tides a little unnerving. These late-fall or winter storms seemed to blow up out of spite, raking across whole swaths of New England or the Mid-Atlantic, leaving nothing but pain in their wake.

As was his habit, he drove through the darkened streets of Paradise in his old Ford Explorer before heading home. He wanted to get a few hours sleep before going back to work. Maybe a drink, too. The storm wasn't supposed to make landfall until about midnight, but the winds were bending trees back against their will, sleet already pelting his windshield. Jesse shook his head thinking about that. About how storms in the east warned you they were coming. About how they told you when they were coming and then kicked your ass.

It was different out west. He remembered how, when he was a kid in Tucson, a few inches of unexpected rain would morph into the cascading wall of a flash flood, washing away everything before it. One minute people would be horseback riding or hiking through bone-dry arroyos and the next they'd be swallowed up by waters squeezed between canyon walls and ground sunbaked so mercilessly hard it could not soak up a drop of rain. Jesse remembered that he had once gone out with his dad, searching for some missing hikers after one of the floods. How they had come upon the body of a drowned horse. It had been many years since he had thought of that horse, its carcass rotting in the Arizona sun.

Then in L.A. there were the choking Santa Ana winds that would blow across the mountains, swoop down into the valleys and through the canyons from the Mojave. The Santa Anas brought destruction with them, too, sucking the moisture out of the vegetation, wildfires following in their path. Fires that would consume whole hillsides, one after the other. Sometimes the winds blew so strongly through the canyons that they howled. His ex-partner used to say it was Satan whistling while he worked. At the moment, Jesse felt about as far away from those Santa Anas as a man could get, but he thought he could still hear Satan's whistling in the winds that buffeted his SUV.

There weren't many cars on the road, but a few brave or stupid souls dared the weather. Jesse knew most of the vehicles. Robbie Wilson, the fire chief, was out in his red Jeep, looking for trouble. Jesse didn't have much patience for men like Wilson, guys who liked being big fish in tiny ponds. Little men with big chips on both shoulders. Men with something to prove, always on the prowl for a chance to prove it. Jesse could never figure out what it was Robbie Wilson had to prove. He also hated that Wilson refused to call him by his first name, always calling him Chief or Chief Stone.

Alexio Dragoa, one of the few commercial fishermen who still sailed out of Paradise, was coming from the docks in his ancient F-150. That damned pickup was nearly all rust. The thing was like an old married couple who stayed together more out of habit than anything else. No doubt Alexio had been securing his boat, the *Dragoa Rainha,* in anticipation of the storm. Jesse gave the fisherman a wave in passing. Dragoa, a gruff Portuguese SOB, couldn't be bothered to return the gesture. *Par for the course,* Jesse thought. *Par for the course.*

Bill Marchand was out in front of his insurance brokerage on Nantucket Street, wrestling the wind for control of a storm shutter. Jesse pulled over to lend him a hand. Bill and Jesse were friendly, if not exactly friends. Jesse didn't have friends, not the way other people had friends. But Marchand sponsored the police softball team and was generous with local charities. In all the years Jesse had served as chief, there hadn't been many town selectmen who'd earned his respect. Most selectmen had proven themselves craven and spineless, rarely backing Jesse or the department in tough situations. Bill Marchand was the exception. He was a thoughtful man who had usually based his support not on the direction of the political currents but on the facts before him.

"Let me get that for you," Jesse said, pinning the shutter to the wall.

"Thanks, Jesse. It's gonna be a bad one,

this nor'easter. You been through enough of these, you can smell it on the wind."

"One is enough of these." Jesse used his free hand to lift up the fleece-lined collar of his jacket against the sleet. The wind was gusting more intensely. "Ready for the shutter?" Jesse asked.

"I've got the latch ready."

Jesse forced the shutter closed, Marchand helping the last foot or two. When the shutter was in place, the insurance broker latched it closed.

"I hope the damned thing holds. I've had to replace these shutters twice," Marchand said, raising his voice above the wind.

"I'm sure your insurance will cover it."

"You're a funny man, Jesse Stone. Thanks again," Marchand said, offering Jesse his gloved right hand. "It's gonna be a bad one, all right. I'll be busy for weeks after this. We'll have to call adjusters in from all over the States. You watch yourself out there."

But it was Jesse's job to watch out for everyone else. He waited for Marchand to get into his massive Infiniti SUV and drive off before pulling away himself. As Jesse was about to turn for home, he caught sight of another vehicle he recognized. It was John Millner's beat-up Chevy van. Millner was a career criminal, a petty thief who'd been in and out of commonwealth correctional facilities during Jesse's tenure as chief. Millner was from the Swap — Southwest Area of Paradise — the only rough part of town. But even the Swap was changing. It was turning into a hipper, more ethnically diverse part of Paradise. Millner's family was old-school Swap and John was more a lowlife than a tough guy. A parasite, an opportunist, not a mastermind.

Jesse followed the white van at a distance up into the bluffs that overlooked the ocean and the rest of town to the south. The Bluffs were where the rich founders of Paradise had built their big fussy houses more than a century and a half ago. Most of those families were gone, their manses knocked down, properties long since sold off. A few, like the Salter place, remained as summer homes. Many had fallen into disrepair.

Millner's van pulled off the road by a darkened behemoth of a house: the old Rutherford place. It had been vacant for Jesse's entire tenure in Paradise. For years there had been efforts by the town's historical society to get it named to the commonwealth's register of historical places, but those avenues had finally been exhausted, and come spring the Rutherford place would be demolished. Jesse had a pretty good idea of what Millner meant to get up to. Giant old houses were lined with miles of copper wiring and other metals that could be sold off to scrap dealers at good prices. The problem for crooked scavengers like Millner was opportunity. You needed time to break through plaster walls and lath to get to the wiring. And a big storm had opportunity written all over it. Emergency situations stretched the cops thin, especially small-town forces like the Paradise PD.

Normally, Jesse would have given Millner enough rope to hang himself. He would have let him break into the condemned house before arresting him, but Jesse didn't have time for that now, not with the storm blowing in. When Millner, all six-foot-six of him, got out of his vehicle and went to swing open the van's side door, Jesse shined his Maglite in the thief's face.

"Who the hell is that?" asked Millner, holding his hand before his eyes to block the light.

"It's Chief Stone, John. What are you doing here?"

Millner hemmed and hawed, thinking of any reasonable lie.

"Don't bother," Jesse said. "I'm not in the mood for your crap. Consider yourself lucky I don't want to deal with you tonight. Now,

13

get out of here and don't let any of my people catch your ass up here again."

Millner didn't say a word, just got back into his van and drove away down toward town. Jesse watched the van's taillights until they disappeared. Then he stepped to the edge of the bluff on which the Rutherford house stood. He looked out at the vast blackness of the Atlantic. He listened to the bones of the old house creak in the wind, listened to the wind whistling through the broken windows. He thought he heard the devil at work. He decided he really needed that drink.

2

He supposed they were all thinking the same thing: This can't be happening. Not again. Not after all these years. But it *was* happening, only this time they weren't a bunch of kids with too much Southern Comfort and Thai stick in them. That first time, it was some innocent fun gone sideways. Severely sideways, plunging them into a paralyzing hell with slick, jagged walls from which there would be no escape. None. Not ever. That they were here to kill their old friend proved as much.

They had been given a temporary reprieve, a cruel reprieve, lasting just long enough to fool them into believing they had put real distance between that old evil and the fragile lives they had built in the meantime. Lives that included wives and lovers, children, careers, small successes, and grander failures, but haunted lives just the same. Haunted because distance from evil is a myth of time, because they were never more than one restless night or, worse still, a tainted moment of joy away from it.

The wind rattled the windows and the loading bay door. The plinking of sleet was less urgent now that the snow was falling in sheets and collecting on the corrugated metal roof. Raw, cold air seeped into the maintenance shed like an accusation and made heaving clouds of their breath. Small plumes of breath came from the mouth of the nude man on the floor at their feet. His wrists and ankles were trussed behind him and his sun-streaked brown hair was caked with the drying blood that had leaked from the welt at the base of his skull. His broken lower jaw was unhinged, his mouth a wreck of splintered teeth and bone. After the pipe had been laid into him, the spray of blood had given the air a coppery tang that the two other men could almost taste. But the blood had settled out of the air like silt out of water. Now the place smelled only of burnt black motor oil, gasoline fumes, and antifreeze.

"What'd you do with his clothes?"

"The furnace in the church."

"His duffel bag?"

"It's a big furnace. Burnt that up, too. Nothing but old, smelly clothes and a Bible,

16

anyways."

"Okay, drag that canvas over here and wrap it around his head."

"You really gonna do this?"

"*We* are."

"But that's Zevon, man. He was our friend once."

"Friends don't come back to town to fuck up everyone else's lives. If he wanted to stay my friend, he should have stayed lost. You may not have anything to lose, but I do."

"But —"

"But nothing. We talked this through. We all agreed. It's too late now, anyway. He's already more than half-dead. Now, get the canvas and do what I told you. The storm's blowing in faster than we thought and he's going to be here soon to get rid of the body. C'mon."

The unconscious man moaned a little as the coarse, mildewed fabric was wrapped around his head.

"What's the canvas for, anyways?"

"Think about it."

"Oh."

"Exactly. You got the tarp ready for him? The rope?"

"Yeah."

Outside, there was already six inches on the

ground and the roads were slick from the layer of sleet that had come before the snow. As he swung around to back up to the bay door, he checked his rearview mirror and saw two quick flashes of lightning and heard two muted claps of thunder. It was done. Zevon was dead. Now the time had come to play his part in keeping the past buried. Yet he understood that this particular episode of thunder and lightning, like their prior sins, was of their own doing and pushed them even further away from heaven than they already were. That the past was unrelenting and that no grave was deep enough to keep it buried forever.

3

Jesse hadn't slept a wink after getting home. He hadn't tried. He did manage to polish off two Black Labels. That's why he'd headed home in the first place. Sleep hadn't ever been a part of the plan, not really. It was always about the drinks. Drinkers are great rationalizers, spinning tales that only they will hear. Tales only they would believe. Jesse kept a bottle of something in his desk drawer at the station, but he didn't generally prefer drink at work or when the sun was up. Coming home, having a drink before dinner, then one or two afterward, was sometimes how he got through the day. He knew his bottle of Johnnie Walker was home waiting for him like a faithful wife. He'd had a wife once, just not a faithful one.

His ritual entailed pouring the drink — sometimes on the rocks, sometimes in a tall glass with soda — stirring it with his finger,

19

licking the scotch off his finger, raising a toast to his poster of Ozzie Smith, and taking that first sip. Sometimes he savored it. Sometimes, like that night, it was open wide and down the hatch. Any confirmed drinker knows that ritual is as integral to the addiction as the drinking itself. Dix was fond of saying that ritual was a secondary reinforcement. Jesse laughed at the notion of secondary reinforcement. He liked the drinking well enough all by itself. He enjoyed the ritual on its own merits. He'd gotten some food in him, taken a shower, and watched a half hour of weather reports before heading back to work.

Whatever sleep Jesse had managed came on the cot in his office. He was still on the cot, staring up at the ceiling, when the first dull rays of light filtered in through his window. He noticed the window was no longer being pelted and the howl of the wind had been reduced to a whisper. Morning had brought with it a soft hush. Then there was a knock at his office door.

"Come," he said.

Luther "Suitcase" Simpson came into the office, a lack of sleep evident on his puffy, still-boyish face and in his bloodshot eyes. He was moving more slowly these days, and not from lack of sleep. It was painful for Jesse to watch. A big man, Suit had been quite the high school football player in his day. But he'd been gut-shot last spring and was only now getting back to work.

"Any coffee out there?" Jesse asked, swinging his legs off the cot.

"Sure, but I wouldn't drink it. Better to save what's left and use it to strip paint."

Jesse stood, stretched the tension out of his muscles. His right shoulder aching from the damp air.

"Making a fresh pot of coffee against your religion?"

Suit reddened. "I'm not Molly, Jesse. You know I'm no good at this stuff. You got to get me back on the street."

Simpson had been on light duty since his return and chafed at working the front desk. Worse, Molly Crane had taken Suit's place in the patrol rotation.

"I know this is tough for you, Suit. I already stuck my neck out by bringing you back this soon."

"I'm sorry."

"No need. I'd be mad at you if you didn't want to get back out there."

Suit smiled that broad, goofy smile of his. Jesse's opinion meant everything to him. He'd always dreamed of living up to Jesse

21

Stone's standards, of being a cop good enough to work in a big city like L.A. Living up to Jesse is what had gotten him shot. He knew it. Jesse knew it, too. That's what worried him.

Jesse asked, "You going to the counseling sessions?"

The smile vanished from Suit's face. He reddened again.

"Yeah, Jesse."

"Getting shot is a serious thing, Suit. It screws with your head. I can't put you back out there if you're going to doubt yourself."

"I'm going. I said I was going."

"Okay, let's talk real police work. The donut shop open?"

Simpson laughed.

"I went and got some at five o'clock on the nose. They're last night's leftovers, but they're good."

Jesse put up a new pot of coffee, ate a hardened jelly donut, and asked Suit to fill him in on the storm damage.

"Storm's almost blown itself out already," Suit said. "We had gusts up to sixty-five, but nothing now. Dumped lots of snow. About a foot, give or take. And it's that real wet, heavy snow. You know."

"Uh-huh."

"You get a lot of that wet snow back in

L.A., Jesse?"

"Cute. You want to earn some more time on the desk?"

For a second, Suit thought Jesse was serious.

"Anyway, there were a few trees and power lines down. I had to dispatch some cars to block roads off and put down some flares while the repair crews did their thing. There were three fender benders. Reports already filed. Only serious thing was a partial building collapse."

"Anybody injured?"

"Nah. It was one of those old abandoned factory buildings on Trench Alley. Molly's over there handling it with the fire department."

Then, as if on cue, Molly's voice crackled through the desk speaker.

"Unit Four to dispatch, over."

"Dispatch, over," Suit said.

"Is Jesse up yet? Over."

"Unit Four, Jesse's right here, over."

Jesse dispensed with protocol. "What's up, Molly?"

"You better get over here, Jesse. Right now."

"What's going on?"

"We've got a body."

"Someone was killed in the collapse?"

"Someone was killed, all right, but not in the collapse. The body's in a tarp."

4

Trench Alley was a dingy, crooked street in the ass end of the Swap. Backed up against Sawtooth Creek and dead-ended by Pennacook Inlet, it was as Dickensian as Paradise got. Even scenic New England villages need garages, body shops, cabinetmakers, plumbing supply houses, welders, and self-storage units.

Jesse pulled up behind a fire truck. Molly Crane's cruiser was parked across the street, half on the sidewalk. The fire chief's red Jeep Cherokee was parked behind Molly's unit. When Jesse walked around the fire truck he was surprised to see Molly, Robbie Wilson, and the entire crew of firemen standing in the middle of the street, boot-deep in snow. But when he looked at the building in question, Jesse's surprise faded away. The building was a squat red-brick affair with plywood where windows used to be, the plywood covered in generations of frayed handbills and posters about forgotten bands and closed musicals at the Village Playhouse. The building's front right corner had collapsed into the street. You could look into the building and see that part of the back wall had collapsed inward as well.

"Robbie," Jesse said.

"Chief Stone."

"Unstable, huh?"

"Badly. If I didn't get your girl out of there when I did, you might've had two bodies on your hands."

Molly bristled at being called a girl. She was only two or three years younger than Wilson and disliked him even more than Jesse did. Jesse could see Molly was about to let Wilson have it. He shook his head no at her.

"Robbie, excuse us. I need to talk to Officer Crane for a minute."

"Take your time. I'm not letting anyone in there, stiff or no stiff."

As they walked toward Molly's cruiser, she kept turning back to stare at Robbie Wilson. Wilson was pretty lucky that looks couldn't actually kill.

"That obnoxious little bastard," Molly said. "I should've kicked his ass in front of his men. Then we'd see who he'd be calling a girl."

26

They sat in the front of Jesse's Explorer, the heater blowing full blast.

"Relax, Molly. Two weeks back on the street and you're already cursing like a sailor."

She smiled in spite of herself. Jesse could do that to her.

"And no matter what he called you, he was right to get you out of that building. I can't afford you getting hurt."

"So you really do love me," she said.

"You know I do, but that's not it. With Suit on desk duty and Gabe Weathers still in rehab for his injuries, the department's two men short."

She punched him in his left biceps. Now it was his turn to smile. Then he wiped it away.

"The body in the tarp," he said.

"A passerby called the building collapse in to the desk. I had the Swap, so Suit sent me over here. It was still pretty dark when I arrived on scene. I had to look inside to see if anyone was hurt. When I got into the building I saw that another part of the roof, toward the left rear of the building, had collapsed onto some metal plates. One of the plates had been dislodged by the debris so that the plate was forced upward like one end of a seesaw. When I shined my flash in

27

behind the plate, I saw the tarp. At first I
didn't think anything of it. Maybe some
forgotten equipment or building supplies or
something. But when I looked at it under
the flash for a minute, I saw that it was
bound up with rope and shaped like a body.
When I kneeled down and stuck my head
into the hole, it was pretty obviously a body.
I couldn't tell much about it from looking. I
pushed the tarp and it felt like flesh
underneath. And before you say anything,
Jesse, my hand was gloved."

Jesse put up his palms. "I didn't say
anything."

"But you would have. I know you, Jesse."

"Maybe. Back to the body in the tarp."

"Funny thing," Molly said.

"What?"

"The tarp was pretty clean and the flesh
gave when I pushed, but pushed back. It
didn't seem frozen or in rigor."

"That's a lot to tell from one push with
your hand. No insult, Molly, but —"

"Did I say it was one push? I pushed a
few times. Then . . ." She hesitated.

"Do I even want to hear this?"

"Probably not." She said it anyway. "I
climbed down into the hole."

"You what? It's a crime scene, Molly. You
know better than —"

"I had to check to see if the victim might be alive."

"Molly!"

"I swear, Jesse. I wasn't trying to be a hero. I thought I was doing the right thing."

"And . . ."

"That's when Napoleon showed up. Suit must have called the FD after he sent me over here. Robbie ordered me out of the building. He had his guys practically drag me out of the hole when I didn't hop to. But for what it's worth, I don't think the victim was alive. He was physically unresponsive to my touch and to my verbal commands. No movement that I could detect. And when I put my hand on where I thought the chest was, there didn't seem to be any respiration."

"Anything else?"

"I think the vic's a male. Would be pretty tall if you stood him upright. Maybe six-three or -four. Broad across the shoulders."

"But you don't think he'd been there very long?" Jesse asked.

"That's my gut feeling. Of course, I don't know these things like you would. In L.A. you must have seen bodies in all sorts of places."

"Not in a snow-covered factory, Molly. We didn't get much of that sort of thing in

L.A. All right, let's get back over there and see if we can't get Chief Robbie to let us retrieve the body."

But she didn't move. There was something else besides Robbie Wilson bothering her. Jesse could see it on her face. He put a hand on her shoulder.

"It's okay, Molly. You did good. I'm proud of you for —"

"It's not that, Jesse."

"Then what?"

"I can't put it in words. It's just when I was down there with the vic . . . I . . . it was just strange. It felt like I had a connection to him."

Jesse nodded. It was like that sometimes. On most occasions, a body was just a body to a cop. It wasn't callousness. It was an attitude born of repeated exposure and self-protection. But there were moments when you couldn't help but feel a kind of weird connection to the victim.

"It happens. I know. Don't beat yourself up over it. Now, let's go," he said.

They got out of the SUV. Just then an inhuman groan filled the air.

"Watch it!" one of the firemen shouted. "Stand back. She's going!"

The ground shook beneath their feet. Jesse and Molly ran around the fire truck and saw that the building was gone. The roof lay halfway into Trench Alley. It had taken down the rusted cyclone fence that had surrounded the empty, rubble-filled lot next door.

"Everybody okay, Robbie?" Jesse said.

"Fine. We're all clear. You both all right, Chief Stone?"

"We're good."

"That stiff of yours is good and buried now."

Not for long, Jesse Stone thought. *Not for long.*

5

Jesse was wrong. It was Friday morning before the body in the blue tarp could be retrieved. The nor'easter had blown in Monday evening. The building had gone down Tuesday morning. It was late Thursday afternoon before the building inspector gave the go-ahead for the site to be cleared. Whoever said that there was less red tape to deal with in small towns was wrong. It had taken a full-court press by Jesse, the medical examiner, and Captain Healy to get the village selectmen to push the building inspector into action. As usual, it was Bill Marchand who did the last bit of persuading.

Now Jesse, Molly Crane, Captain Healy, Chief Wilson, and the medical examiner's crew stood on the corner of Algonquin Street and Trench Alley, just beyond the safety barrier set up by the demolition crew. Technically, there was no reason for Molly's presence, but Jesse knew she would have found an excuse to be there anyway. For all the ass-covering Molly had done for him over the years, for how she looked out for him, he owed her more than he could say. Allowing her to be there was the least he could do, though he was ambivalent about her being back on the street.

Most of it was selfishness. He liked having her at the station with him. They were good together. More than that, he trusted her. She was organized. Unlike Suit and the other guys who worked the desk and dispatch, Molly could do her job and brew a pot of coffee without being overwhelmed. Having her at the station house also made dealing with female suspects much easier. But the truth was that when it came to Molly, Jesse's attitudes were a little old-fashioned. Although she was as good a cop as there was on the Paradise PD, Molly had four kids and a husband at home. Jesse had too many officers killed in the line of duty during his tenure. He had almost lost two more in the last six months and he didn't think he could face Molly's family if anything happened to her on his watch.

Molly had been willing to trade off her desire to be on patrol for a job with a regular schedule, one that allowed her to cook dinner for her family and participate in some of the kids' after-school activities. Now that the kids were older, Molly had been itching to get on the street again. With Suit and Gabe out and no money in the budget for new hires, Jesse had no choice but to let Molly scratch that itch. He only hoped she wouldn't develop a taste for the street.

"Come on, come on," Molly said aloud without meaning to.

"Relax," Jesse said, looking at his watch. "Your pal in the blue tarp isn't going anywhere. Should only be a few more minutes."

"What's your girl even doing here, Chief?" Robbie Wilson wanted to know.

"She's not my girl, Robbie. She's the best cop I've got. Maybe you want to start showing her some respect."

Wilson threw up his hands. "Jeez, so sensitive. All right. All right. I'm sorry, Mol — Officer Crane."

She didn't answer.

"You realize any crime scene evidence is probably screwed beyond hope," Healy said to Jesse. "And what hasn't been tainted has been carted away with the line of dump trucks that have been passing us for the last hour."

Jesse nodded. "That's why I asked your forensics team to handle the crime scene. If there's anything left, your team is better equipped to find it."

A heavyset man in a blue hard hat and reflective lime-green vest over a dust-covered Carhartt jacket came running up Trench Alley. He nearly slipped on the slick pavement. He yammered into a black microphone as he ran. It squawked back at him. By the time he got to the barrier, the fat man was sweating and panting. There was a shocked look on his face.

"Which one of . . . you . . . is Chief . . . Stone?" he asked, bending over, gasping for breath.

Jesse stepped forward. "I'm Chief Stone."

"You . . . gotta come . . . quick . . . There's . . . there's . . ." He was too out of breath to finish.

"Healy, Molly, you're with me. The rest of you stay put."

Robbie Wilson didn't like it. "But I'm —"

"Stay put. This is a police matter now," Jesse said.

The three cops hurried down Trench Alley, around the crooked elbow in the street, and up toward the site of the demolished building. They didn't have their weapons drawn, but kept their hands close to their holsters. The fat man hadn't indicated there was any immediate threat. They hadn't heard any shots. No one was screaming. No one was running in their direction. When they got to where the abandoned building had stood, all the workmen wore the same shocked expression on their faces. The debris from the old factory building was completely gone: bricks, rebar, tar, plywood, glass, steel columns, all of it. All that remained was the cracked concrete slab, though a fine cloud of dust hung in the air. Thirty feet beyond the slab, Sawtooth Creek, swelled with melted snow, flowed by.

"Who's in charge here?" Jesse asked.

A lanky, middle-aged black man in an orange reflective vest walked up to Jesse. FOREMAN was written neatly in permanent marker across the front of his blue hard hat. PETTIGREW was written in the same marker in the same block lettering across the name strip on his vest. He held a radio in his left hand.

"That'd be me, James Pettigrew."

"Jesse Stone. You wanted me?"

Pettigrew removed his glove and shook Jesse's hand.

"We got a situation here, Chief. I think you better come have a look."

Jesse pointed at Healy and Molly. "Is it

safe for all of us?"

"Not a problem," Pettigrew said. "The slab is damaged but stable. This way."

"What's the problem?" Jesse asked.

"You better just see for yourself."

The metal plate that had been dislodged during Tuesday morning's partial collapse had been removed. Bent and twisted by the debris, it sat close off to the side. The body in the blue tarp was clear to see in the morning light. It smelled, too, though not nearly as bad as it would if the temperatures had gotten above the week's high of thirty-seven degrees. Molly was right. Whoever the man in the tarp was, he'd been tall and broad across the chest and shoulders. Loops of red-and-white synthetic rope were tied tightly around the ankles, knees, waist, chest, and neck of the body. But Jesse didn't see what the fuss was about.

"I'm confused," Jesse said, turning to Pettigrew. "Everybody knows about the body."

Pettigrew shook his head. He put his radio in a vest pocket, moved to his left, and pointed at another metal plate a few feet away from the blue tarp. "That's not it. Here, Chief, give me a hand. Help me lift this up."

Jesse and Healy went around to the other side of the plate. Molly helped Pettigrew.

The foreman said, "Ready? Now!"

And with that, they lifted and slid the second metal plate up and back, resting it on the slab next to the other damaged metal plate. Then they looked down into the hole it had covered and saw a frayed, filthy blanket. Jesse knelt down and slowly pulled back the blanket, pieces of it disintegrating in his fingers.

"Jesus, Mary, and Joseph!" Healy crossed himself.

Molly dropped to her knees, crossing herself, too. "Oh my God." She clamped her hand over her mouth.

"You think it's them, Officer Crane?" Healy asked.

She did not answer. He wasn't sure she'd even heard him.

"Them who?" Jesse asked, peering down at the two skeletons.

"Mary Kate O'Hara and Ginny Connolly," Healy said.

Molly pulled the small flashlight off her belt and laid flat on her stomach. She shined it down into the hole. The skeletons were different sizes. One was about five feet in length. The other five-six or -seven. Then Molly gasped. She pushed herself up and ran. She stumbled, fell forward, ripping the knees of her uniform pants. Got up again, limped outside, fell to her knees, and vomited.

When Jesse reached Molly, tears were pouring out of her. He got down beside her, threw his arm around her shoulders.

Healy came and stood over the both of them.

"What is it, Officer Crane?"

"It's them, Captain. It's Mary Kate and Ginny."

"How can you be sure?"

"The ring," she said. "Look at the ring."

6

There had been very few times after his rookie year on the LAPD that Jesse Stone was at a loss. This was one of those times. Jesse wasn't drinking, but Healy was. He was working on his second Jameson, pacing in front of Jesse's desk.

"How's Crane holding up?" Healy asked.

"She'll be fine. I sent her home to get cleaned up. She'll be back here in a little while. You want to fill me in?"

"I was still in uniform back then, just starting out," the captain said. "You were probably taking infield practice in your first season in A ball."

"Long time ago."

"Feels like yesterday, Jesse. Two sixteen-year-old girls, Mary Kate O'Hara and Virginia Connolly, went missing on the Fourth of July. They were supposed to meet a bunch of friends at Kennedy Park to see the fireworks and hang around for a concert

40

by a local band afterward. Their parents said they left their houses around eight. The friends said that Mary Kate and Ginny were there for the fireworks, but that both of the girls skipped out during the concert. They never made it home. Nobody realized they were missing until about three a.m. If I remember right, the parents didn't notify the Paradise PD until they had called all of the girls' friends. So it was maybe five or six before the cops had any idea what was going on. Your department was smaller then. I think it was eight men and the chief. His name was —"

"Frederick W. Tillis," Jesse said, pointing at the wall to his right. "Someday my picture will be up there staring down at the poor fool who inherits this job."

"I knew Freddy Tillis a little bit after I got the bump to detective. Nice enough fella, I guess. Not the most competent policeman I ever came across. I think his major qualification for the job was that he came cheap."

"They hired me because they thought I was a bumbling drunk."

Healy laughed. "They were half right."

"The wrong half. But what about the girls?"

"Tillis waited two days before he called us staties in. By then the trail was icy cold, not that there was much of a trail to begin with. The girls seemed to have vanished. There weren't even many tips. You know, the usual crazies. One said he'd seen them abducted by a spacecraft. There was one credible lead, I think, a drunk guy eating at the Gray Gull. He said he saw a few kids in an overcrowded boat rowing out to Stiles at a time that would fit. His name will be in your files somewhere. It's something like Sabo or Laszlov, like that. Nothing came of it. The guy was plastered."

"The ring," Jesse said. "Molly kept talking about the ring."

"Mary Kate O'Hara's ring. Her class ring from Sacred Heart Girls Catholic. The ring company made a mistake in sizing it. It was too large for her ring finger, so she always wore it on the middle finger of her right hand. Both of the skeletons had Sacred Heart rings on, the smaller one on its right middle finger. Be a hell of a coincidence."

"I don't believe in coincidence, but let's wait for the autopsies before we get ahead of ourselves."

"It's them, Jesse." Healy gulped the rest of his drink. Held the empty cup out for another. "Don't make the same mistake Freddy Tillis did. Go dig the file out and start working it."

Jesse poured.

"Why is this the first I'm hearing about these girls, Healy? I've been chief here for over a decade now. I've heard about almost everything else that's come down the sewer pipe in this town. Why not this?"

"You're from where? Tucson, right? You played ball in Albuquerque. Worked LAPD for ten years. Paradise is a small town. I been in all sorts of small towns since I came on the job. And if there's one thing small towns protect, it's their darkest secrets. It's shame. They're ashamed, Jesse. You may be chief, you may live here, but you didn't grow up here. It's one thing to be from a place. Something else to be of a place. Talk to Crane about it. She'll tell you."

Jesse nodded.

"What do you make of the guy in the blue tarp?" he asked.

Healy laughed. It was a laugh that had no relationship to joy. "You just said you don't believe in coincidences."

"Would be a hell of a coincidence for three bodies to end up in the same abandoned building, buried in utility holes ten feet apart."

Healy shook his head. "So you think there's a connection?"

"One way or the other."

43

"What's that supposed to mean?" Healy asked.

"That the bodies being ten feet apart means more to me than the passage of time."

"We'll know soon enough."

"Uh-huh," Jesse said, finally pouring himself a drink.

7

The files were buried and forgotten, much as their bodies had been. It had taken him nearly a half hour to dig them out of a back storage room, a room Jesse had spent precious little time in since his arrival in Paradise. He didn't want to think about the other secrets Paradise kept buried there. Now he sat with an array of the girls' photos laid out on his desktop, the photos dulled by time and carelessness. In spite of their faded images, Jesse could see enough to get a sense of the girls and to glimpse the past.

Mary Kate O'Hara was the smaller of the two girls. Copper-haired and freckle-faced, more cute than pretty, she had fire in her eyes. They looked hazel in the faded photographs. The paperwork said they were green. What did it matter now? Virginia "Ginny" Connolly was the taller of the pair. She was strawberry blond and blue-eyed. In her tenth-grade graduation picture — taken in February of that year — there was still some awkwardness in her features. A nose a bit too big for her face, a mouth full of braces, slumped shoulders to hide her height. But in the photos of her taken in the months leading up to her July fourth disappearance, she'd shed her braces, grown into her face and body. *She would have been a beautiful woman,* Jesse thought. Both girls had been good if not remarkable students at Sacred Heart. Both had been good athletes, particularly Ginny. Neither had gotten into much trouble, though Mary Kate was a bit of a pistol. She'd been a prankster, according to her school records.

When Jesse took out the other photos from the files, the ones that weren't just of the two dead girls, he was taken aback. Several of those pictures featured Ginny and Mary Kate with their arms around a third girl. That girl was quite pretty, with dark, wavy hair and an infectious smile. She had a look in her eyes that was quite familiar to Jesse. He had gazed at that expression, at that face, for five or six days a week, for more than ten years. It was a face more familiar to him than Jenn's, his ex-wife, or Sunny Randall's, or Diana Evans's, or any of his other lovers, recent or past. It was Molly's face.

He put the photos aside and began seriously reading through the files, such as they
were. Jesse shook his head at how
haphazardly the investigation seemed to
have been handled, at least at the start. He
knew he shouldn't judge a small-town PD's
investigation the way he would judge one
handled by a big-city police department,
but he couldn't help but compare his LAPD
experiences to what had gone down in
Paradise when the girls went missing. He
recalled how he had been taught to keep
extensive and thorough notes, especially
during a homicide investigation. Jesse's
murder books were legend. No detail was
too small to escape mention, because you
just never knew what would lead you to the
killer.

That didn't seem to be the philosophy of
the Paradise PD back in the day. Of course,
he had to allow that it was never really a
murder investigation. In fact, from what he
could glean, there didn't seem to have been
a working theory of the case or, more ac-
curately, there seemed to be any number of
working theories. From the interview notes,
Jesse could infer the questions the cops were
asking and could thereby reconstruct what
the cops were thinking. Early on, they apparently believed Ginny and Mary Kate

went off on an adventure together, possibly hitching down to Boston or to New York City. Then that shifted to a runaway scenario based on the fact that Ginny and her mother had recently been at odds. It was only after the state police came in to help that the girls' bank records were checked — something a big-city department would have done immediately. And only when no unusual activity turned up, no big withdrawals the week before they vanished, did the working theories take a darker turn.

When the state came into it, they rounded up all the usual suspects: local sex offenders, ex-cons with a history of violence, especially a history of violence toward women. There were a few suspects the state police kept an eye on, but it came to nothing. And it took the better part of a week for a physical search to be mounted. It was a pretty thorough search, too. People had combed over the Bluffs, Stiles Island, the marina, and the rest of town. Unfortunately, there had been a few days of heavy rains in the interim and the feeling was that if there had been any less-than-obvious physical evidence to be found, it had been washed away with the rains.

The most fascinating parts of the reading for Jesse were the interviews with the teenagers of Paradise. It was fascinating on many levels because the kids interviewed back then were people Jesse had known only as adults. Molly and her husband among them. In fact, Molly had been interviewed three times. Bill Marchand and two other selectmen, Robbie Wilson, the mayor, and several of Paradise's other citizens had been interviewed. Just as fascinating for Jesse was seeing names he didn't recognize. A good number of the teens back then had stayed and made their lives here, but many had not. He wondered where those kids had gone and why they had gone and what they were up to now. The bottom line was that the interviews, like everything else in the case, led the cops nowhere. No one knew who Ginny and Mary Kate were meeting in the park. No one remembered seeing them.

Jesse had little difficulty believing what he read. He had been through several Fourth of July celebrations in Paradise and it could get pretty chaotic. There were always fireworks and bands in the park, usually Aerosmith, Boston, or the Cars tribute bands. Drugs and underage drinking were never much of a problem in town, but the one exception to that rule was the Fourth celebration. He could only imagine how chaotic it was twenty-five years earlier when the department was even smaller than it is now. When he was done reading through the files, he was drawn back to the old photos, especially the ones of Molly. Then, as he looked up from the photos on his desk, the grown-up version of that girl was standing in front of him.

"Sit down, Molly. You want a drink?"

"More than you know, but I don't think my stomach can take it," she said, sitting across from him.

He handed Molly all the pictures from the two files and watched her in silence for the next ten minutes. Watched her as she traveled back in time. For a few moments, Molly looked sixteen again, the years melting off her, the lines on her face fading away. But when she finally looked back up, she was herself again, the lines etched into her face more deeply than they'd been when she had come into Jesse's office. She tried handing the photos back to Jesse, but he waved her off.

"Make plenty of copies of those. If it turns out that we've found Mary Kate and Ginny and that they were, in fact, murdered —"

"It's them. I'm telling you, it's them. And what do you mean, *if* they were murdered?" Molly said, her voice loud enough to be heard in the squad room. "They didn't bury themselves under that blanket under that metal plate."

Jesse stayed calm. "If it's them and they were murdered, we're going to be working an old double homicide. We're going to have to re-interview people. Those pictures may help refresh memories, maybe spark new ones."

"What about the guy in the tarp?"

"No doubt about his being murdered," Jesse said. "When they got him back to the ME's and unwrapped him, half his face was blown off. There was an entry wound behind his left ear and one right in back of his head. Until we get an ID, he's another John Doe."

"But it's no accident, us finding his body there next to Mary Kate and Ginny."

"I doubt it."

"What do you think it means, Jesse?"

"We follow the evidence around here."

She wasn't going to let it go. "But if you had to guess."

Jesse said, "You already know the answer to that, too."

"He's connected to Mary Kate's and Ginny's murders."

"That's where the smart money would be."

"You think the guy who murdered the

girls murdered —"

Jesse walked around his desk, stood close to Molly, and brushed his hand across her cheek.

"Listen, Molly," he said, his hand resting on her shoulder. "I can only guess at how hard this is for you. As fine a cop as you are — and you're the best I've got — you need to be an even better, more professional cop than usual. If I could afford to, I wouldn't let you anywhere near these cases, but I can't. Even if I could, you wouldn't stay away."

"Mary Kate was my best friend, Jesse. Ginny Connolly grew up two houses away from me. Their disappearing the way they did helped make me want to be a cop."

"Then use that, Molly. Don't let it cloud your judgment. I've always trusted you. Don't give me a reason to start doubting you now."

"I'm sorry . . . . about before, I mean, at the building site, losing it like that. It was unprofessional."

"That badge and uniform don't make you immune."

"It made me look weak."

"It made you look human."

"What do we do first?" she asked.

"We wait until the identities are confirmed

and CODs are established."

Molly stood up. "Okay. I better make some copies of these photos and get back on patrol."

"Not so fast," he said. "Sit another minute."

She didn't sit. "What is it?"

"Unless I'm way off, these missing girls were the biggest unsolved mystery in Paradise's history."

"I guess that's right. It's also probably the only unsolved mystery in Paradise's history." She laughed. It was a nervous, staccato laugh.

"Then why is today the first I'm hearing about them?"

Molly looked everywhere but at Jesse. Her face reddened.

"I can't answer that, Jesse. I don't know."

Jesse got the sense there was something Molly wasn't saying, but he let it go. Pushing her now wouldn't do either of them any good.

8

After Molly left, Jesse went out to talk to Suit. But Suit spoke first.

"Molly okay? She's acting weird."

Jesse nodded.

"Word's spreading, Jesse . . . about the bodies. Stu Cromwell from the paper just called for you."

"I figure we've got about an hour before it goes national. Then the phone's going to ring off the hook."

"What am I supposed to say?"

"For now, say that there won't be any comment until we get autopsy results and official IDs on the bodies. I'll scribble something out that we can release as an official statement. I'll call over to the mayor's office to see if we can't get someone to answer the station house line, so you can do your job. I'll handle Cromwell."

"Thanks, Jesse."

"How old were you when the girls disappeared?"

"I was a kid. I wasn't even sure what was going on, really. All I can remember about it was how freaked-out my mom and all the other moms on the block were. She made all of us stay close to the house that summer, especially my big sister."

"Did your mom or dad talk to you guys about what happened?"

Suit laughed. "My folks weren't great communicators, Jesse. But you know how grandmas talk about bad things? You know, like when they talk about cancer and they whisper it or call it the C word? It was like that. We could always tell when the parents on the block were talking about what happened to those girls because they would whisper or look . . . I don't know."

"Ashamed?"

Suit shrugged his big shoulders. "Like I said, I don't know."

"Anybody ever talk about it after that summer?"

"The next summer, I think. Around the Fourth, maybe. But after that, I can't remember people ever bringing it up. Until this morning I had forgotten about it. I guess there's some shame in that."

"You look hard enough at anything," Jesse said, "and you'll find some shame in it. You recall anything else about that summer, you come to me with it."

"You mean don't talk to Molly about it."

"That's exactly what I mean."

"Guess I'm not as dumb as I look," Suit said, but only half jokingly.

"You keep handing me straight lines like that and I'm going to start calling you Luther. And no, Suit, I never thought you were dumb."

"Thanks, Jesse."

"Forget it. Do me a favor."

"Sure."

"Call the paper and get Stu Cromwell over here."

Suit tilted his head, furrowed his brow. "I thought you hated the press."

"They have their uses," Jesse said, a smile on his face.

"You going to give him an interview?"

"We'll let him think that."

Suit punched the paper's number into the phone.

9

There was a knock at Jesse's door. He knew who it was just by the size of the shadow behind the pebbled glass.

"Come on in, Stu," he said, standing to greet the newspaperman.

Stu Cromwell strode into the office. He was in his sixties, but still an imposing figure. Tall, lean, and fit, he had piercing blue eyes and a mop of white hair. He was a favorite son of Paradise, a local boy who'd made a name for himself on the world stage and come back home to settle down. Unfortunately, the local papers he'd most recently worked for failed as regularly as Hollywood marriages. He'd gotten so fed up with his employers going under that he and his wife had bought out the last failing paper with their own money. Now the *Paradise Herald* belonged to them.

Jesse waved his arm at the chair across from his desk. "Sit."

"Thank you, sir," Cromwell said, shaking Jesse's hand. "I appreciate the invitation."

Jesse liked that about Cromwell. He had manners.

"How's Martha?"

"Not so good. The chemo's been rough on her and the prognosis isn't great."

"Sorry to hear that."

"Thanks, Jesse, but I suspect you didn't call me over here to ask about my wife."

Jesse shook his head.

"Is it them, Jesse, Mary Kate O'Hara and Ginny Connolly?" Cromwell asked, easing into the chair. As he sat, he flipped open a notepad.

"Officially or off the record?"

Cromwell said, "Let's start with officially."

"Until the medical examiner determines their identities, it would be foolish of me to speculate."

Cromwell laughed. He closed his notepad. "Okay, how about off the record?"

"Maybe."

"Maybe what?"

"Maybe it's the missing girls."

"Maybe probably or maybe unlikely?"

"Maybe probably."

Cromwell rubbed his clean-shaven chin, opened his notepad. "Their remains are skeletal, so why probably?"

"Nice try, Stu." Jesse clapped his hands together. "If I answered the question in that form, I'd be confirming something that's not been officially acknowledged."

"It was worth a shot," Cromwell said. "But everybody in town knows you found two skeletons in close proximity to the body in the blue tarp. If you're not going to talk to me about this stuff, why did you call me over here?"

"Did I say I wasn't going to talk to you?"

Cromwell closed his notepad again. Laughed again. "A little squid pro quo, huh, Jesse? You scratch my octopus and I'll scratch yours."

"Uh-huh."

"Who's going to scratch whose octopus first?" Cromwell asked.

Jesse never had much use for the press. And his attitude toward the media only got worse after his ex, Jenn, a failed actress, had risen from the weather girl at a Boston TV station to a reporter on a syndicated magazine show. Jenn was smart, but she wasn't the most savvy person about world affairs and politics. The only subject Jenn was an expert on was herself, but it wasn't only Jenn's narrow focus that fueled Jesse's contempt for the press. He had found her colleagues to be a bunch of self-important boobs. Stu Cromwell was neither self-important nor a boob. And it was Jesse's sense of things that reporters, especially newspaper reporters, always knew more than they would or could say. They were like cops in that way.

"I wasn't here when the girls went missing," Jesse said, "so I'm operating in the dark. I could use someone who knew the landscape back then the way you would have known it."

"What about your cops? Some of them grew up here and have never left."

"I'll talk to them. I *have* talked to some of them already."

Cromwell cleared his throat. "You are aware, then, that Molly Crane was close to both girls?"

Jesse nodded.

"I heard she pretty much fell apart this morning."

"Please, Stu, don't put that —"

Cromwell raised his palm up. "It has no bearing on the story, Jesse. Don't worry. It won't be in the paper tomorrow — not mine, anyway. But I still don't know what you want from me."

"Your notes from back then," Jesse said. "Your files."

"Sorry, Jesse. That's a nonstarter. I've

never shown anyone my notes and files outside of my editors, and not always then. Even if you were willing to show me all the official files, local and state, I wouldn't make that trade."

"How about this, then. You act as an unofficial consultant to the department."

"In what unofficial capacity exactly?" Cromwell drew air quotes around the word *unofficial*.

"First, I'd like to sit down with you and talk about how Paradise was back around the time the girls went missing. After I start doing my investigation, I'd like to be able to run things by you. I'll need a way to test what I'm being told against what the reality of Paradise was. I am not going to know the players like you know them or knew them."

Cromwell was curious. "And for this I get what?"

"Exclusives."

"You do realize that you're going to get swamped by the media once this gets out there. You'll have more satellite trucks here than ever before. You sure you want to go promising exclusives to a small-town paper?"

Jesse nodded.

"Okay, then," Cromwell said. "Exclusives like . . . ?"

"Sacred Heart Girls Catholic class rings were found among the remains."

"Did one of them have the ring on the middle finger of its right hand?"

Jesse said, "Possibly."

Stu Cromwell stood up and stuck his right hand out to Jesse. "Aren't you going to shake the hand of your new unofficial consultant?"

Jesse shook Stu's hand.

"About the ring . . ." Cromwell said.

"Middle finger of the right hand."

Cromwell smiled.

"Until I say different, Stu, quote me only as an unnamed police source. Agreed?"

"Agreed."

Cromwell stood, thanked Jesse, and left.

10

He had seen human bodies in all states of disrepair, but the face of the man in the blue tarp was a particular mess. Jesse was beyond sickness or disgust. He accepted that about himself. He found looking at bodies in the morgue to be more difficult than doing so at the crime scene. A body was just one element of a crime scene, one part of the activity. The morgue, with its somber, antiseptic chill and stainless steel, was a different experience. Somehow the sterility of the place, the forced distancing of the bodies from their humanity, had a paradoxical effect on Jesse. They became more than cases to him here.

Jesse found himself looking from the near-faceless body on the metal table to the face of the ME. Hers was an attractive face, somewhere between pretty and striking, not beautiful. She had high cheekbones, a strong, square chin, and polished-copper eyes. Her nose was slightly flattened, her lips were thin, but nicely shaped. She wore her dark brown, impossibly curly hair pulled back so tightly that it seemed as if she was trying to make a statement. It was hard for Jesse to know what she was trying to say. And he wondered if her spare use of makeup was part of the same statement or whether there was a different message in that.

He'd run into Tamara Elkin a few times since she'd taken the job in early summer, but they hadn't really exchanged more than hellos. Their conversations had been such that Jesse hadn't gotten any sense of her. It wasn't easy getting a sense of her, though there was a hint of mischief and flirt in her eyes. She didn't talk much and she seemed pleased to wait for him to speak first.

"His face is in bad shape," Jesse said.

"Your powers of observation are keen ones, Chief Stone. Next you'll point out the victim's farmer tan."

"I did notice that. And it's Jesse, not Chief Stone."

"How nice for you."

"I could live without the sarcasm, Doc."

"And I could do without the flirting."

Jesse laughed. "If asking you to call me by my first name is flirting, you've got a low threshold, Doc."

She smiled, and there it was, he thought, that mischief in her eyes.

"Whatever. Entrance wounds from very near the rear of the skull here," she said, tapping the back of Jesse's head with the tip of her index finger, "and here." She touched Jesse behind his left ear. "The shots were from very close range."

Her touch was gentle and lingered a beat longer than he expected. In spite of her denial, it felt like flirting. If it was, he was flattered by it. Under a different set of circumstances, Jesse might have encouraged her and pursued things. But he was still carrying a torch for Diana Evans, the former FBI agent he had been involved with last spring. She was back in the D.C. area, still getting her life back in order. He'd been with a lot of women during his long breakup with Jenn, but before Diana, only Sunny Randall had really lit the spark in him. Unfortunately, Sunny had been as entangled with her ex as Jesse had been with Jenn. He wasn't about to throw another chance at love away, whether Tamara Elkin was flirting with him or not.

"We found charred and soot-laden canvas fibers in the entrance wounds and bloodied canvas fibers elsewhere. We've sent it all to the state crime lab."

"The shooter didn't want a mess," Jesse said. "Two wounds and all that damage, must have been large-caliber. Maybe hollow-points."

"Definitely hollow-points. Sounds like you've done this once or twice."

"Once or twice."

"Yes, I've heard all about you, Chief Stone," she said, and left it at that. "Unless your department is willing to pay for forensic facial reconstruction, there's little hope of photo identification."

"Or dental. What's left of his mouth is a train wreck," Jesse said. He pointed to an indentation and nasty dark mark on John Doe's lower jaw. "That wasn't caused by gunshots."

"Blunt-instrument trauma prior to death. He was bound as well. Look at his wrists and ankles."

"Ligature marks."

She nodded. "It's in the report. Other marks, too, but of his own making," she said, running her gloved fingertip along the body's left forearm. "Intravenous drug user, but not recently. The scarring looks to be several years old. He had been a heavy drinker at some point as well. His liver was almost as much of a mess as his face."

"Any identifying marks, Doc?"

She smiled. It was a crooked smile, one with a surprising amount of playfulness in it, Jesse thought.

She said, "Lift up his left arm."

Jesse saw the tattoo: a two-headed rattlesnake, forked tongues extended, its body wrapped around the horizontal beam of a cross, the snake's rattle sticking skyward at one end of the cross. The snake's heads hung below the other end. The cross was done in dark blue ink, the snake in bright red. It was about four inches long by three inches wide and ran from the bottom of the dead man's left armpit along the top of his rib cage.

"That can't be a very common tattoo," she said.

"We'll find out soon enough. Can I get a photograph of —"

"Already done. There's a hard copy with the file and I can send you a JPEG. Let's go into my office and I'll get you the reports of the girls."

As Jesse followed Tamara Elkin down the hall, he found he had as many questions in his head about her as he did the dead.

11

In his capacity as police chief of the Paradise PD and as the catching detective on cases for the LAPD's Robbery-Homicide Division, Jesse Stone had done this sad Kabuki dozens of times. Sometimes he was forced to do it over the phone. More frequently, he performed the soul-crushing duty in person. Today it would be done face-to-face with Molly Crane at his side.

The O'Hara house wasn't much. Like many of the older homes in that part of Paradise, it had started out as a simple, cedar-shingled cottage. Then, over the decades, rooms and dormers had been added to meet the owners' needs or whims. The O'Hara place, with its split shingles gone almost black with age and a garage sagging with snow and neglect, was the poor relation on the street. The kind of place the old neighbors shook their heads at in pity and new neighbors shook their heads at in contempt.

Jesse, riding shotgun, flung open the cruiser door but didn't get out of the cruiser.

"How long since you've been here, Molly?"

"Feels like forever."

"You sure you're up for this?"

Her jaw clenched. "No, I'm not sure, but I have to be here with you. It's the right thing to do."

"For the O'Haras or for you?"

"Both."

Jesse had no intention of arguing with her. Of course Molly was here because she felt it was right. He sensed it was more than that. Way more. Guilt probably only a fraction of it. They got out of the cruiser. Molly came around and stood by Jesse.

"Both parents still alive?" Jesse asked.

"I think so. I know her mom is. Mary Kate's parents split up about a year after she went missing. Mr. O'Hara, Mary Kate's dad, couldn't take staying here, being surrounded by reminders of his favorite girl. My mom told me he felt like he was drowning. Mom said she didn't blame him for leaving. I don't think anyone did. He was a great guy, Mr. O'Hara. We used to call him Johnny. He'd pile all of us girls into his big old station wagon with the fake wood on the sides and take us to the park or to the beach. He taught us how to play ball and catch frogs. How to fish. We all loved Johnny."

There she is again, Jesse thought. *Young Molly.* There was something so happy and pure about her joy in speaking about the past, he couldn't help wishing he had known her then.

"Johnny sounds like a pretty friendly guy," Jesse said. "Ever get too friendly?"

Molly tilted her head in confusion, stepped away from him. "What?"

"Man surrounds himself with a bunch of pretty young girls. Spends a lot of time with them —"

"Johnny was a good man. He never did anything inappropriate with us."

"No hugs that lasted a little too long? No pats on your ass when you got a hit? No special time or attention paid to any of you girls?"

"Nothing like that."

"And Mary Kate, did she ever say anything about —"

Molly turned to Jesse, her face red with anger. "Nothing."

"Sorry, Molly, but we have to know what we have to know."

"I get it. I don't like it, but I get it," she

said. "Without obvious suspects, we work from the family out."

"The mom stayed."

"Yeah, Tess — that's Mary Kate's mom — she stayed. Like Johnny couldn't stay, Tess couldn't leave."

"Happens all the time," Jesse said.

"What does?"

"Tragedy."

"What about it, Jesse?"

"Blows families apart."

"Or brings them closer together," Molly said.

"Uh-huh. Tell me about the mother."

"Tess, right. She was quieter than Johnny. More religious. I think Johnny would've been fine with his kids going to public school, but Tess wouldn't stand for that. She used to go to Mass every morning and volunteered at the church. But she was — is, I guess — a very sweet person. I haven't seen her in years. She was always nice to us, too. Just not in an outgoing way like Johnny was."

"So Mary Kate was more like Johnny?" Jesse asked.

Molly nodded. "She was just like her dad," she said. "She even looked like him. Her sisters were like their mom, in looks and temperament."

As they took the short walk up to the front door, Molly nodded at a street-facing window on the second floor.

"See that, Jesse?"

"Electric candle in the window? Hard to miss."

"That was Mary Kate's room. I guess Tess was hoping Mary Kate would come home someday."

Jesse shook his head. "Turns out she never really left."

12

Molly rang the bell. As they waited, Jesse noticed the front shades were pulled down. They were frayed and sun-bleached as if they were always drawn. Several years' worth of rotting leaves clogged the rain gutters, the gutters pulling away from the house under the weight of the leaves. A pane of glass in the front window was missing and had been replaced by cardboard and duct tape.

The door pulled back. A short, frail woman stood at the threshold. She was gaunt and ashen-skinned. She held a rosary in her hand, the cross dangling in the cold air like an unasked question and its unspoken answer. She was dressed in a pilled gray sweater and blue polyester pants, both long out of fashion and too large for her by several sizes. Her brown eyes were dull and unfocused. Jesse supposed she was sixty or so, but looked much older. Then a light seemed to snap on behind her eyes. A smile came across her bare lips.

"Little Molly Burke!" Her voice was surprisingly strong. "Is that you?"

"It's Molly Crane now, Mrs. O'Hara. And as you can see, I'm all grown up. This is Chief Stone. He'll want you to call him Jesse."

Tess O'Hara nodded at Jesse, her smile fading. "Jesse."

"We need to come in, Tess," Molly said. "Would that be all right?"

Tess O'Hara didn't speak. She simply walked into her living room, leaving the front door open behind her. They followed her in, Jesse closing the door. Tess had taken a seat in a big recliner in front of an old TV set. The recliner was a study in duct tape and the TV set was a big, bulky beast in a chipped wooden cabinet. The paneled walls were bowed and warped, but were covered in photos of children and grandchildren. At the center of the photo display was a large framed shot of Mary Kate at her tenth-grade graduation ceremony. There were crosses and/or crucifixes on every wall. There were religious sayings painted on wooden plaques, too. The kinds of things you might find at flea markets or church sales. One in particular caught Jesse's attention.

Now faith is the assurance of things hoped
  for,
the conviction of things not seen.
                              HEBREWS 11:6

Mrs. O'Hara noticed Jesse notice, but didn't say anything.

Jesse and Molly sat on a lifeless sofa at an angle to Mrs. O'Hara. Molly recognized the sofa as the same one she'd sat and watched TV on a hundred times. When they were little, Mary Kate and Molly would play with their dolls together on that couch. Those memories made Molly smile. Remembering why they were here made it disappear.

The thing Jesse noticed most was the smell of the place. Beneath the overwhelming odor of the morning's burnt coffee and overcooked eggs, there was a dank, musty scent. Colonies of black mold must have been thick beneath the carpeting and walls. Her daughter was dead, but it was Tess O'Hara who had entombed herself. Jesse wished he hadn't seen the phenomenon before, but he had.

"Do you know why we're here, Tess?" Molly asked.

Tess didn't answer. She started to rock slightly, rolling the rosary in her fingers, mumbling a Hail Mary almost to herself.

Jesse opened his mouth to speak. Molly shook her head. Jesse closed his mouth. When Tess repeated the prayer, Molly joined in.

". . . full of grace, the Lord is with thee. Blessed art thou among women. Blessed is the fruit of thy womb, Jesus. Holy Mary, Mother of God, pray for us sinners, now and at the hour of our death."

"Amen," Jesse said loudly with the two women.

The women crossed themselves.

Molly repeated the question.

"You've found my Mary Kate."

"We have," Jesse said. "I have some hard things to say, Mrs. O'Hara, but I have to say them. Do you want us to call anyone for you? Would you like anyone to be here with you while we talk? One of your daughters? A neighbor?"

Tess reached out and took Molly's hand.

"Molly was my Mary Kate's best friend in the world. Who else could I want here? So say your hard words, Jesse. Ask your questions."

"I've read the police reports from back when Mary Kate went missing," Jesse said.

"At the time you said you had no idea where she might have gone or who she might have gone off with."

Tess nodded.

Jesse nodded, too. "Okay, but it happens that with the passage of time things come to us. We think of things or we hear something that makes us rethink what we thought we knew for sure."

"Sorry, Jesse," she said. "I have searched my mind every day since that July fourth. I have prayed on it, but nothing has come to me. I've asked my other girls so many times they won't even talk to me about it anymore."

"Did you ever suspect anyone in your own family of having anything to do with Mary Kate's disappearance?"

Tess O'Hara looked up and stared into Jesse's eyes as if he had asked the question in a foreign language.

Molly said, "What he means is —"

"I know what he means, Molly," said Tess. "I know what he's really asking and the answer is no."

Jesse didn't push her. Not out of delicacy, but because he knew it would be a waste of time.

"You said back then that Mary Kate had no boyfriends. Is that right?" Jesse asked.

"That's right." There was an air of proud defiance in Tess's voice.

This time Jesse didn't surrender quite as quickly. He was silent for nearly a minute, hoping the discomfort would work on Tess, but clearly this was a woman used to long silences.

Then he said, "I don't know, Tess. She was an awfully cute girl with beautiful eyes. Sometimes girls don't tell their moms things, but moms know better."

"Not my Mary Kate. Just ask Molly. She'll tell you."

It went on like that for another half hour. After the conversation, Molly and Jesse knew nothing more about the circumstances surrounding Mary Kate O'Hara's disappearance and subsequent homicide than they had when they'd entered the house. In her years of grief and unanswered prayers, Tess had turned her daughter from a cute and mischievous sixteen-year-old girl into a saint. No surprise there. The human heart is an amazing editor. Jesse had witnessed it before. He'd seen murdered gangbangers, men who had themselves tortured rival gang members to death, turned into innocent lambs by their grieving families. Why not Mary Kate O'Hara? Molly and Jesse did get the addresses, phone numbers, and e-mail addresses for the rest of the family. Tess hadn't granted her husband a divorce, but it hadn't stopped him from abandoning his family. She had no idea where he was, nor did she seem to care.

Before they left, Jesse told Molly to show Tess O'Hara the photograph they'd brought along.

"What's this?" she asked, staring at the photo.

"It's a tattoo," Jesse said.

"I can see that, but what's it mean?"

"We were hoping you might recognize it, Tess," Molly said. "It was on the chest of the man we found alongside Mary Kate and Ginny."

"Looks like a two-headed snake twisted around a cross. Blasphemy!" She threw the picture onto the floor.

Molly picked it up. "So you don't recognize it?"

Tess O'Hara shook her head violently.

Jesse nodded that it was time to leave. They may have been done with Tess, but she wasn't done with them.

"How was Mary Kate killed?" Tess asked, swallowing hard.

Molly went pale.

"I'm afraid Mary Kate's remains were skeletal, Mrs. O'Hara," Jesse said. "So while the medical examiner is fairly certain of her findings, they are not —"

"How?"

"Multiple stab wounds. I saw the evidence myself last night."

Jesse could see Tess wondering if she should ask for specifics. She decided against it, though she did ask another question.

"You're certain it's her?"

"It's her," Molly said, kneeling down by Tess's side. "But she wasn't alone, Tess. Ginny Connolly has been with her this whole time."

Molly's words didn't seem to register.

"The medical examiner has released Mary Kate," Jesse said. "If you tell us where you'd like her taken, we can arrange that for you."

Again, nothing.

"Give us a minute, Jesse," Molly said.

Pacing as he waited for Molly to finish up, Jesse thought about how someone like Tess O'Hara reconciled her faith with her daughter's murder. He knew that if it had been Jenn or any of the children he'd never had found murdered and left to rot in the floor of an abandoned factory building, chalking it up to God's plan wouldn't have been answer enough for him. But his curiosity or satisfaction wasn't the point. Those two girls found down there needed a voice, and he meant to give it to them.

13

That night Jesse found he didn't have much appetite for anything but amber liquid swirling around two clear ice cubes. Ritual was part of the joy, sure, but so, too, was the beauty of it. The sound of the cubes tinkling against the glass, against each other. The smoky aroma. The earthy hints of peat. Then there was the heat. The pleasant burn on the back of his tongue. The burn in his throat going down. The warmth in his belly. The electricity on the surface of his skin as the warmth spread over him. There had been a time in his life when he'd been able to enjoy the full experience of it, the permission Johnnie Walker granted him to surrender to his lesser angels. He had once been able to drink without hearing Dix's voice in his head. No more.

They had been round and round about Jesse's drinking so many times that he was dizzy from it. They had dissected the reasons, tossed the pieces up into the air, reassembled them a hundred different ways, but there was Jesse with another scotch in his hand. And there was Ozzie Smith on the wall. And the world spinning around in its own good time. One reason Jesse convinced himself that he drank was that it helped him with his silence. Silence was a great asset for a cop. He had learned that early on. If you keep quiet, the people you're interviewing can't bear it. They will fill up the empty space with their own chatter and sometimes, if you're lucky, they fill it up with answers. When they would yammer, Jesse would think of drinking. Of course his drinking had helped him to an early retirement from the LAPD. He wasn't thinking about that now.

There had been many instances over the course of his time in Paradise that he had given up drinking for weeks, even months, at a time. During those times, was he a better chief? Worse? He couldn't say. He was certainly an unhappier one. Because during those weeks or months it was just a show, to prove something either to himself or to someone else. When he realized no one was applauding or handing out cash rewards for his efforts, he went right back to it. But there were nights that he knew exactly why he was drinking. Nights like this night.

The case was getting to him in a way that few cases did. He wasn't a man to let things get under his skin. He prided himself on it, but this case had gotten under his skin, deep under it. And it wasn't just one thing. It was everything. It was that he had been blindsided by it. That neither Molly nor Suit nor anyone on his own force had ever bothered mentioning it to him. It was Tess O'Hara burying herself alive. It was that they still didn't have an ID on the guy in the blue tarp. It was the sight of the skeletons juxtaposed with the photos of the girls. It was that these girls had known Molly. That Molly had been part of their lives and now part of their deaths. It was what the case was doing to Molly.

For his decade-plus in Paradise, Jesse had been able to count on Molly to be Molly. Sure, he loved her, but it was love at arm's length. Sure, he knew her husband and kids, but he didn't involve himself in their lives. It was love born of his need for routine, and no one, not even Johnnie Walker, was more reliable, more rock-solid, than Molly. Until now. She had always been there when he needed her. He trusted her. Her judgments. She wasn't anything like the other women Jesse had been attracted to in appearance or attitude. She wasn't blond or classically beautiful. She wasn't needy. She didn't need or want to be rescued. Suddenly, that had all seemed to change.

It was more than that, too. More than Molly. It was that Jesse had always been good at seeing cases for what they were and what they were not. He had the knack of perspective. Not all cops do. He could almost immediately see how a case would come together, which pieces were missing and which ones were solid. Not with this case. And there was his sense that even though the investigation had only just begun, everyone was holding something back. Molly included. That didn't bode well for a case where the entire town had a twenty-five-year head start on him.

Angry with himself for his self-doubt, Jesse poured himself another. He raised the glass to Ozzie.

"You were the better shortstop, Oz, but not even you would know what to make of this case."

It wasn't all bad. He had finally met the new ME and there was something about her that had gotten his attention. Something more than her sarcasm. Maybe it was that one smile she'd deigned to share with him. He had to admit that he found it hard not to stare at her face.

"What do think, Ozzie? Was I flirting with her?"

Ozzie kept his opinion to himself.

14

They met at the Rusty Scupper in the Swap. The Scupper — a shot and tallboy chaser joint — was as close as Paradise came to a dive bar. It wasn't the kind of bar where you could order an appletini and not draw stares. The Scupper stank of past accidents, of spilled beers, of overturned ashtrays, and of emptied stomachs. It was also a place that kept its secrets. The two of them sat at a wooden booth covered in generations of carved graffiti: mostly the names of drunk men and the women they loved, longed for, or lamented. There were a lot of four-letter words, too. Even the first two lines of a limerick.

There once was a girl from Japan
Who searched the streets of Tokyo for a
    man

That was as far as the poet had gotten.

One of the men at the booth read the lines as he had many times before and laughed as he always did.

"Why you think the guy stopped there?" he asked his booth mate. "I always think about that, whether he just couldn't think of nothing else to write or if he got too drunk or his arm got tired or something. Maybe he got into a fight or the tip of his knife broke off. What do you think?"

But the other man was lost in his own dark recesses. He fidgeted, spinning his beer bottle like a prayer wheel. Peeling off pieces of the bottle's wet label, then rolling the wet, sticky paper around on his fingertips and flicking the balls away.

"So what do you think?"

"Huh?" the fidgety man asked.

"About the girl from Japan."

"I don't know about no girl from Japan," he said, scratching at the label with his dirty thumbnail.

"But what do you think?"

"I think we're fucked." He patted his jacket pockets. "I need a smoke."

"Chill, man. We're okay. There's nothing to connect us to Zevon."

"Nothing but that they found his body right next to the girls. Why did he do that, stick Zevon next to the girls?"

"How could he know the building was gonna go? Shit happens, man."

"But why always to us? I didn't even want to go to Stiles that night."

"Yeah, you said that, like, a million times, but you're full of it. You wanted a piece of her like we all did. It was her friend that screwed everything up. We shouldn'ta let her come."

"Now who's full of it? She wouldn'ta gone with us if —"

He stopped mid-sentence when the waitress stopped by the table to ask if they wanted another round.

"Sure," they both said, just to get rid of her.

"Look, what's done is done. We messed up. This will blow over, too."

"It's never done. And we just killed —"

"Keep it down. Keep it down, man. Take it easy."

Their second round came, though neither of them had half finished their first beers. The fidgety man stood up, again patting his jacket for cigarettes. When he felt them, he let out a loud sigh. He pulled a bent cigarette out of the semi-crushed pack and rolled it around in his fingers.

"I got to have a smoke," he said.

"Go ahead, man. Do it already."

When he was certain his friend was out of the Scupper, he went to the men's room. He slid the little metal bar into the crude hole in the doorjamb and dug his cell out of his pocket.

"Yeah, it's me. I think we got a problem."

When the conversation was over, he went back out to the table and reread the limerick's first two lines, but this time he didn't laugh.

15

The following morning Jesse was sitting in his office, waiting for Healy to show so they could finally get the real police work under way, but they had to get the press conference behind them. Jesse had wanted to notify both sets of parents before going public with the autopsy results, but Ginny Connolly's mother wouldn't be getting into Logan until that afternoon. Molly was going to meet her flight and then drive her back to Paradise. Maxie Connolly had moved out of state six months after her daughter's disappearance. Molly told Jesse that Ginny's father had left before his daughter could walk.

"I don't even remember Ginny's dad," Molly said, "and there were no pictures of him in their house."

Jesse had also hoped to get an ID on John Doe before he spoke to the media, but that wasn't going to happen. It seemed John Doe hadn't been a popular guy. His fingerprints hadn't gotten any hits from the local, state, or federal databases and his DNA sample was at the back of a long line at the state crime lab. The only tangible thing they had to work with was the tattoo.

As he passed the time, Jesse pounded a baseball into the pocket of his old Rawlings glove. Some men paced. Some prayed the rosary. Jesse pounded the ball. Variations on a theme. He had once been an inevitable phone call away from Dodger Stadium. Funny how inevitability is a bit more elusive than the word implies. Jesse's dream of Dodger blue came crashing down during a meaningless exhibition game in Pueblo, Colorado. In the course of a few seconds, his future took a permanent detour away from Dodger Stadium. The team doctor said he'd been unlucky. That if only Jesse had landed on any other part of his shoulder, they probably could have fixed him up like new. *If only,* Jesse thought. *Two of the most dangerous words in the English language.* Without that powerful arm, Jesse's career was shot. All the baseball savvy in the world won't help you throw a runner out at first from deep in the hole. And deep in a hole was where Jesse Stone had found himself.

Jesse was still pounding the ball when Bill Marchand came into the office. Square-jawed, blue-eyed, with black and silver hair that seemed to fall into place of its own accord. About Jesse's height, but more slender, he was one of those men whose clothes hung on him just so. It was no wonder to Jesse that Marchand had succeeded in business and politics. He had the rare combination of good looks and unforced charm that appealed to men and women alike. When Jesse saw that Marchand was close to his desk, he wrapped the fingers of his glove around the ball and put the glove back in its customary spot on his desk.

"Bill."

"Jesse."

"You here as friend or foe?" Jesse asked.

"Both, I suppose."

"Those shutters hold during the storm?"

Marchand smiled. "They did. Thanks for the help."

"What can I do for you, Bill?"

For one of the few times since they'd known each other, Marchand looked uneasy. He'd been sent to talk sense to Jesse about the murders. If it was any of the other selectmen or some other town functionary, Jesse might've been tempted to let him twist in the wind for a while. But Marchand usually had his back and Jesse wasn't a what-have-you-done-for-me-lately? kind of guy. He valued loyalty and friendship even if he wasn't very good friend material himself.

"Boys in town hall nervous?" Jesse said.

Marchand exhaled, laughed. "If you've forgotten, Jesse, Mayor Walker is a woman."

"I haven't forgotten. Bill, it will be easier if you just say what you've come to say."

"She's worried. We're all worried."

"With what's going on, it'd be hard not to be worried."

"Look, Jesse, it's not that. We've had a fair share of crime around here since you came on board. Worse than in some nearby towns, much better than in some others. And you've gotten to the bottom of all of it. But this . . . this strikes at the core of things."

"Tough to sell Paradise as the Best Little Seaside Town in Massachusetts when you've got the skeletons of two murdered girls and an unidentified body with half its head blown off all over the national media."

Marchand nodded. While he didn't always love Jesse's lack of diplomacy, he appreciated Jesse's ability to cut through the bull and get to the point.

"Town hall wants it to all go away quick," Jesse said.

The selectman smiled. "That's about right."

"Quick isn't my job. Doing right is."

"How did I know you were going to say that?"

Jesse shook his head, a sly smile on his face. "Because it's the same answer I give everyone who's ever walked through my office door and tried to tell me how to do my job, from Hasty Hathaway on down."

Marchand raised his palms up in front of him. "Hold on a second, Jesse. I'm a long ways away from that corrupt little prick, Hasty Hathaway. You know I've always erred on your side of things when matters come before us."

"Uh-huh."

"So why give me the treatment? We're friends. I'm only the messenger."

Jesse stood up from his desk chair, turned his back on Marchand, and stared out his window at the water and Stiles Island.

"It's because we're friends that I'm telling you this, Bill. This isn't a parking ticket I can make go away with a wave of my hand. I've got three murders to deal with, two of which are twenty-five years old. Everyone in this town over the age of forty is a suspect for the old murders, and probably the new one, too."

"Including me?"

"Including you," Jesse said. "So tell Her Honor and her minions that I have a job to do and I'll do it my way."

"She can always fire you."

"That's her prerogative, but you'll make sure she doesn't do that."

"I will?" Marchand asked. "Why would I do that?"

"Because you like winning softball championships and you've got no shot without me."

They both laughed at that.

"And," Jesse said, "you know it would look even worse if she tried to get rid of me in the middle of this mess."

"Okay, Jesse, I'll talk them off the ledge, but I can't promise they won't walk back onto it."

"Understood."

"Is there anything else I can do to help?"

Jesse nodded.

"What's that?" Marchand asked.

"New softball uniforms. The old ones are beat-up."

"Anything else?"

"An obvious suspect might be nice."

Marchand laughed. "I'll see what I can do about the uniforms."

They shook hands and Marchand left.

Jesse went back to staring out the window and waiting for Healy to show.

16

The station was ill-equipped to handle the glut of reporters crowded into the small conference room. That suited Jesse fine. When he noticed that most of the reporters weren't wearing their coats, Jesse instructed Suit to shut off the heat in the building, then delayed the beginning of the press conference for twenty minutes. He'd already made sure there were no seats in the room. The more uncomfortable the media were, the sooner they'd stop asking questions and the sooner he could get on with his job. Jesse began with a brief statement about how all the resources of his department and those of the state police would be brought to bear on the cases. His main focus was on the body in the blue tarp. He gave as many specifics as possible on his John Doe.

"Finally," Jesse said, holding up an enlarged print, "we have this. The tattoo is four inches long by three inches wide and is located under the victim's left arm." Jesse put the print down and raised his left arm. "It runs from here to here. Officer Simpson will distribute copies of this image as you leave the premises and it will also be available on ParadisePD.gov, as will many of the facts we discuss here today. The Paradise Police Department would appreciate your help in identifying the deceased."

Jesse was purposefully less forthcoming about the girls. He did confirm that the bodies found at the abandoned factory building were those of Mary Kate O'Hara and Virginia Connolly. He mentioned that the ME believed Mary Kate's death was caused by numerous stab wounds, any of which might have been fatal. That there were notches and scrapes on several of her ribs, scapula, and clavicle that were consistent with wounds from the same knife. He didn't elaborate beyond that. He noticed that even before he opened the floor to questions some of the reporters were rubbing their hands together and blowing on them for warmth. He almost smiled.

A Boston TV reporter Jesse recognized because he had worked with Jenn said, "You didn't give the cause of death for the Connolly girl."

"You're correct."

"Will you give it to us now?"

"No."

After that, the questions came rapid-fire.

"Have you officially notified both sets of parents?"

"I spoke with Mrs. O'Hara yesterday afternoon and Mrs. Connolly will be arriving in town later today."

"Does the ME have any idea how long the blade on the knife was that killed the O'Hara girl?"

"She does. Next."

"Does she have an estimate as to how long the girls have been buried there?"

"We believe the girls have been where they were discovered since shortly after they disappeared."

"You believe that based on what?"

"Science."

Jesse was at his irksome best.

"Is it your theory that the John Doe is somehow connected to the murder of the girls?"

Jesse shrugged. "I'm not in the theory business. I'm in the evidence business."

"Do you have any suspects?"

"Yes."

"Who?"

"That would be telling. Next."

The sparring went on for about fifteen

minutes before Jesse turned the mics over to Healy, who was equally vague, just less annoyingly so. After ten minutes of Healy giving the press the runaround, they surrendered to the cold and left.

Jesse and Healy shook hands. Healy said he had to get back to the office, but that he could return to town tomorrow if Jesse needed him.

"I'll let you know," Jesse said. "Today I've got to talk to Ginny Connolly's mother. Molly's picking her up at Logan. Then it's due diligence time. Going back and re-interviewing everyone mentioned in the old reports."

At the mention of Ginny Connolly's mom, Healy rolled his eyes.

Jesse asked. "What's that about?"

"When you meet Maxie Connolly, you'll see."

17

The minute Maxie Connolly came through his office door, Jesse understood why Healy had rolled his eyes at the mention of her name. She didn't just come through the door. She blew in like a force of nature. Watching her walk toward him, Jesse half expected to hear the blare of trumpets. It didn't take a trained detective to get that Maxie was all about herself. But persistent narcissism catches up to the best of them. It had definitely caught up to Maxie Connolly and had started taking its toll. Time, too. The skin of her face was too tanned and taut. Her hair, too blond and brassy. Her sunglasses were too big, her full-length mink too outrageous, and her jewelry too tasteless. All the knobs on her were turned up to ten. Jesse expected to see Molly trailing behind, but Molly was nowhere to be seen.

"You're cute," Maxie Connolly said in her two-pack-a-day voice. She threw herself in the chair facing Jesse's desk.

"Thank you. Where's Officer Crane?"

She tilted her head in confusion. "Officer Crane? Who's Officer — Oh, Molly. Jeez, little Molly Burke turned out to be some piece of ass, huh? Who woulda figured that? I mean, she was a cute girl, but I never figured she'd fill out like that. I bet you have trouble keeping your hands off that ass of hers."

Jesse stood up and came around the desk. He held out his right hand.

"I'm Chief Stone, but I'd like it if you'd call me Jesse."

She took his hand.

"I'd like it if you would call me yours."

He laughed, but not at her. He'd been around grief and its many forms long enough to give Maxie Connolly a break.

"I'm too old for you," he said. "I'd never be able to keep up."

She bowed her head and smiled.

"Where *is* Molly?"

"She's dropping Al at the hotel."

"Al?"

"Husband number three. Traveling's rough on him. Molly said she'd be here as soon as she got him settled in. Hey, Jesse, you got anything to drink in here?"

"I can get Officer Simpson to get you a

glass of water."

"That the big fella out by the desk?"

"That's him," Jesse said.

"Hunky as he is, I was hoping for something a little stronger than water."

Jesse reached into his bottom drawer and pulled out the bottle of Jameson that someone had given him as a gift last Christmas. He didn't prefer it. Bourbon was usually his backup after Johnnie Walker, but Healy liked it and Healy was the one he most often shared a drink with in the office. He took out a red plastic cup and poured a finger or two for Maxie Connolly. After pouring, he put the bottle away.

She raised the glass to him. *"Slainte."* Maxie took it in a single gulp. "Thank you, Jesse."

He nodded.

They sat there like that for a few seconds, in silence. Cracks were starting to show in her armor. They both knew what was coming next.

"Maxie — may I call you Maxie?"

Now it was her turn to nod.

"I'm going to ask Officer Simpson to come and sit with us."

"Does he have to be in here?" she asked, her raspy voice quivering, her hands shaking.

"I think he does, Maxie. Usually I'd have Molly in here with us. It's that I want someone to take notes when we're talking. I need to pay careful attention to you, and if Officer Simpson is in here with us, I can do that more effectively."

That wasn't it at all. Jesse wasn't comfortable being alone in his office with women he wasn't acquainted with: not suspects, not women he was interviewing. These days it was just too easy for people to make accusations that were impossible to contain or disprove. He had already taken a big risk by giving Maxie a drink and he had no intention of taking any risks beyond that one.

"Can't we wait till Molly gets back?"

"Let me check something."

Jesse went to his door, poked his head through, and asked Suit to see where Molly was at. Just as Suit pressed the button on the mic, Molly walked into the station.

18

Molly Crane's contempt for Maxie Connolly grew exponentially as her dead friend's mother spoke to Jesse about her daughter. Jesse caught on to Molly's ire quickly enough — not that she hid it — but he needed Molly there to listen. She'd grown up on the same street with Ginny and Maxie. She'd been witness to some of the events leading up to the girls' disappearance. Maxie broke down briefly when Jesse assured her there was no mistake about her daughter's remains. She asked for another drink and Jesse gave it to her. The second drink seemed to loosen her up even more.

"She was a lot like her father, Ginny was, all quiet and to herself," Maxie said. "I don't know what I saw in that father of hers to begin with. Sure, Steven was a handsome man, but I swear, the minute after he said 'I do,' it was, like, 'Not anymore.' Nuh-uh. I couldn't get him to do anything. Not go to the movies. Not screw. I'm not even sure how Ginny was even conceived. Musta been a blue moon or something. And believe me, Jesse," she said, putting her hand on his thigh as he leaned against the front of his desk, "I've never had trouble getting men interested in me."

Jesse waited a beat and then went to sit behind his desk.

"All he wanted to do was to go to work, come home, eat dinner, and sit in front of the TV and watch his beloved Sox. I think the only way I could have gotten him interested in doing me was to dress up like Oil Can Boyd. Instead I went and wasted my money on garters and bustiers."

"When did he leave?" Jesse asked.

"Not soon enough." She saw Jesse wasn't amused and gave him a serious answer. "When Ginny was a baby."

"Where'd he go?"

"First to the Dominican to get a quickie divorce, then . . . who the hell knows. Who cares?"

Jesse asked, "Did he ever show any interest in Ginny at all after he left?"

"He wrote to her for a few years, no return address. Then that stopped when Ginny was ten. The letters just stopped coming. Never another one after that."

"Did you ever read the letters?"

"Never. Steve was dead to me."

"Did Ginny ever discuss what was in the letters with you?"

Maxie shook her head. "Me and Ginny . . . we didn't have that kind of relationship. She wouldn't talk to me about stuff like that. Jeez, it near killed her when she started bleeding to come to me and let me explain the facts of life."

Jesse came back around the desk. "Why did you leave town so soon after Ginny went missing?"

"For the same reason Johnny O'Hara split," she said. "I needed to breathe. Without Ginny here, I had nothing to hold me in Paradise any longer. Nothing except pain, and I don't like pain, Jesse. I'd always wanted to get out of this place anyway. Paradise! Yeah, right. If Ginny turned up, I was a phone call away. You think I wanted to bury myself alive like Tess? She never had much use for me, Tess, but I heard she's like a ghost these days. She's still in that little crumby house over on Crestview. Still goes to Mass every day. That was never for me."

Molly couldn't hold her tongue. "But you sent her to Sacred Heart all those years."

"My folks paid for it. Said they didn't

want Ginny to turn out like me. Imagine my own folks saying that. Really knew how to hurt a girl. You got another drink there, Jesse? Suddenly I'm not feeling so chipper."

Jesse poured her another short one just to get her through the remainder of the interview.

When she was done, Jesse went back to the interviews Maxie Connolly had done with the police in the immediate wake of the girls' disappearance. Although the years had eroded her memory somewhat, her statement was consistent with what she had told the police back then. She was watching TV when Ginny went to meet Mary Kate and her other friends at the park for the fireworks and concert. She met friends for dinner. Had a few drinks. Got home around eleven-thirty on the Fourth. She went to bed and was woken up by a panicked call from Tess O'Hara early in the morning.

Jesse explained that he could release the remains to her as soon as she could arrange for a place to take Ginny. That did it. Maxie fell off her chair onto her hands and knees and wailed. She was shaking uncontrollably. Jesse turned to Molly for help, but she was frozen. Molly's eyes were as distant as Jesse had ever seen them.

"Molly!" he said as he knelt down beside

Maxie Connolly. He threw his arm over her shoulders. "Molly! Get her a glass of water or something. Then take Mrs. Connolly into the ladies' room."

Molly finally snapped out of it, though her eyes were still very far away.

Twenty minutes later, Suit was driving Maxie Connolly to her hotel. Molly was sitting across from Jesse. He said nothing. Molly knew all about Jesse and his silence. She was determined not to talk, but somehow words came out of her mouth.

"I'm sorry, Jesse. I hate that woman. I guess I always have. I thought maybe it would have gone away after all these years. That's why I didn't say anything when you had me go pick her up. But it's worse now."

Jesse nodded.

"Maxie never gave a rat's ass about Ginny. Ginny did everything for herself. Made her own meals, washed her own clothes. She cleaned the house. Shopped. Got herself up in the morning. The only real parenting she ever got was from my folks. She raised herself. So of course it killed her to go to her mother about her first period. You won't understand this, Jesse, but when a girl gets her period it can be special or terrible. It's a little bit of both, I guess. Especially for a Catholic girl. We're raised in such a schizophrenic way about that stuff. Sex is made so taboo, but having children is so meaningful. I don't know."

"What aren't you saying, Molly?"

"About what?"

"You tell me."

"Maxie Connolly was a whore and a drunk. Still is, as far as I can tell."

Jesse opened his mouth to speak, but Molly cut him off.

"And don't even bring up Crow to me. That was different. It was only once and it was only about sex and curiosity."

Jesse shook his head. "That's not what I was going to say."

Molly flushed.

"All I was going to say was that everybody is entitled to their grief, Molly. Even Maxie Connolly. You don't have to like her to give her that. Now, get home. We've got an early start tomorrow."

As he watched Molly walk away, Jesse realized just how little he knew about her.

19

Stu Cromwell kept a bottle in his drawer as well. Officially, cops and reporters were wary of the other, but they often shared common vices.

"Hope you like rye," Cromwell said, sliding the glass across his desk to Jesse. "It was my dad's drink. For years I wouldn't go near the stuff for just that reason. Now I can't stay away from it."

"When it's the only thing on the drink menu, it's my favorite."

They clinked glasses.

After a sip or two, Cromwell said, "I didn't expect to see you so soon."

"And I didn't expect to be here."

"You here to talk or to drink?"

"A little bit of both, Stu."

"Well, we drank some. Now you want to talk some?"

Jesse said, "What did you make of all those reporters at the press conference today?"

Cromwell screwed up his face. "Reporters! Those weren't reporters. They were leeches. Most of them will disappear in two or three days. Once the next starlet has an affair or shows up at a club holding hands with another woman, they'll clear out and move on."

"You sound bitter, Stu. That the rye talking or you?"

"Guess I'm a little jealous. Guarantee you any one of those jackals makes more money than I ever did or will. None of them have any real journalism training. Most are failed actors, but it's tough to knock them taking the money. And there's no real future for newspapers. Let's face it, Jesse, this paper might not be long for this world. I spend more time on the phone with my creditors than with Martha's oncologists."

"You seem to know a lot about the enemy," Jesse said.

"Journalism is a small fraternity that's shrinking by the day. When I was in college, I didn't like all my fraternity brothers, either, but I knew a lot about them."

Cromwell poured them both a little more rye.

"Anything else, Jesse?"

"Maxie Connolly."

Cromwell gave a tight-lipped smile. "What

about her?"

"Was she always such a — such a brassy —"

"I believe the word you're struggling for is *broad.*"

Jesse laughed. "I was thinking *character,* but *broad* works."

"She got around."

"Stu, you just called her a broad. This is no time to go polite on me."

"She screwed around and she wasn't choosy about her bedmate's marital status, but the cops looked into that back then. You must have it in your files. They interviewed all of her beaus. Most of them didn't even know Maxie had a daughter. At least she had the good taste to keep the men out of her own house."

"Any men the cops didn't know about?" Jesse asked.

Cromwell hesitated for a beat, then turned his palms up. "None that we could find, and we looked hard," he said, his voice strained.

"Did you know her?"

"Maxie Connolly?" He cleared his throat. "By reputation only until the girls disappeared. You'd see her around town. She was hard to miss, if you know what I mean. Back in the day, she was quite a looker, in a cheap and loud sort of way. How's she look-

114

ing these days?"

"Still loud, but she's forsaken cheap. She was wearing a mink coat and jewelry worth more than a few years' worth of my salary. But after I told her she could pick up Ginny's remains, she wasn't looking so well."

The newspaperman nodded. "I think everyone assumed Maxie didn't really give a tinker's damn about her daughter, but you can never know how someone feels just by looking from the outside in."

Jesse stood. Shook Cromwell's hand. "Thanks for the drink. Next time, the drinks are on me."

"Now I've got a question for you, Jesse. If you don't mind?"

"Shoot."

"Why did you withhold Ginny Connolly's cause of death? It was easy enough for me to find out the likely COD was a severely fractured skull. Besides, you know that stuff will become public knowledge soon enough. Were you going to use it to sort out the crazies?"

"Bingo! The crazies come in waves. We've already had a few come in and call in. Just makes it easier to eliminate the first set. Do me a favor, Stu, don't publish that for at least another day."

"As long as you keep me in the loop, okay?"

When Jesse stepped outside, the weather had turned from crisp to damp and raw. The cold wind that had earlier felt bracing now cut through his exposed skin to the bone. He turned up his collar and walked back to his Explorer. He didn't get far before he was surrounded by some of those reporters Cromwell had just warned him about. They shouted questions out to him as they stuck digital recording devices in his face. The questions were run-of-the-mill and so, too, was Jesse's answer.

"No comment."

When Jesse made it to his Explorer and drove away, he shook his head as he looked at the reporters in the rearview mirror. He hoped Cromwell was right, that they would disappear with the next whiff of celebrity scandal or mayhem. He was a patient man, but he didn't suffer fools gladly. He didn't suffer them at all.

20

Down below, the crests of the waves were chopped white by the wind. When they came ashore, they came barreling in with nasty intent. But that hadn't stopped Maxie Connolly from putting her husband to bed and coming to that old familiar spot on the Bluffs. It had always been their special place. She was hungry for distraction, hungry to get relief from the gnawing guilt, hungry to escape the grief that, until tonight, she had so long kept at bay. All she had been able to picture in her head since leaving the police station was Ginny and Mary Kate clawing at the dirt being shoveled onto them, choking them. It didn't matter that Chief Stone had assured her that the girls were both already dead before the blanket was placed over them and covered in a shallow layer of dirt. She wanted to get that image out of her head at whatever cost. And she wanted to see him again maybe more than anything she had ever wanted, second to having her girl back.

Of all the men she had used and who had used her, he had been the one. It wasn't only about the sex. That's how she knew it then. That's how she knew it now, twenty-five years on. She wanted to feel his arms around her again. Wanted to hear the sound of his voice. To smell his peppery cologne. Just recalling the way his cologne meshed with their sweat and the smell of their sex excited her. It had been a long, long time since a man, any man, had made her feel this way. Certainly not that limp old fool asleep in their hotel room.

In spite of the cold. In spite of the guilt and pain, she didn't know how much longer she could contain herself. She thought she might orgasm at the sound of his tires spitting out gravel as his car approached, but she told herself she had to hold it together. She had to. She couldn't scare him away again. No, she had done that once, and now that she was back she knew she couldn't risk doing it again. Losing him that first time, then losing Ginny, almost killed her.

She turned back toward the ocean, the wind whipping her hair against her cheeks. She listened to the sound of his footsteps as he came near. She couldn't bear to watch him for fear of falling completely to pieces. Then she heard his voice. A voice she thought she would never hear again.

"Hello, Baby," he said. It was what he had always called her.

She finally turned around to look at him. "Hello yourself, Loverboy," she said, as she always had.

As soon as she turned around, she knew things were different. He had changed. Of course he had. How could he not? But there was something in his eyes that frightened her a little. Her fear melted away when he took her in his arms and the smell of his cologne mixed with the sea air.

"I've missed you, Loverboy," she said, her cheek pressed against his coat. "I was hoping you'd call."

"You knew I would."

"You've changed, Loverboy," she said.

"Lots of things have changed since you went away, Baby."

"I had to go."

"I know," he said, brushing her cheek with his thumb. "I know."

"I'm sorry about what happened between us before. I didn't mean to —"

"Shhh, Baby." He put his index finger across her lips. "It's okay. That's all over now."

"I can't lose you again."

"Did you bring them with you?" he asked, cradling her head to his chest.

He felt her nod. "In my bag."

"I want you, Baby."

"Right here? Out in the cold? Can't we go back to your car like we used to? You used to love it when we'd come up here and be together in your car."

"Now, Baby. Right here. The way I like it. Turn around."

"But I —"

"That wasn't a request, Baby. You made me walk away from you once —"

"Please don't be mean to me tonight. Just kiss me one time and then you can do anything you want to me."

He leaned down and kissed her hard on the mouth.

"Thank you, Loverboy." Black tears ran down her cheeks.

"Don't thank me yet, Baby. I'm going to make it all right and take away all your pain."

She turned toward the ocean, lifting up her coat and skirt, sliding her panties down to her ankles, and stepping out of them. It was all she could do to choke back her tears. She had wanted this for so long. With all the men she had been with since, she had pictured him. Imagined it was his touch, not theirs. She hadn't wanted it like this. But he was right, she had made him walk away from her once. Not again. Never again. He yanked her by the hair and shoulder, though instead of lifting up her coat and skirt, he grabbed her throat and pulled her close to him. He placed one hand firmly against the side of her jaw and the other hand firmly against the opposite side of the back of her head. And suddenly she knew she had been right to be afraid. Then, with a sharp snap, he kept his promise, taking all of her pain away forever.

21

Jesse was stirring a good-night drink with his index finger, looking out the window and wondering why he'd moved out here, away from town, in the first place. He wasn't a second-guesser by nature, but since last spring he'd occasionally found himself rethinking past decisions. Not regretting them. Not beating himself up over them, not exactly. But dissecting them, trying to follow how he'd reasoned them out. To see if he had actually reasoned them out at all or whether he had simply reacted.

He'd discussed it with Dix. Sometimes he hated bringing up new subjects with Dix because the man turned everything into a struggle. "What do *you* think it means?" There were moments when he swore he would strangle Dix if he asked him that again. But such was the nature of their relationship. Whenever a new topic came up, it was nearly impossible to get Dix to talk. Then it was impossible to shut him up. At least, that's the way it felt. But it had been different when Jesse mentioned his recent bout of introspection. They seemed to have switched roles.

"How does it make you feel, questioning your decisions?" Dix asked.

"Uneasy."

"Uneasy. Is that all you've got?"

"Uh-huh."

"First you say you don't know when I ask you what you think it means. Then this? Uneasy. That's one word, Jesse. That's terse, even for you."

Jesse shrugged.

"One word and a shrug."

"What do you want me to say?"

"C'mon, Jesse, have I ever answered that question?"

"There's always a first time."

"Indeed there is, like you walking in here and admitting to mulling over past decisions about something other than alcohol and Jenn."

Jesse shrugged again.

"You feel uneasy," Dix said. "Is it the introspection that leads to the unease or is it feeling uneasy that's making you introspective?"

"I don't know."

"Yes you do. You know. There's only one expert on Jesse Stone in this office and it isn't me."

Jesse said, "I think I'm feeling uneasy."

"Good."

"Good?"

"Discomfort means something is going on."

"What?"

"Same answer as before. I can't know what's up, but my sense is that you're changing."

"Changing?"

"Isn't that what you're really talking about, Jesse, changing? Isn't that why you come here?"

"Maybe."

"When did you start this new pattern of behavior, this looking at your decisions?"

"Late last spring."

"And what happened late last —"

But Dix never got to finish his question.

"Suit," Jesse said.

"What about Suit?"

"You know the answer." Jesse's voice changed.

"I do, but I think you need to hear yourself say it."

"Suit was shot. There."

"You sound angry, Jesse."

124

"Do I?"

"Very. Who are you angry at? At me? At the man who shot Suit?"

Jesse ignored the question. "I've had men killed under my command before."

"But you're not here talking about before or other men. What is it about Suit?"

Jesse hadn't answered. He'd sat there in silence for the remainder of the session and he hadn't gone back to see Dix for weeks. Even now, in the midst of a case where Dix's insight and perspective would probably have been beneficial, Jesse hadn't scheduled an appointment. Jesse hadn't answered Dix that day, not because he didn't know the answer. He knew the answer. He had known the answer before he ever walked into Dix's office. He just didn't want to admit it to himself, let alone say it aloud.

Jesse looked down at his drink and noticed the ice had completely melted. Before he could move to do something about it, his doorbell rang.

22

Tamara Elkin stood on the welcome mat, an unopened bottle of Johnnie Walker Black Label in her hand.

"You going to ask me in, Chief, or am I going home to drink this alone?"

"If you stop calling me Chief, I'll consider it."

This wasn't the first time a woman had shown up unexpectedly at his door, but he'd never been shocked by their presence. Surprised? Sometimes. Not shocked. This was different.

"Jesse, may I please come in?" Dr. Elkin said, adding a sarcastic curtsy.

"Please."

As she passed him, he caught a blast of her grassy, sweet perfume. Her curly hair, freed from its bonds, bounced as she walked. The way it moved and framed her face reminded Jesse of a lion's mane. She placed the bottle at her feet and removed her parka to reveal a low-cut white sweater over tight jeans and black cowboy boots. He was staring at her again, as he had when they first met. She noticed, but just smiled that mischievous smile of hers. A smile, Jesse thought, full of promise and trouble.

"What should I do with this?" she asked, holding up her coat.

He took it from her and hung it on a standing coatrack next to his jacket.

She picked the bottle up from the floor and wiggled it. "And this?"

"Follow me."

Tamara Elkin liked her scotch neat. Jesse decided he'd go with it that way, too, as he hadn't had much luck with ice before her arrival. They clinked glasses and sipped. Jesse sat down in his leather recliner. The doctor made herself comfortable on the sofa. And she did seem awfully comfortable, stretching herself out, propping herself up on an elbow. She had long legs and a runner's body, not the kind of build that usually got Jesse's attention.

She pointed at the full highball glass on the coffee table. "I see you've had a head start."

"It's untouched, but not for lack of trying," Jesse said. "I got distracted, then you showed up."

"If you'd like, I can go." Her face lost its smile.

"Don't. I'm glad you're here. And speaking of that . . ."

"I was curious," she said.

"About?"

"You."

"What about me?"

"You don't get a job like mine and not hear about Jesse Stone. You've got quite a rep there, Chief — excuse me, Jesse. Almost from the day I got into the office, you seemed to be a popular topic of conversation. And your popularity seems pretty gender neutral there." She raised her glass to him. "The guys talk about your ball playing mostly and about you and the ladies." There was that smile again. "The women talk about your looks and your . . . I don't quite know how to put it. Your self-containment, maybe? It's like the cowboy thing down in Texas."

"The cowboy thing?"

"I got my medical degree at the University of Texas and interned in El Paso."

"Now the boots make sense," Jesse said.

"Texas, as you might've heard, is big on mythmaking. The biggest and most enduring myth of all is the cowboy myth. You know, the lone man riding the range. The man who needs nothing more than his horse and what he came into the world with. Maybe he's nursing a broken heart or he's out there searching for the right gal."

"And is that going to be you, Doc, the right gal?"

She laughed. It was a deep laugh, deeper than her voice would have suggested.

"Not likely, Jesse. I don't think I've ever been anybody's right gal for more than a few months. Usually, I'm the right gal until the sun comes up. See, I'm a lot like you."

"Are you?"

"More than you know."

Jesse freshened their glasses. "Really?"

"Really. I was a world-class distance runner, five and ten thousand meters, mostly. Got me a full ride at Vanderbilt. I might've made the Olympic team if I hadn't tried to run a steeplechase for fun. I came over a hurdle, my foot hit the water pit, and I slipped. Broke my left femur in four places and wrecked my right knee in the process. Good-bye Olympics. Hello recreational jogging and medical school."

"Ouch."

"How's that right shoulder, Jesse?"

"Gives me a lot of trouble on raw nights like this," he said.

"Don't I know it. I've got a failed marriage under my belt, too. Great guy, just not great for me. Handsome son of a bitch. He was used to a lot of attention. Guess there wasn't enough of me to give him all the attention he needed."

"Okay, Doc, you're batting a thousand so far."

"Heard you've got a weakness for this stuff." She shook her glass, then took her drink in one gulp.

"Do I?"

"That's what the cops from the surrounding towns talk about, your drinking. They tell me you got hired here because you were a drunk."

"They're right. Long story for some other time."

"I'm not judging. I've got my issues, too, if you hadn't figured that out. Got me in some trouble."

"That how you wound up as ME of this corner of the world?"

She nodded. "It'd take some prodigious pretzel logic to explain how coming here from the Office of the Chief Medical Examiner of the City of New York is career advancement."

"You've got my attention," he said.

"Long story for some other time."

"So why are you here, Doc? In my living

room, not in Massachusetts?"

"Not because I'm the right gal," she said, "but because I've been very alone for a very long time and I could use a friend."

She stood up from the couch, walked over to Jesse, bent over and kissed him hard on the mouth.

Jesse was a lot of things, but he wasn't a liar, especially not a liar to himself. He was severely tempted for lots of reasons, not the least of which was the way Tamara Elkin smelled. He liked the way her hair felt against his cheek. Her kiss was also sweet and skillful. He, too, had been alone for months, having seen Diana only once since last spring. But there had been all sorts of temptations he had learned not to give in to.

He stood up even as she kissed him. He clamped his hands around her thin but well-defined biceps and gently pushed her away.

"A friend?" he said. "I could use a friend."

"How about a friend with perks?"

He shook his head. "Bad timing."

She didn't wilt or blush or run. Jesse liked that. She'd taken a risk and didn't shrink when it failed to work out.

"There's someone else?" she said.

He nodded. "There would have to be for me to turn you down. At least, to turn the perks part down. I'm up for the friend thing if you are."

"Could sure use one of those," she said.

"Then I'm your man."

She leaned over and kissed him again, only this time it was softly on the cheek.

23

Jesse rubbed the sleep out of his eyes and rolled out of bed. He threw on some clothes because Tamara Elkin had spent the night in the guest bedroom. She hadn't wanted to drive home after all the drinking they'd done. Jesse was fine with that and he figured the ME was also testing his resolve on the friendship front. So far, so good. He'd managed to keep to his own bed and she to hers.

When he knocked at the guest room door there was no answer. Thinking Tamara might still be asleep, Jesse stepped in to wake her up. But there, reflected in the full-length mirror on the bathroom door, was Tamara Elkin, nude as the day she was born, her slender, muscular body damp and shining, her curly hair somewhat tamed by water. Without the curls, her hair stretched almost to her mid-back.

"Whoa! Sorry," he said, and backed out of the room.

She followed him out a few seconds later, a towel wrapped around her body.

"Don't apologize, Jesse. I didn't plan it, but I guess I wouldn't have minded if you closed the bedroom door behind you instead of going back through it."

"Like I said, under different circumstances . . ."

"Right. This woman of yours —"

"Diana."

"Diana must be something special."

Jesse winked. "She would have to be."

"That's a lovely thing to say. Give me ten minutes and I'll come downstairs and cook us some breakfast."

She was good to her word. Ten minutes later Tamara Elkin was standing in Jesse's kitchen. She was dressed, her hair still damp, her face made up, though she didn't use a whole lot of cosmetics. She didn't have to and it wouldn't have suited her, Jesse thought.

"What do you like for breakfast?" she asked, her head scanning from side to side, studying the layout.

"Scrambled eggs. Hash browns. Toast. Orange juice. Coffee. A donut, too, if one's around."

"For goodness' sakes, Jesse Stone, how do you stay in shape eating like that?"

"You asked me what I like for breakfast, not what I eat. Two different things."

Tamara didn't say anything, but Jesse could tell she was making a mental note. She would be more careful in the future about the questions she asked him and how she asked them.

"How about some eggs, then? I make a wicked morning-after omelet."

Jesse took the bait. "Morning after what?"

"Morning after a bottle of scotch."

He laughed. "Sure."

"Thank you, Jesse," she said.

"For what?"

"It's been lonely for me here. Really lonely."

"I've been kind of alone my whole life," he said. "No matter where I've been or who I've been with."

"I can see that, but alone and lonely are different."

He nodded.

Before either one of them could speak again and just as Tamara was reaching into the fridge for the eggs, Jesse's house phone rang. His cell phone buzzed, too. Tamara Elkin held up her cell to show Jesse she was also getting a call.

Jesse picked up his cordless house phone and walked into the living room. Tamara picked up her phone.

"Jesse Stone," he said.

"We got trouble, Jesse." It was Suit.

"What kind?"

"Jogger found a woman's body at the foot of the Bluffs by Paradise Dunes Road."

"ID?"

"She didn't have any on her, but she's blond and she's wearing a full-length fur coat."

"Maxie Connolly," Jesse said in a whisper.

"You think it's a suicide?"

"We don't even know it's her yet. Who's down there with her?"

"Peter Perkins. I alerted the ME's office, too."

"Good work, Suit. Call Healy and give him the heads-up. I'll be there in twenty minutes."

Jesse hung up. Picked up his cell phone and saw that there was a voice mail from Peter Perkins.

He sent a text of his own to Stu Cromwell, then stepped back into the kitchen.

"What was the call about?" she asked.

"Treed cat."

She shook her head. "Not a dead blonde at the base of the Bluffs?"

"My mistake. Yeah, a dead woman."

"Any idea who it is?"

"Pretty good idea."

"Want to share."

"I think it's better if I don't."

"Okay, you're probably right," she said.

"Get used to that, Doc."

She looked confused. "Used to what?"

He gave her a half-smile. "To me being right about things."

24

It was Maxie Connolly's body. Jesse was sure of it from thirty feet away. The second he caught sight of that blond hair, a shade that wasn't on God's original color palette, he knew. Even if he hadn't recognized her hair, he saw that ridiculous mink coat. But there was nothing ridiculous about Maxie Connolly in death. All the brassiness, the come-on, the crudeness, was gone to wherever those things go when the life is sucked out of you. It was evident from the rips, mud, and twigs caught in her coat that she had come to rest at the base of the bluffs after a long, hard tumble.

Oddly, though, she had come to rest on a long rock, almost as if she were napping. One arm at her side, one bent across her chest. Her legs, separated by only a few inches, were straight ahead of her. Jesse might have been able to accept the illusion of sleep but for two factors impossible to ignore: her head was twisted at an angle that only an owl might achieve and her eyes were open and unseeing. Perhaps because of the cold temperatures or because she hadn't been dead very long, Maxie Connolly's blue eyes hadn't yet taken on the milky, opaque quality of the dead.

It wasn't yet eight o'clock and the narrow slit of beach was pretty deserted in winter. Jesse liked it that way. He was glad to see that Peter Perkins had followed Jesse's long-standing rule against his cops using their sirens or light bars unless they absolutely had to. It was Jesse's experience that all flashing lights did was slow traffic and attract unwanted attention. The only people there were Tamara Elkins, Peter Perkins, the jogger who'd found the body, and Stu Cromwell. Jesse understood that Maxie's death was going to complicate his life and the case. Texting Stu Cromwell accomplished two things: It would help Jesse control the details that got out to the public and it showed Cromwell that Jesse was a man of his word.

Jesse walked over to the ME.

"Do you know the victim's ID?" the ME asked, her demeanor completely professional, her mouth once again neutral.

"Maxie Connolly. Ginny Connolly's mom."

"Holy shit!"

"Uh-huh." Jesse pointed at Maxie's body. "What do you think, Doc?"

"I think she snapped her neck on the way down. My guess, without opening her up, is that C-five or C-six, maybe both, are broken. And although she may look intact, I bet I find a whole host of broken bones and internal damage when . . . you know. Mink coats may cover a multitude of sins, but she took a long, hard fall, Chief."

So it was Chief again. He let it go. "Suicide?"

The ME looked up to the top of the Bluffs, shrugged. "Probably. I don't know that I'll be able to make a definitive determination unless I find evidence indicating something else killed her."

"Evidence like what?"

"Bullet wound, stab wound, ligature marks, like that."

"Did you find a note on her?"

"I just got here a few minutes ago," she said. "But there doesn't seem to be anything on her except her clothes."

Jesse shrugged. Then he said, "I have to treat it as a homicide until you tell me different. So that's what I'm going to do. I'll let you get back to work."

He walked over to where Stu Cromwell was standing. "Give me a few minutes to talk to my man and to the jogger and I'll have a statement for you."

"Okay."

Jesse turned his back on the sea spray. The air was a bit warmer and clearer than it had been the night before, but it was still pretty cold and the icy ocean water didn't help. He called Peter Perkins over.

"What's the deal?"

"Suit dispatched me after he got the call," Perkins said. "I checked the body. She was cold, unresponsive. Did the initial forensics, but it's pretty clear this is where she landed."

Paradise had no budget for a dedicated crime scene unit, so a few of Jesse's cops had been certified by the state to do basic forensics. Jesse didn't love the setup, but he'd given up trying to convince the powers that be to spend the necessary funds. It had been hard enough to get the county to fund a certified ME. When the situation called for it, as with the remains of the girls and John Doe, Jesse asked Healy's people to do the forensics. They had the training and the resources to do it properly.

Jesse asked, "Any sign of a struggle?"

"None that I could see. The scene was pristine around the body and the only footprints near it were the jogger's."

Jesse turned, tilted his head at the jogger. "What's his story?"

"Name's Rand Smythe. Age forty-seven. Retired. Lives down the beach on Falmouth Circle with his wife."

"Retired?"

"Made it big in the computer software business," Perkins said. "One of the big companies bought him out. Says he runs this stretch of the beach beneath the Bluffs every day."

"What happened?" Jesse asked, eyeing the trim, silver-haired Smythe in his cold-weather running getup and two-hundred-dollar running shoes.

Perkins pointed behind him. "Smythe says he came around the elbow there where the bluff juts out and the beach narrows at five-fifty-seven."

"Pretty sure of his timing, isn't he?"

"Watch." Perkins tapped his wrist. "He's got one of those fancy runner's watches, shows the actual time and the time of the runner. Measures his heart rate, all stuff like that. He was checking his time when he noticed the body. He touched her neck. She was cold and there was no pulse. Then he called it in. He didn't hear or see anyone or anything."

Shielding his eyes with his hand, Jesse looked at the sky over the water. Then he turned back to the Bluffs and to the jogger.

"That time of the morning it would just be the gulls," he said. "Tell Mr. Smythe he can go and that we'll keep his name confidential, but that we might need to speak to him again."

"Okay, Jesse."

"And, Peter, when you're done with Smythe, call Molly and get her down here."

As Peter walked away from him, Jesse kept looking up at the Bluffs.

25

Captain Healy and Molly Crane showed up at the crime scene at about the same time. Jesse had just finished giving Stu Cromwell his statement.

Yes, the dead woman was Maxie Connolly, but that's not official until the next of kin is notified and he identifies her. No, there were no obvious signs of foul play. Yes, her death would be investigated as if it were a homicide. Yes, you can quote me on that.

It wasn't much of a statement, but Cromwell would have it first. Though Cromwell knew Jesse wasn't giving him anything he couldn't have figured for himself, he had a statement he could attribute to an official source. That would make all the difference when it came to peddling the finished story.

Jesse made sure Cromwell had left the area before he went over to talk to Healy and Molly.

"This is a mess," Healy said. "You think she killed herself?"

Jesse shrugged. "Seems to be the question of the day."

Healy and Jesse stared at Molly.

"What do you think, Molly?" Jesse asked.

She shook her head and walked to the edge of the water.

Healy was curious. "What's with her?"

"Catholic guilt. She didn't like Maxie very much and didn't do a good job of hiding it."

"What do you think, Jesse?"

"When Maxie first walked into my office, I would never have figured her for this. But by the time she left, I would have changed my opinion. She took the official notification about her girl pretty hard."

"Guess even bad girls live in hope," Healy said. "When you take the hope away, they crash like everybody else."

Jesse wasn't sure what to say to that, so he said nothing.

Healy pointed up. "You think she threw herself off the Bluffs?"

Jesse shook his head. "I don't like it." There, he said it out loud. "I didn't know the woman. Spent a half hour with her, but it seems too *Wuthering Heights* for me, her throwing herself off the Bluffs like that. And how did she get up there? Molly picked her up at the airport and we drove her back to her hotel. A fist full of pills and half a bottle of bourbon, okay, I'm buying. But this . . . I don't like it."

"Yeah, you said that."

"Molly," Jesse said, "come over here a minute."

"What is it, Jesse?"

"Did Maxie mention renting a car to you?"

Molly laughed, then caught herself. "She lost her license. She had a few DWIs down in Florida. Told me about five minutes after she got in the car, like she was proud of it."

"Go get the husband and bring him in to the station. Don't tell him anything, but keep him there. Tell Suit to call the cab companies in town and see if we can't find out if one of them brought her up here. Call Connor Cavanaugh at the hotel and tell him I'll be by later this morning to look at his security tapes from last night and early this morning. And I want any record of phone calls in and out of their room last night."

"That it?" Molly asked.

"For now. Hold on a second," Jesse said, grabbing her arm as she started away. "Healy, can you give us a minute?"

Healy turned and headed toward the body.

"You okay?" Jesse asked, letting go of Molly's arm.

"Fine."

"No you're not."

"I will be."

"Better answer," he said. "I bet you wished Maxie dead a few times when you were younger, huh?"

Molly clenched her jaw.

"I don't know if Maxie suicided or if she was murdered, but there's one thing I'm sure of."

"What's that, Jesse?"

"Your wishes had nothing to do with it. Now, go get the husband."

26

Healy and Jesse circled around to the other side of the bluff and climbed the switchback stone steps up to the top. Healy was pretty winded when he finally made it, a full thirty seconds after Jesse. But both of their lungs burned as they sucked in gulps of frozen air. When Healy caught his breath, he turned to face the ocean.

"Helluva a view from up here with the sun low in the sky," Healy said. "The ocean, Stiles Island, the harbor, and the town. You can understand why all the rich families built their places on the Bluffs. Probably seemed like heaven."

"Just another name for Paradise. Come on."

They walked around to the spot on the bluff above where Maxie Connolly's body had landed. They were careful as they approached, checking the ground for footprints, drag marks, signs of a struggle, but there wasn't much to see except for some snapped branches on the winter-bare hedge that outlined the ledge of the bluff. This spot, the highest point of the Bluffs, had become a popular spot for visitors, as it offered the best view of Paradise and the rest of the area. On a very clear day, you could look south and see all the way to Boston. The town fathers hadn't seen fit to put up a protective fence or guardrail, but had gotten a local nursery to plant some waist-high hedges along the perimeter of the bluff.

"Looks like that spot there's where she went over," Healy said, pointing at the snapped branches. "No handbag or anything left behind."

Jesse nodded. "None by the body, either. Can we get a forensics team up here? Peter did the basics by the body, but I want a more thorough job done where she went over."

"They're already on the way."

"That's why they pay you the big money," Jesse said.

"Looking more and more like a suicide."

"Maybe."

"I know, Jesse. You don't like it."

"I don't, but I have to admit that it looks like suicide."

"Let's see what the ME has to say."

Jesse shook his head. "I already spoke to her. She doesn't think she's going to find anything definitive to say it's not suicide. A suicide note would be nice. Would make our jobs a lot easier."

"Got a pen and a piece of paper?" Healy asked.

"Why, you thinking of jumping, too?"

Healy just laughed.

They moved about twenty yards to the right of where they assumed Maxie Connolly had gone over and stepped close to the edge of the adjoining bluff. When they looked down they could see the activity below. Maxie's body was being bagged and the ME's wagon had arrived to take her back to the morgue.

"Mother and child reunion," Healy said to himself.

"What?" Jesse asked.

"Nothing. It's just that Maxie and her daughter will be in the same place together after all these years."

Jesse turned to look at his friend.

"You feeling okay, Healy?"

"Why?"

"You're being pretty philosophical this morning."

Healy grunted, then changed the subject.

"I don't think I could do it this way. You know, jump," he said.

"Uh-huh."

"You eat your gun, it's over. There's no time to want to take it back. Regret isn't an option. You jump and there's that fear and panic, even if it doesn't last long. I wouldn't want to die like that."

Jesse kept silent. After he'd discovered Jenn cheating on him and his drinking had gotten out of control, he'd had a few bad moments, moments when he'd considered eating his gun. But that was a long time ago and he had no time for bad memories at the moment. He had four bodies on his hands, three separate cases, and almost nothing to go on.

"I'm heading back to Paradise," Jesse said. "I've got to tell the husband. Call me if you find anything."

Healy gave Jesse a careless salute. "Aye, aye."

Now nearly back on the beach, Jesse looked behind him at the zigzagging stone steps he'd just come down. Maxie's trip down had taken much less time.

Al Franzen didn't look so much confused as defeated. Franzen sat on the other side of Jesse's desk dressed in an expensive pair of gray wool slacks, a darker gray sweater, a black blazer, and black loafers. But the clothes hung off him, the way clothes often hung off gaunt old men. He had a hangdog expression on his tanned face. Yet as thin as he was, Franzen's jowls and the skin of his neck had long ago succumbed to gravity. He wore his wispy gray hair in a bad comb-over and sat stoop-shouldered, with his bony hands in his lap. His hands were covered in brown splotches. But Jesse could see in Franzen's age-faded brown eyes that he already knew Maxie was dead. It had been his experience that the next of kin often knew before they were told.

"Mr. Franzen," Jesse said, "I'm afraid I have some bad news for you."

Al Franzen nodded as Jesse spoke the

words he had repeated many times before. He had once tried to think of a different way to start these conversations. He had since given up trying. There was no good way to say it.

"Maxie is dead," Franzen said.

Jesse nodded.

"I knew it."

"How did you know it?" Jesse asked.

"I'm old, Chief Stone, not stupid. Even at my age I can put two and two together to make four."

"I meant no disrespect."

But Franzen seemed not to hear. "I was a millionaire five times over by the time your mother changed your first diaper. I'm not the old fool Maxie thought I was. I knew she thought she was taking me for a ride, but, God help me, I loved her. She was the most exciting woman I had ever met, and just being around her . . ." Then he gathered himself. "I'm sorry, Chief Stone, forgive me."

"No need to apologize. But I have to ask you, how did you know Maxie was dead?"

"She wasn't in the room when I got up. Her pillows were cold and untouched. Her side of the sheets was smooth and cold. And then Officer Crane comes to my door and asks me to get dressed and come with her, but won't tell me why. Like I said, it's simple math."

Jesse asked, "Did she receive any calls or visitors last night? Did she make any calls?"

"I don't know. I'm afraid I am not a well man and I take medication that makes me a very sound sleeper. A bomb could have gone off in the next room and I wouldn't have heard it."

"But why did you assume she was dead, Mr. Franzen? She might just have gotten arrested or simply gone missing or run off."

Franzen shook his head. "No, I knew. I knew from the minute we got the call for her to come back to this town that Maxie wasn't going to ever leave it again."

Jesse didn't ask how or why he knew. He asked, "Do you think your wife was capable of suicide?"

The old man looked at Jesse as if he had spoken to him in Japanese.

"Suicide! Maxie? That's crazy. You're telling me she killed herself?"

"A jogger found her on the beach at the bottom of an area of Paradise known as the Bluffs. It's way too early on in the process to draw a conclusion, but there are no signs of a struggle. Preliminary indications point to suicide."

Maybe Al Franzen wasn't defeated after

all. He stood up and slammed a hand on Jesse's desk. "Nonsense! Maxie was the most alive person I ever met. She wouldn't."

But instead of feeling boosted by Franzen's reaction, Jesse sagged. He remembered how Maxie had reacted the day before. The truth was, you couldn't ever really know what was in someone else's heart. It was difficult enough to know what was in your own.

"She took the news about Ginny pretty hard," Jesse said. "Yesterday, she fell apart sitting in that same chair when I told her she could collect Ginny's remains."

Al Franzen slumped back in the chair. He had put up a fight, a good fight, but Jesse could see that the truth was dawning on Al as it was dawning on him. Maxie probably *had* killed herself.

"When you said you knew Maxie was never going to leave Paradise again," Jesse said, "what did you mean?"

But Jesse had lost him. Al Franzen had retreated into himself, his eyes as unseeing as Maxie's. Jesse waited a few minutes to let Franzen collect himself before explaining to the old man that he would have to identify his wife's body.

28

Rod Wiethop lived in a crappy two-room apartment above a deli in the Swap. He wasn't happy about being woken up by the pounding at his door and he was even less thrilled when he pulled back the door to see who had been doing the pounding. He sneered at the badge on Jesse Stone's jacket.

"Yeah, what?" he asked, a freshly lit cigarette dangling from his lips.

"I'm Jesse Stone, chief of the Paradise PD. Can I come in, Mr. Wiethop?" Jesse pronounced the *th* in Wiethop's name like the *th* in Thursday.

"It's Wiethop, like *Wee-top,*" he said, his voice all gravelly from smoke and sleep. "And no, you can't come in. What's this about?"

Jesse didn't react, not immediately.

"You drive the six-to-six shift for Paradise Taxi?" he asked.

"What of it?"

Jesse gave Wiethop the cold stare and asked, "Is that yes or no in asshole-speak?"

Wiethop shook his head. "Jeez, cops. It's too early for this crap. Come on in."

Jesse stepped into what passed for the living room. It had all the charm of a holding cell. Jesse guessed Wiethop had probably spent a fair amount of time in holding cells.

"What can I do you for, Chief?"

"You had a fare last night. A blond woman wearing —"

"A fake fur coat. Yeah, I'm not likely to forget her. She was a pretty hot piece of skirt for an old working girl. Something to drink, Chief?" Wiethop asked, holding up a half-empty bottle of cheap vodka.

"No, thanks. Little early in the day for vodka."

"You mind if I do? It's the only thing I can drink."

Jesse said, "Knock yourself out."

Wiethop filled a dirty coffee mug and took a gulp, blowing cigarette smoke out his nose as he did.

"About this woman you're not likely to forget."

"What about her?"

"Where'd you pick her up and where'd you drop her off?"

"Easy." He took another gulp followed by

157

a deep drag on the cigarette. "Paradise Plaza at about eleven-thirty and dropped her at the Gray Gull maybe five minutes later."

Jesse was already shaking his head before Wiethop was halfway done with his answer.

"Try again."

"Check my trip sheet if you don't believe me," Wiethop said, lighting another cigarette with the one he was still smoking. Jesse had already rattled him.

"Did that. Checked your trip sheet. Been to the Gray Gull. You're full of it."

Jesse could see the wheels turning in the cabbie's head. Wiethop poured himself some more vodka, took all of it at once, and winced.

"Okay, all right." He crushed the second cigarette out without even taking a hit. "The old babe gave me fifty bucks on the arm if I said I took her to the Gull."

"That's a start. Where'd you really take her?"

"The Bluffs, over by the old Salter place. I told her she could wait in the car until her trick showed up. She didn't like that too well. Threw the fifty and a ten at me and told me to shove it."

"You thought she was a hooker?"

"C'mon, Chief. Made sense, right? Getting picked up at a hotel and then asking to

158

get driven up to some deserted place on the Bluffs. Shit, you knew she was gonna get in somebody's car after that. She's wearing that big fake fur and she was all made up and smelled like a million bucks' worth of perfume, too."

"That was no fake fur, Wiethop, and she was no hooker."

"You're kidding me." He shrugged. "I didn't figure that. But I'm telling you she was meeting somebody. I'd stake my ass on it. She could hardly sit still in her seat. I thought she was going to make a big score."

"You're sure you left her by the Salter place and not further up the Bluffs?"

Wiethop held his hands out at Jesse. "Why would I lie to you about something as stupid as that?"

"All right. Thanks." Jesse turned to go.

"Listen, Chief, you ain't gonna tell my boss about —"

"About the extra fifty and lying on your trip sheet? Not unless I find out you were lying to me. I find that out and it won't be your boss you'll have to worry about answering to."

"I wasn't lying to you. I swear."

Jesse wasn't sure he believed him.

29

Connor Cavanaugh was an old football buddy of Suit's. He was head of security at the Paradise Plaza, the one full-service hotel in Paradise. The rest of the accommodations in town were a patchwork quilt of quaint inns and fussy Victorians converted into B-and-Bs by overwrought Bostonians or New Yorkers with fantasies of simpler lives. Winter was the dead zone for any place with vacant rooms in Paradise. There was the regatta in summer, the changing foliage in autumn, and the antiques sales in spring to lure outsiders to town. Usually, there was no equivalent winter magnet to draw people to Paradise, but this year there was murder.

Cavanaugh perked up when Jesse strode into his basement office. He stood up and gave Jesse a big handshake. Though Cavanaugh had put on some weight since his playing days, his belly creeping over his beltline, he was strong. Jesse flexed his hand to get feeling back into it once Connor had let it go.

"How you doing, Jesse? All these bodies can't be good for anyone but us. We got a run on rooms. A lot of the news crews are staying here."

"I'm doing okay, but I need to get these cases solved."

"I hear you," Cavanaugh said. "You remember how to use the system?"

"Uh-huh."

"I'll go do my rounds, then. I got it all queued up for you."

"How about incoming and outgoing calls?" Jesse asked.

"Right. I almost forgot about that." Cavanaugh took a slip of message paper out of his back pocket. "There was one incoming call at ten-forty-seven and an outgoing call at eleven-twenty. Anything else?"

"Do you have the numbers?"

Cavanaugh hesitated. "Technically, we're not supposed to keep track of this sort of thing. Our guests have a right to their privacy."

"Tell it to the NSA. Do you have the numbers? It will be between the two of us."

Cavanaugh handed the slip of paper to Jesse. "That's the incoming number there. I don't have the outgoing. Guests can dial out directly. It only comes up on our records as local, long-distance, or overseas."

"That's fine," Jesse said. "I'll take it from here."

Jesse waited for Cavanaugh to leave. He looked at the number of the incoming call. He didn't recognize it, though he didn't have any expectation that he would. He was confident he already knew the outgoing number. That was Maxie calling Paradise Taxi for her cab. He had gotten the time of that incoming call when he'd been to the cab company's offices earlier that morning. The times matched up. He called Suit, gave him the incoming number, and told him to trace it. He also told Suit to make an appointment for him with Lance Szarbo, the only viable witness to the girls' disappearance.

Jesse got to work on the hotel's video surveillance footage. He knew that there would be coverage in the hallway outside Maxie and Al Franzen's room, in the elevator, all entrance and exit points, the lobby, and all other public areas of the hotel. He began with hallway footage, speeding through the video until he saw Suit accompanying Maxie back to her room. From that point on, he watched the footage at a slower rate, though he didn't figure he

162

would see Maxie appear again until after her phone call to Paradise Taxi. He was wrong.

Maxie came out of her room at nine-twenty-three p.m. She wasn't wearing her full-length mink, or any other coat, for that matter. And without the coat on it was easier to see what men had seen and still saw in her. At sixty-plus years of age, she had the body of a forty-year-old. And she carried herself with a kind of ferocious sexuality that some men found irresistible. Jesse marveled at it because there was no one there to watch her. She might have had some work done, but so what? She was wearing a satiny silver blouse, a not-too-short black skirt, and black stilettos. She went directly to the elevator. Exiting the elevator, she went to the Whaler Lounge. She ordered a drink at the bar. It wasn't two minutes before several men approached her. Though it was difficult to see her facial expressions, it wasn't difficult to see Maxie Connolly was in her comfort zone.

It went on like that for about a half hour: men coming, toasting, flirting, and going. Then at ten-oh-nine another man approached her, but unlike the other men, Jesse recognized this one. It was Alexio Dragoa, the fisherman. Although Jesse had spotted the fisherman at the bar, he hadn't had any reason to connect him to Maxie Connolly. He wasn't sure he had one now. That was until he enlarged the images and saw that Maxie was less than pleased to see Dragoa. She tried standing, moving away, but he grabbed her by her arm, pushing her back down onto the bar stool. That wouldn't have been difficult for Alexio. He was a powerfully built man with incredibly strong forearms, wrists, and hands. Still, Alexio didn't appear to be assaultive. It was almost as if he was pleading with Maxie, gesturing with his arms and hands. After a few minutes of that, Alexio backed off. Maxie stood and walked by Dragoa. She headed for the elevator. Alexio remained in the bar, had three drinks in short order, then left. Maxie went straight back to her room and didn't reappear until eleven-twenty-two, this time in her fur coat. She seemed in a hurry. *But for what?* Jesse wondered. *For what?*

30

Suit had gotten back to Jesse even before he had finished going through the surveillance footage. The incoming call to Maxie's room had come from one of the four remaining pay phones in Paradise. At that time of night, there wouldn't have been any open businesses, nor much street traffic in the vicinity of the phone. The incoming call was a dead end. The other thing Suit had to say was even less encouraging. Word about Maxie Connolly's "suicide" was out and the phones were ringing off the hook.

"What should I tell them, Jesse?"

"Confirm the death. Tell them that pending the ME's report we have no comment and that we don't speculate. As soon as we have the ME's findings, we will release a statement to the press."

"Will do, Jesse."

After the call, Jesse rode the elevator up to Al Franzen's room. During his conversation with Suit, it had occurred to him that Maxie Connolly must've had a cell phone. Yet the call had come to her room and she had used the room phone to call Paradise Taxi. Was it significant? He didn't know. Might be, might not. He was also curious about her handbag. Like her coat, Maxie's bag had been expensive but too much. He noticed it the second she blew into his office. It was by some Italian designer. Jesse knew that because it was fairly covered in the designer's name. The thing was huge and had all sorts of gold studs and diamond accents on it. But it hadn't been found on the beach below the Bluffs or at the place where Maxie had gone over. His best guess was that when he found the cell phone, he'd also find the bag. And it was a good bet he'd find them both in the hotel room.

He knocked at Al Franzen's door. When there was no response, Jesse worried that things were going to go from terrible to worse. That he was going to have to call Connor Cavanaugh upstairs and use his passkey to get in. That they would find Al Franzen dead, a victim of his own frail health or with the aid of an outside party. But Jesse relaxed when he heard stirring from inside the room.

"Coming," he said. "Coming."

Franzen's already sad face fell to the floor at the sight of Jesse Stone. He couldn't imagine that the police chief at his door meant anything good. He gestured for Jesse to come in.

"I'm sorry to bother you, Mr. Franzen."

The old man seemed not to hear. "I've made arrangements for Maxie and Ginny's burial for when they release Maxie's body. I think they should both stay here, together."

Jesse said, "I can make sure the ME holds on to Ginny's remains until she releases Maxie to you. Please let me know when the service happens. I'd like to be there."

Franzen nodded his appreciation.

"You know, Chief, people thought Maxie didn't care about Ginny, but she did. She told me what people here thought of her. Sometimes I would catch her holding her girl's picture and crying. Old men know grief. I have buried a wife and a daughter myself. Now two wives."

"Sorry."

"We all grieve in different ways. Maxie, I think, has been grieving her whole life, even before Ginny. I don't claim to understand it. I don't know what the pain was in her life before what happened to Ginny. Maxie would never talk about it. But there was a hurt there. Deep-as-a-mountain-is-high

167

kind of hurt. And Maxie would go from man to man to ease the pain. I knew she did, maybe even the day after we were married, but it wasn't about cheating. It was about escaping."

"You're a wise man, Mr. Franzen."

"I'm an old man. Sometimes those are the same things. What can I do for you?"

"We didn't find Maxie's handbag with her," Jesse said. "Is it here, do you know?"

"That silly thing," Franzen said, shaking his head. A sad smile on his face. "So big and showy. If Maxie could have gotten neon on it, she would have. That was my Maxie. But no, Chief, it's not here. I looked."

"Did she have a cell phone?"

"Sure. She kept it in that bag of hers. Why, you didn't find that, either?"

"You should have been a cop."

Franzen shook his head. "No money in it."

Jesse laughed.

"Can you give me her cell number?"

Al Franzen recited the number, which Jesse entered directly into his cell.

"Did Maxie ever talk about the people she knew in town? Did she mention old friends?"

"You mean old boyfriends?" Franzen asked.

"I mean anyone."

"Not really. She used to talk only about how people here didn't like her very much, but she never talked about anyone in particular, though . . ."

"What?"

"I don't know. Maybe it's just my old mind playing tricks on me or my mistaking it for her missing Ginny," Franzen said.

"It might help."

"I got the sense that there was always somebody here for her. You know, like the one true love that got away."

"But she never said anything or mentioned a name?" Jesse asked. He had thought about mentioning Dragoa's name, but decided against it. Once a name got out there, he wouldn't be able to take it back. And if there was a name even an old man might remember, Dragoa was one that would stick.

Franzen didn't hesitate. "No, I'm sorry. Like I said, it was just a sense that I got. When Paradise would come up occasionally, Maxie would get a faraway look in her eyes. I'm not so old or feeble that I don't remember what that kind of look means."

Jesse shook Al Franzen's hand and left. Again, with more questions than answers.

31

None of the yachting club membership were pleased about Alexio Dragoa docking the *Dragoa Rainha,* the *Dragon Queen,* at the marina. They weren't pleased about any of the few remaining commercial fishing vessels left in Paradise operating out of there, but they were most displeased with Alexio. The other fishermen had, at least, made an attempt to keep their boats freshly painted and presentable for the tourists and visitors to town. They made sure to sell some of their catch at dockside during peak tourist season to lend an air of authenticity to Paradise's alleged seagoing past. Those had been the stipulations Alexio's dad and the other fishermen had agreed to in order to be grandfathered in when ownership of the marina changed hands. But Alexio, like his father before him, paid them little mind.

Neither of the Dragoas, father nor son, much cared for appearances. They were real men of the sea, workingmen, tourism be damned. With each passing year, there were fewer working boats. Most of the fishermen had given up years ago, either getting out of the business altogether or refitting their vessels to service tourists for game-fishing excursions or for corporate outings.

Jesse stood dockside, watching as the *Dragoa Rainha* was skillfully maneuvered into her berth. Dragoa's boat was kept far away from where the fancier yachts were docked during the season. Most of the leisure craft were either already out of the water for the winter or had been sailed to warmer climes by their owners. Even the few other holdout working boats had been out of the water for weeks. Only the *Dragoa Rainha* remained. Jesse was no sailor, so he just stood aside when Alexio's crewman threw ropes onto the dock. The crewman then jumped onto the dock and used the ropes to secure the boat. Jesse nodded at the crewman, who returned the nod before getting back on board.

Ten minutes later, Dragoa and the crewman unloaded three red-and-white coolers and a hand truck onto the dock. The crewman stacked the chests onto the hand truck.

"Remember, the bottom two are for the Lobster Claw. The top one is for the Gull,"

Dragoa said.

"Aye, Skip."

"And collect the money. Cash. I don't want to hear no bull from them about —"

"No checks. I got it, Skip."

Jesse waited for the click-clacking of the hand truck's wheels along the boards of the dock to quiet before talking to Dragoa.

"Skeleton crew," Jesse said.

"No need for more men this time of year."

Dragoa was a good-looking man. Some men are beaten down by rugged, outdoor work. Some are honed by it, their features chiseled and set by the cold, the wind, and the water. That was Alexio Dragoa. Beneath a sea-tousled mop of ink-black hair, he had fierce brown eyes, a square, cleft chin, and a nose that had seen more than one bar fight. But it was the kind of nose that added character to his looks. *Good thing he has looks,* Jesse thought, *because he has no manners.* It was also good because Alexio smelled perpetually of fish, cigarette smoke, and exhaust fumes.

"What can I do for you, Stone?" he asked, lighting up a cigarette.

Jesse didn't bother asking Dragoa to call him by name or Chief. Alexio's range of public grace wavered between impolite and downright rude. And he had no love for

Jesse or any town official. With Jesse, Dragoa's dislike was more straightforward. He didn't appreciate the Paradise PD arresting him every time he got into a tussle at a local bar. With the other town officials, Dragoa's distaste was more amorphous and ingrained. Almost as if it had been passed down from his late father, Altos. The Dragoas had been feuding for decades with the selectmen and every other regulatory agency in town. They wanted to do their work, run their business, and live as they pleased. Whether it was Alexio's rust-bucket F-150, the condition of his boat, or his refusal to sell a part of his catch dockside during tourist season, he did everything he could to flaunt his distaste for the powers that be.

"Small haul," Jesse said, pointing at the retreating crewman.

"What, you come to bust my chops about not selling part of my catch to the stupid tourists?"

"I don't see any tourists."

Dragoa laughed, smoke billowing out his mouth and nostrils.

"Stupid rule," he said. "The tourists don't even cook the stuff they buy. They end up throwing it out. Wasting it. It's a sin to waste the fruit of the sea that way."

"Uh-huh."

"So what is it, Stone?"

"Let me buy you a beer."

"No, thanks. You're okay, not like the other pricks in this town, but I don't drink with cops."

"We can have a beer and talk or we can talk at the station. Your choice, Alexio."

"I don't have to talk to you at all."

"True, but I can make you come down to the station anyhow," Jesse said.

"What for?"

"To talk about Maxie Connolly."

Jesse thought he caught a twitch at the corner of Dragoa's lip.

"Why you wanna talk to me about Mrs. Connolly?"

"Because she's dead."

There it was again, that twitch. The cigarette fell out of the fisherman's mouth. That was about the most emotionally expressive thing Jesse had ever seen Dragoa do. Alexio was good at expressing anger, but not much else. Clearly, Maxie's death hit him hard.

"How about that beer?" Jesse said.

"Maybe something stronger."

"Sure."

Dragoa pushed himself off the boat and began a slow walk toward the Gull.

32

In winter, the Gray Gull was empty at that hour of the afternoon. Even so, they tried to stop Dragoa from entering.

"I can't let him in here, Jesse," said the hostess, looking a little panicked. "He's been banned by the boss. He's caused too much trouble in here."

"What, you buy my goddamned fish but I'm not good enough for this —"

Jesse cut him off. "It's okay. He's with me. It's official police business. He misbehaves, I'll just shoot him."

The hostess, looking even more panicked, stepped aside. She pointed at a two-top at the rear.

"I'll send a waitress over."

Jesse had club soda with lime in a tall glass. Dragoa had a double bourbon, which Jesse let the fisherman drink in silence. It was only after he ordered them a second round that Jesse spoke.

"You confronted Maxie Connolly in the Whaler Lounge last night. What was that about?"

"I don't have to talk to you."

"You don't, but I have video of you shoving Maxie Connolly back onto her bar stool last night. A few hours later, she was dead. You want to leave that with no explanation, fine," Jesse said, purposely not mentioning how Maxie had died.

"I was in the bar drinking already."

"I saw that. Did you know Maxie Connolly? Were you friends with Ginny?"

Dragoa got a sick look on his face. "No. No. I was older than Ginny. Why you bring her up?"

"You living in a cave these days, Alexio? We just found Ginny and Mary Kate's bodies. That's why Maxie was back in town, to bury her girl."

"Yeah. Yeah. I know." Dragoa waved his hand dismissively. "First I hit on her. I had a few in me and every guy in the bar hit on her. I figured, why not? I used to have a thing for her when I was young. Every guy in town did. Then when she blew me off and I got all mad, I felt bad. So I grabbed her arm and apologized. Said I was sorry to hear about Ginny. That's all."

Jesse bought Dragoa's story as far as it

went, then asked, "Did you know Ginny?"

"Small town, Chief. It was smaller back then."

"That's not much of an answer."

"I was older than her, but I seen her around school. Everybody knew everybody."

Jesse didn't ask a follow-up. He let the silence speak for him. He looked out the glass doors at the wind chopping the water, thought of Maxie's body at the base of the Bluffs. Silence could often be more effective than threats, even with the men like Dragoa, but the fisherman seemed determined to say not another word. Jesse finally broke the quiet.

"So what did you figure was going to happen between you and Maxie when you approached her? That you were going to get a room together?"

"I don't know what I figured. I wasn't thinking with my head. I had a few in me."

Jesse asked, "And what did you say about Ginny?"

Dragoa got that look on his face again, like just before and when the cigarette fell out of his mouth. "I said I was sorry about what happened to her."

"Why should you be sorry? I thought you said you didn't know her."

"That was a bad time in Paradise, Chief.

Bad for everybody. People think my poppa and me, we don't care about nothing. I care."

Dragoa took a mouthful of bourbon. Went to light a cigarette. Jesse grabbed the lighter out of his hand.

"Not in here."

Alexio asked, "What happened to her, anyways?"

"In a minute," Jesse said. "Where'd you go after you left the Whaler?"

"Helton."

"Why'd you drive all the way over to Helton?"

"I got a room with somebody didn't mind getting a room with me," Dragoa said.

"A hooker?"

"Yeah. I ain't married no more."

"How long were you with the hooker?"

"All night. I paid for the night. Drove straight to the *Rainha* this morning."

"What motel?"

"First you tell me what happened to Maxie."

"A jogger found her at the base of the Bluffs early this morning."

Dragoa bowed his head. "That's too bad," he said. "How?"

"She either jumped or was pushed off."

"You think it was me?" Dragoa snorted.

"Wasn't me. I was at the Helton Motor Inn from about eleven o'clock on with a blonde called herself Trixie. Go check."

"I will."

"Can I go now?"

"Finish your drink," Jesse said.

"Nah, I don't feel like drinking no more."

With that, Dragoa stood and drifted out of the Gull. Jesse watched him go. He would check the fisherman's alibi, but Jesse didn't think he was lying. Still, there was something about Dragoa that didn't sit just right.

33

Darkness had settled over Paradise by the time he got back to the station, but it wasn't dark enough to hide him from the press gathered outside. Jesse waded through them without bothering to say "No comment." A TV type Jesse recognized from a national morning show stood in his path and shoved a microphone in his face.

"Do you think Maxie Connolly's death is connected to the other murders?"

Of course it is, you idiot. It's connected whether Maxie committed suicide or was herself murdered. It's not a question of if, but of how.

"No comment" is what Jesse said, then gave the correspondent his coldest stare, the stare he used to give pitchers who had thrown at his head. The TV guy withered under it, stepping out of Jesse's path. Jesse made sure none of the reporters followed him into the station.

"Everything confirmed for tomorrow in Boston?" Jesse asked Suit.

"He's expecting you around ten o'clock at his office."

"Heard from the ME?"

"I checked. She says sometime tomorrow."

"You're getting good at this, Suit. I don't know. I may have to keep Molly on the street permanently even after the town doctor clears you for active duty."

Suit slumped in his chair. "Just kill me now."

"Relax. I was kidding."

"Don't kid like that, Jesse. I'm going nuts in here."

"Anything else?"

"Molly's in your office and . . ."

"And what?"

"I don't know if this is legit or not, Jesse, but I got a call from a guy who says he might be able to help us ID our John Doe."

"Let's get him in here."

Suit waved his palm back and forth. "This guy sounded a little crazy to me. You want to waste your time with some nut?"

"We haven't had any luck otherwise. Get him in here."

"That's the other thing."

"Suit, come on. Don't make me pull teeth."

"He lives in some weird little town in Arizona. Diablito, he said. Says he saw the story on the news. He says he recognized the tattoo."

"Name?"

"Wouldn't give it to me. Said he would only give it to my superior officer."

Jesse shook his head.

"See what I mean, Jesse?"

"Okay. Give me his number and I'll call him."

Suit handed him a slip of paper that Jesse put in his back pocket as he headed for his office, where Molly was pacing a rut in the floor.

"What's up?" Jesse asked, sitting himself down in his chair.

"You smell like cigarette smoke."

"Compliments of Alexio Dragoa. We had a talk."

She made a face. "Him? What did you have to talk about with him?"

"He says he knew Ginny Connolly. That the town was smaller then. That all you kids knew each other. True?"

Molly shrugged. "I guess so. Twenty-five years ago we weren't as connected to Boston. People didn't commute to work from here like some do now. We were more of our own town. All of us kids knew each other or knew of each other. Like I said, Jesse, Paradise was a different town then."

"But you can't say definitively about Alexio and Ginny?"

"I was best friends with Mary Kate, not Ginny. I didn't keep track of Ginny the way I did with Mary Kate. What did you talk to Dragoa about?"

"Seems he was one of the last people to see Maxie Connolly alive. Forget about Alexio Dragoa for now. Let me ask you something, Molly, how many times were you interviewed by the cops when the girls disappeared?"

"Three times, I think. Once by Freddy Tillis and twice by the staties. Isn't it in the files?"

"Tell you the truth, the file's pretty spotty. Looks like they interviewed just about every kid in town, but none of the interviews went anywhere and there wasn't any follow-up to speak of. Seems like the Paradise PD bought into the theory that the girls actually ran away."

Molly made a face.

"Words, Crane. What's with the face?"

"Freddy was a nice man, but he wasn't much of a cop," she said. "Even as kids we knew that."

"That's what Healy says."

"I guess I can't blame people in town for wanting to believe that Ginny and Mary Kate ran away. It's easier to live with that thought than that one of your neighbors is killing teenage girls. And there was no evidence of foul play back then."

Jesse took it all in. As off balance as Molly had seemed to him since the discovery of the three bodies, this was the Molly he had come to rely on. Her assessment was honest and untainted by her closeness to the case.

"I'll pick you up at your house at eight-thirty tomorrow morning," Jesse said, changing subjects. "We're going to Boston to interview Lance Szarbo."

"Who?"

"He's the one witness who claimed he saw the rowboat heading out to Stiles the day the girls disappeared."

That got Molly's attention. "He was blasted, wasn't he?"

"Uh-huh."

"Are you sure it's worth the trip, Jesse?"

"Won't know until we speak to the man. You just said that Freddy wasn't much of a cop, and by the look of the file I'd have to agree. And because we don't have much else to go on."

"Okay," she said without much enthusiasm and headed for the office door.

Jesse called after her. She stopped, turned. "Yeah, Jesse."

"Don't wear your uniform."

"What should I wear?"

He said, "Not your uniform."

"That's not very helpful."

"Dress like a detective."

"How does a detective dress?"

"I have faith in you, Molly. You'll figure it out."

"I thought the Paradise PD couldn't afford detectives."

"If we could, you'd be one."

"What would the job pay?"

"Not enough. Go home and get some rest. Be with your family."

"Yes, Your Highness. Anything else?"

He smiled. "Your Highness . . . I could get used to that."

"Don't."

Jesse took the slip of paper Suit had given him out of his pocket, looked at his watch, and dialed. The phone rang six times before someone picked up.

"Diablito Motel. Paco speaking."

Jesse introduced himself. Titles didn't seem to impress Paco, nor did Paco seem to know anything about a guy calling the Paradise PD earlier in the day. The only thing Paco seemed interested in was getting off the phone.

"Where is Diablito?" he asked, sensing Paco's impatience.

"Between Tubac and Nogales."

"East or west of I-19?"

"Towards Sasabe," Paco said, testing Jesse.

"So you're west of 19."

"How you know that?"

"Grew up in Tucson."

"Me, too," Paco said with a big smile in his voice.

"So can you help me out here, Paco?"

"Wait a second."

Jesse held on.

"A call was put through to your number from Cabin Twelve this afternoon. Lasted about seven minutes."

"What's the guy's name?"

"John Smith," Paco said. "We get a lot of Smiths and Gonzaleses in here."

"I bet. Can you put me through?"

"I can, but it would do no good. He split. Checked out a half hour after the call."

"Can you tell me anything about this Mr. Smith?"

"Ex-military, I think. Tattoos everywhere, some from prison."

"How can you be sure?"

"I been in both," Paco said without hesitation. "Trust me. I know."

"How was he?"

"Loco with a big *L*. Looking for enemies under the mattress and in the mirror. Paid me in pennies and crumpled-up singles. I was happy to see him go."

After he hung up with Paco, Jesse put in a call to the Helton police chief. Jesse figured it was the Helton PD's turn to have a chat with a motel deskman.

34

Jesse didn't get into Boston much anymore since Jenn had left for good. When he did make it into the city, it usually wasn't to visit people who kept suites in glass-and-steel office towers. He wasn't sure how often Molly got into Boston. Probably about as often as she wore a gray blazer, black slacks, and black pumps. Though she was very pretty dressed that way, her curves less well hidden than in her uniform and winter jacket, she seemed utterly uncomfortable. Jesse thought she looked like a woman with a thousand itches to scratch but no idea where to start.

They hadn't exchanged ten words before they got into the elevator at 111 Huntington Avenue. It was Molly who spoke first.

"What am I supposed to do?"

"Nothing."

"What?"

"I'll talk," Jesse said. "You listen, observe.

If you have any questions, ask them. Don't ask too many. You're here to unnerve him."

Molly smiled in a way she hadn't since before the nor'easter. "I'm the bad cop."

"Uh-huh."

The elevator opened up directly into the offices of Commonwealth Colonial Capital, Inc. The receptionist sat at a green granite kiosk, the company logo — a triangle of three interlocking frosted-glass *C*'s — displayed on the matte black wall behind her. After a minute of false pleasantries, they were shown to Lance Szarbo's office.

Thin, hazel-eyed, and silver-haired, Szarbo was a handsome man of fifty-five, unashamed to display the perks of wealth. From his Patek Philippe watch to his hand-tailored suit to his custom-made shirt and shoes to his perfect and square white smile. The three walls of glass behind his desk offered a panoramic view of Boston.

Szarbo asked, "So how do you like the view?"

"Impressive," Jesse said.

Molly was cool. "All that glass must make it tough to hang pictures."

"Yes," Szarbo said, head tilted. "I confess to never having thought of it that way."

Jesse struggled not to laugh and asked, "What sort of firm is Commonwealth

189

Colonial?"

"Venture capital, but I don't believe you're here with a business plan to beg funds. Please sit," he said, gesturing at the chairs that faced his desk. "Can I get you something to drink? Some coffee or tea, perhaps? Water?"

Jesse said, "Nothing. Thank you."

Molly shook her head, barely acknowledging their host.

"So you're here about the missing girls," Szarbo said. "I've been keeping up. Terrible thing about the one girl's mother killing herself that way."

"It's not officially a suicide," Jesse said.

"Makes sense, though, doesn't it?" Szarbo asked.

Neither Jesse nor Molly reacted. Instead, Jesse removed a folded sheet of paper from his inside jacket pocket. He waved it at Szarbo and then placed it in front of him.

"That's a copy of the statement you gave the police twenty-five years ago," Jesse said. "Take a minute to read it over."

Szarbo did as he was asked, muttering parts aloud. "Yes," he said, looking up. "That's about it. I wish I could have been more helpful, but as you are no doubt aware, I was several sheets to the wind at the time."

"Celebrating?" Jesse asked.

"I suppose I was, yes. I was doing mostly real estate investment back then and I had just gotten the news that my first considerable deal was going to pay off rather handsomely."

Jesse said, "This was in Paradise?"

"Stiles Island. Until that time, the island wasn't much to speak of. There were several old, larger houses scattered around the island, but no real community. A group of fellow investors and I supplied the funds for the first meaningful development. By May of that year, all the plans had been approved and the permits issued. So a few of us in the investment group decided to go to Paradise on the Fourth of July to celebrate."

Molly said, "But you were the only one looking out the window of the restaurant?"

"I can't say, Detective Crane. I can only tell you what I saw."

"And what was that?" Jesse asked.

Szarbo gave an impatient look at his visitors. "You read the statement."

"Many times, but humor me, Mr. Szarbo. I've been at this a long time. Sometimes when you speak about the past, new details come to light."

"I was staring out at the island because that deal meant a lot to me and you know

191

how you get when you're so hammered. You just fix your gaze and you don't even realize it. Well, in any case, it was dark, but the marina was lit up and I think there was a full moon. I might be misremembering that, but I seem to recall being able to see pretty well in spite of the dark. There were a lot of motorboats out on the water to watch the fireworks. A little while after the fireworks ended, I noticed —"

"How long after?" Jesse said.

Szarbo shrugged. "Ten minutes, a half hour, an hour. Who knows? I had no sense of time by then. I can't even tell you how long I was staring out at the island. I was so hammered that I hadn't even noticed that the woman I'd come with had taken a ride back to Boston with one of the others."

"Go on."

"After the fireworks had ended, I caught sight of a rowboat headed toward Stiles Island."

"How do you know it was headed toward Stiles?" Molly asked. "Couldn't it have just been in the harbor like all the other boats, there to watch the fireworks? Then when the fireworks were over, it was circling back to the mainland?"

"No. No. It was definitely headed directly toward Stiles." There was no doubt in Szarbo's words or in his voice.

Jesse said, "In your statement you mentioned that the rowboat was low in the water and that the people in it were kids."

"What I said was that there were a few kids in an overcrowded boat rowing out toward Stiles Island."

"Kids?" Jesse asked. "How did you know they were kids?"

"I don't know that. They just seemed like kids. To say anything else would just be speculation."

"Boys? Girls?"

"Both, I think," Szarbo said. "I can't be sure. Again, I don't know why I think that. Look, Chief Stone, you have all of this —"

"Just a few more questions and then Detective Crane and I will be out of your hair."

Szarbo looked relieved.

"Close your eyes and try to picture the rowboat. Just focus on the boat, not the people on it, not on the water, not on anything else."

"Okay."

"Just answer quickly. Don't think about it. What did the boat look like?"

"It was too dark, Chief Stone. I'm sorry."

"Was it old or new?"

"Old, I think."

"How many people were rowing, one or two?"

"Two."

"Boys?"

"Yes, boys. I'm not —"

"How many people were on the boat?"

"Four . . . no, five. I don't know. I think I'm just making that up."

Szarbo opened his eyes.

"Thank you," Jesse said.

"I don't see how any of this helps," Szarbo said. "The only thing I know for sure is having seen the boat rowing out to Stiles. The rest is . . . I don't even know what to call it. Guessing?"

Jesse offered Szarbo his right hand. After Szarbo shook it, he shook Molly's as well.

In the elevator on the way down, Molly seemed to have withdrawn even further into herself than she had on the ride to Boston.

35

Sitting there with the contents of Maxie's bag spread out on the floor, a suffocating wave of panic overwhelmed him. Not guilt. Panic. He was faint, nauseated, breakfast forcing its way back up into his throat. He was sweating, too, through his shirt so that it was clinging to the lining of his sports jacket. He opened a window and sat back on his knees. He sucked in hungry lungfuls of cold air until he could push the panic back down. And when he'd gotten control of the nausea and the light-headed feeling had gone, he sat back against the wall. The icy air from the window hit the sheet of sweat on the back of his neck, giving him the chills.

Killing Maxie had been easier than he anticipated it would be. How odd, he thought, given how he'd once been so obsessed with her that he could not get her out of his head. How at times he'd risked everything just to catch a glimpse of her from across the street or to smell her too-sweet perfume or to brush against her in passing during a "chance" encounter at the market. And God, when they finally got together — Maxie having approached him — it was like nothing he'd ever experienced, not before and not since. She had once been a fantasy to him. Then she was everything to him. But she just had to ruin it, pushing him too hard to do things he wasn't ready to do. She was like that, always pushing for more. More was the only language she had seemed to understand. If she'd only been a little patient and let him get his legs underneath him, it might've worked. Patience wasn't one of Maxie's virtues.

No, he was long past the guilt. Maxie's blood on his hands was of her own making. If she hadn't forced him away with her crazy demands, there might have been a future for them both, a way to see each other and still get on with their lives. He hated to admit it, even to himself, but Ginny's vanishing the way she had had been a kind of blessing. It had gotten Maxie out of town and removed the dangling sword from over his head. But no, she had to come back, climb the ladder, and rehang the sword. That's why it had been so easy to snap her neck, drive her farther up the Bluffs, and push her body down onto the beach. All the years of yearning and resentment were sufficient to make him want to end her, but when she degraded herself in front of him, calling him Loverboy — how could she do that after twenty-five years? — he wanted to rip her to pieces. How could she think he would want her? She was nothing but a pathetic old whore with her satin panties, stinking of perfume and desperation.

He closed the window and crawled on hands and knees to where the contents of Maxie's bag were laid neatly out; he went over each of them again as he had already done three times before. He turned her empty bag upside down and shook it so that his shoulders ached. Nothing. He turned the bag right side up, stared into it. Empty. He rubbed his latex-gloved palms along the inside of the bag, feeling for a hidden pocket, for a slight rectangular bulge, for something, anything. But again, there was nothing. No matter how many times he went through her things or searched her bag, he could not find the one missing letter. That damn letter, written in his moment of despair and pain, was the only thing that tied him to her. She had promised to bring it. All the others were there. Now they were gone forever. Shredded. Burned. Nothing more than ashes and smoke. But the one missing letter would be enough to ruin him and bring what little was left of his world crashing down around his head.

He had been concerned about her cell phone, too, but those fears proved to be unfounded. Over the years, there had been the occasional late-night call to his house, the number blocked. When those calls went unanswered, no messages were left. When his wife picked up, the person at the other end would hang up. The number of calls had dwindled, averaging maybe one or two a year for the last five years or so. Maxie had an old-style flip phone and it was easy enough to scroll through her call records. He was relieved to see that none of her recent calls were to any of his numbers. He was even more relieved to see none of his numbers were listed in her phonebook. There was little doubt Maxie's death would be declared a suicide, so it was unlikely the cops would dig into her phone records. And even if they did, so what? He could explain those calls away easily enough if he had to. Now her phone was history, too. Crushed beneath the wheels of his car, its pieces scattered along the road to Boston. No, it was that damned letter he had to worry about.

That was on him.

There was a knock at his door.

"Give me two minutes," he said, collecting the contents of Maxie's bag and shoveling them back inside.

"There's someone here to see you."

"Two minutes," he repeated.

"Okay."

In a day or two, under cover of darkness, he would drive back up to the Bluffs and leave the bag in a nook between some rocks for the cops or a passerby to stumble on. In the meantime he slid the bag in a drawer and locked it. He sat at his desk for a few seconds, trying to regroup. It was only when he stood to open his office door that he realized he had been holding Maxie's satin panties against the freshly shaven skin of his cheek. In that moment he realized both the depth of his obsession and hatred where Maxie Connolly was concerned. To be human was to be a contradiction. He threw her panties in the same drawer as her bag, but even as he did he knew he would have a much more difficult time leaving them somewhere to be found by a stranger.

36

Instead of stopping at the station, Jesse swung his Explorer toward the bridge to Stiles Island. Molly, who'd been silent during the ride back from Boston, took notice, sitting up in her seat, her head swiveling left and right.

"What are we doing?" she asked, her voice strained. "Where are we going?"

"That's up to you," Jesse said.

"I don't understand."

"I think you do. I think you understood the minute Szarbo said there were boys and girls on that rowboat."

"He wasn't sure about anything he said. You heard him."

"I did."

"I don't —" Molly went quiet.

"Where would they have taken the boat to, Molly?"

"I don't know," she said.

"C'mon, Crane."

Her eyes got a faraway look in them. "Humpback Point, I guess," she said, her lips turning up at the corners.

"Where?"

"No one calls it that anymore. It's not there anymore. I mean, it's there, but there's a house on it now."

"Which house?"

"The Sugar Cube," she said.

Jesse knew the place. Everyone on Stiles and in Paradise knew it. And owing to the fact that it had been featured on the cover of several magazines, people all over the world knew it, too. They called it the Sugar Cube because it looked like one. The only thing that broke up the white exterior was a continuous horizontal line of blue glass panels that ran around all four walls of the home. It was all very minimalist. There were no fencing, no stone walls around the property, no formal driveway, no formal landscaping to speak of. Just some well-kept lawn, a Japanese rock garden, a few pieces of abstract sculpture. The lot's one signature outdoor feature was a twenty-by-twenty black stone square with a central fire pit surrounded by four long slabs of gray granite. There was a rectangular white marble pool and white cabana as well. Jesse thought it was pretty enough, but about as cozy as a mausoleum. The place was owned by a New York City architect who used it as a summer home and to impress potential clients. It had been closed for the season, the owner having notified local security and the Paradise PD that he wouldn't be back until after Memorial Day.

Jesse parked his Explorer on the shoulder of the road that ran past the north side of the property. He hopped out and waited for Molly to follow. She came around and stood next to him. The sun was up and strong, but no matter how strong the sun, it wasn't the time of year to be standing on a finger of land sticking out into the Atlantic. The winds whipped cold sand into their faces.

"Show me," he said.

"This way."

Molly walked across the road, through the straw-colored dormant dune grasses, over the low dunes and onto the narrow strip of beach that bordered that part of Stiles. She turned right and led Jesse to a V-shaped outcropping of rocks that nearly bisected the beach.

"You could take a boat out here and tie it up," she said. "And if it was dark, there was no way you could see a boat tied up here from the water. Then you could climb over the rocks." She pointed. "See, the rocks kind of form a natural ladder. There wasn't a paved road here back then, just a kind of a berm between the beach and the field. This lot didn't used to be elevated the way it is now. When we were kids, the field sloped down below the berm."

"So passing boats couldn't see anyone up here."

Molly nodded.

"Was it called Humpback Point because of the berm?" Jesse said.

She nodded again.

Jesse said, "You smiled before when you called it Humpback Point."

"I did?"

"You did. There was another reason you guys called it that. Emphasis on the *hump* in Humpback."

"You should be a detective," Molly said.

"Like you."

She smiled. "That's just pretending."

"So kids came here to get high, drink, make out?"

"Sometimes more than make out," she said.

"Did something happen to you here, Molly?" Jesse's voice was low and serious.

Molly looked up and saw the pained expression on his face.

"Oh, no, Jesse, it wasn't like that," she

said. "It was kind of awkward. I guess it always is, right? Was it like that for you?"

He smiled at her. "*Awkward* doesn't quite describe it. *Quick and awkward* is more like it."

She laughed. "With us it was really sweet and beautiful."

"It wasn't your husband?"

She clenched her lips together and shook her head. "I guess I hoped it would be, but I was a sixteen-year-old Catholic high school girl. What did I know about anything? But he was really sweet and gentle."

"Do you think Mary Kate and Ginny were on that rowboat and do you think they were coming here?" he asked.

"We found their remains in the Swap, Jesse. That's all the way off the island at the western end of town. And I think the cops searched the island after it was reported they were missing. Didn't they?"

"They did. Doesn't mean they weren't here or that they weren't killed here."

"I guess not," she said. "But . . ."

"But what? Come on, Molly. You're not that girl anymore. You're a cop, the best one I've got."

"The killer crushed Ginny's skull and he stabbed Mary Kate multiple times. That's a lot of blood and a lot of deadweight to transport, even if they weren't very big. How did he get them off the island and over to the Swap without anyone noticing?"

"Good question."

Jesse's phone buzzed in his pocket. He checked the screen. It was the ME. He looked over to Molly. "I've got to take this," he said.

Molly walked back down the beach toward Jesse's SUV.

"What you got for me, Doc?"

"The proximate cause of death was a fractured cervical vertebrae, likely resulting from a violent fall. Several of her vertebrae were broken, so take your pick. As I suspected, she was pretty badly broken up internally. I am listing it as a probable suicide," the ME said with some hesitation in her voice.

"Probable. Why probable, Doc?"

"It's her panties."

"Her panties. What about her panties? Were they on backwards or something."

"That's just it, Jesse. They weren't on her at all."

"What?"

"She met her maker commando-style," Tamara said. "Takes all kinds."

"Let's keep the missing panties between us, okay? Fax the report over."

"Already done."

"You up for a little more friendship tonight," he asked.

"As long as that's what it is, sure. If you're looking for love, you're looking in all the wrong places."

"I got the message, Doc. You're nobody's right gal."

"Nice to meet a man who can handle his scotch and pay attention."

"I've never been flattered like that before."

"Call me later."

When Jesse got back to his Explorer, Molly had retreated back into herself and her past. He had some other questions to ask her, but let them slide. Molly's debut as a detective had already been a tough one.

He dropped Molly back at her house before heading to the station.

"Take a little while, then get yourself back to the station," he said.

"In uniform?"

"Up to you, but it will really get Suit crazed to see you dressed like that. I've let him play detective once or twice, too."

"That's okay, Jesse," she said. "I think I'll get my uniform back on."

37

He pulled up to the maintenance shed on the grounds at Sacred Heart Girls Catholic just as he had on the night the nor'easter blew into town. This time there was no flash and roar of gunfire, no need for him to back up into the delivery bay. No body for him to dispose of.

"It would creep me out, working here. Doesn't it ever get to you?" he asked.

"Why?"

"Because the girls went to school here."

"Yeah, I guess. Sometimes," he said, draining the oil from the old red tractor they used to plow the snow off the sidewalks in front of the school. "Mostly, I don't think about it. I can't afford to be choosy. With my record, I'm lucky I got a damn job at all."

"Which one of you shot Zevon?"

He turned, looking over his shoulder at his visitor. "Who do you think?"

"You?"

" 'Course. I didn't like Zevon that much to begin with and I liked him even less that he came back to town. Besides, our other pal talks a good ball game, but underneath, Mr. Tough Guy's . . . you know him. He was the one that caused all this shit to begin with. You know what he had the nerve to tell me at the Scupper the other night? That he didn't even wanna go to Stiles the night we . . . you know, that night."

"I call bullshit on that!"

"That's what I said. You hear about Maxie Connolly?"

"Sure," he said. "Looks like she killed herself. Threw herself off the Bluffs, but that doesn't mean you were wrong the other night. Our friend's definitely a problem."

"He'll be all right. You know how Alexio gets sometimes, all hot-blooded and crazy. We just got to keep him calm, hold his hand a little. That's all." He turned around again. "Come over here and help me with this filter a second. The guy who put it on didn't lube it and then put it on so tight —"

"Do it yourself. I've got to get back to my office. I can't get dirty."

"No, that's right. You don't like getting dirty."

He ignored the dig. "It's too late for hand-holding. Jesse's already had a talk with him."

"With Alexio. Shit!" He dropped his wrench, sent it clanging against the concrete floor. "What? What happened?"

"Alexio was in the Whaler Lounge at the hotel and Maxie Connolly walked in. First he hit on her and then he got all stupid, telling her how sorry he was about Ginny. A few hours later, she was dead."

"You don't think Alexio —"

"He didn't. But Jesse Stone is smart. Alexio's on his radar screen now and he's not coming off it until the chief has somewhere else to look."

"Hey, don't even think about putting Stone on me. I'll give you —"

"Don't be an idiot," he said. "How far would it get any of us to throw suspicion at you? No, we've got to think of a way to get Jesse to look someplace else. You think Alexio still has the knife from that night?"

"Sure he does. You know how cheap he is. He's still got his grandpa's first nickel. He won't sell fish to the tourists because he thinks it's a waste."

"Okay, give me a day or two. I think I might have an idea of what to do."

"What should I do until then?"

"Nothing. Not a thing. Finish changing the oil. Go about your job. Do what you always do. If Alexio calls, keep him calm and tell him we've got it all under control."

"Do we?"

"Do we what?"

"Have it all under control."

"Not all of it, not yet, but we will."

"You sure about that?"

"I've gotten us this far. Let me worry about it. Don't call me unless it's an emergency. I need time to set things up. I'll be in touch when I'm ready."

"You got someone in mind?"

"I do."

"Okay, then. You better get out of here."

He left without another word. He knew what had to be done, but in spite of his urge to just get it over with, he knew he had to keep his wits about him and wait for the right moment. Unlike that night on Stiles, he couldn't let this spiral out of control.

38

He had decided on a spot he thought would make sense, a place where someone walking along the Bluffs might eventually stumble onto Maxie's handbag. It wasn't too far from where they used to meet when he thought all he wanted was her. Even now, having murdered her and coldly tossed her body off the Bluffs, he flushed at the memories of their stolen moments in his car, of the times they could sneak off to a Boston hotel for a night. Then there were the times they had pushed their luck beyond all reason, like when they'd run into each other outside the restrooms at the Gray Gull. He remembered getting weak at the sight of her, then his fury at the thought of her being at the bar with another man. How Maxie fanned the flames by rubbing up against him and taunting him.

"Do you want me, Loverboy?" she'd say, her lips brushing his ear, her warm cigarette breath against his neck. "Get rid of that stuck-up fiancée of yours and meet me here in an hour."

He exploded, pushing her into the men's room, locking the door behind them, taking her in the stall. It was all over in an instant, but was so much more exciting than anything he had done with any other woman before or since. His heart raced at the thought that he had ever been so stupid or so impulsive. Thinking back on it, he wondered if Maxie hadn't set him up. *Was she really there with another man or did she follow me to the restaurant?* He'd been so blind back then that he had never considered the possibility she was lying to him. That was all so long ago, but it felt alive in him.

Before leaving the spot and going back to his office to retrieve Maxie's bag, he smiled at the cleverness of his plan. How he would fashion a kind of suicide shrine out of Maxie's bag, a file photo of Ginny, and a couple candles. The cops, even Jesse Stone, would eat it up. He knew the press would. He was sure of that. He envisioned the headlines:

MOTHER PRAYS AT
DEAD GIRL'S SHRINE
ENDS IT ALL

He was still feeling the rush of pride as he pulled up in front of his office. All he had to do was get the stuff, head back up to the Bluffs, and it would be over. He'd worry about the missing letter when the time came. If it came. For now, it was one thing at a time. The street was quiet when he stepped out of his car and put the key in the office door lock.

"Hey!" a man's gravelly voice cut through the quiet and the dark.

He startled, fumbling his keys.

"Relax," said the voice, and a man stepped out of the shadows of a nearby storefront. He was a rough-looking guy with a face full of dark stubble and a dangling cigarette. "I'm here to do you a favor."

"Really?" he said. Removing the keys from the lock, he worked them between the fingers of his right glove. He didn't want a fight. Hadn't studied or sparred in years, but he hadn't forgotten his training and one blow with a fist full of keys was better than just a fist if it came to that. "You're here to do me a favor. And do I get to know the name of my benefactor?"

"Cut the crap, mister. We need to talk."

The keys were in place. He forced his body to relax, preparing to strike with his right arm if the guy got too close. "About what?"

"About how I seen you drive up to the Bluffs the other night to snuff the blonde."

"I'm sure I don't know what you're talking about."

"Cell phones are great things, you know, especially 'cause they come with cameras. I got a nice shot of your car, plate and all, with you behind the wheel. I thought it was real weird, her having me drop her off up there alone like that in the freezing cold. I figured I might snag me some married guy going up there to meet her for a little backseat bingo."

"Look, whatever your name is, I'm sure —"

"Forget my name and forget the stalling. See, here's the thing, I was going to leave it alone. I figured, how much could I hit some poor working stiff up for 'cause I caught him meeting some old broad up in the Bluffs? It didn't seem worth the trouble. Why am I going to screw up some guy's marriage for a few hundred bucks? But when the police chief shows up at my door and starts busting my chops about the blonde, I got kind of curious, you know? Then when I find out the blonde offed herself, going over Caine's Bluff, I'm thinking maybe she had a little help with the takeoff. Funny thing is, I got a way of tracking down plate numbers and when I traced yours . . . man, I really got interested."

"Damn it!"

"You got that right. See, like I said, I'm here to do you a favor."

He put on a brave act. "Even if you do have a photo of my car going up to the Bluffs, so what? It's evidence of nothing. I could have gone up there two weeks ago, last year, last evening. In any case, electronics are easily tampered with. There's nothing tying me to that unfortunate woman or to her suicide. Sorry, you'll have to go squeeze some other orange to get your juice."

Rod Wiethop pulled something out of his pocket and held it in the yellowish beam of the streetlight. "You know, I don't think so, mister. I think I'm gonna be able to squeeze all the juice I need outta you for as long as I'm thirsty. See, after the chief come talk to me, I went down to the garage and went over my cab. People are dropping all kinds of stuff in the cab all the time: drugs, groceries, gifts, underwear . . . all sorts of things.

And the blonde, she dropped this."

"An envelope. Why should I care —"

"You know, I'm losing my patience with you now," Wiethop said. "I ain't your wife. Deny, deny, deny might work with her, but not with me. See, I got this letter here from you to the blonde that would pretty much blow your life up. Man, what were you thinking to put that stuff down in writing?"

"I wasn't thinking at all. That was the problem. Perhaps you're right, let's discuss your terms over a drink. Come in."

Wiethop smiled. "That's more like it. I guess I could use a friend."

"Yes," he said, "friends."

39

Tamara Elkin tried pouring Jesse another drink, but he waved her off. She decided she'd had enough as well and put the bottle back in the kitchen. When she came back into Jesse's living room, she plopped herself down in his recliner across from the sofa on which Jesse had kicked up his feet. Neither of them spoke and neither seemed the least bit uncomfortable. Then she became aware of Jesse staring at her hair.

"Many men have tried to figure out the enigma that is my hair, Jesse Stone," she said, a laugh in her voice. "And many have failed."

"Any live to tell the tale?"

"The lucky ones."

He shook his head at her, smiled. But she noticed something off in his smile.

She asked, "What's wrong?"

"Nothing."

"Come on, Jesse, we've been friends for,

what, two days? And no offense, but you're not as inscrutable as you'd like to believe you are. So let's hear it." She crooked one of her long, tapered fingers at him and wiggled it. "Something's bothering you. Besides, isn't sharing part of the whole friendship thing?"

"The panties," he said.

"I don't know about you. You're sending me mixed messages there, Chief. I thought discussing my underwear was off-limits if we were going to be pals."

"Not yours. Maxie Connolly's."

She laughed that deep laugh of hers. "You, sir, are a unique individual. Given my chosen career, you can imagine I've had some strange discussions in my time, but discussing a dead woman's missing panties is a first."

He smiled, but again it was a troubled smile. "It's more than her panties," he said. "Her handbag and cell phone are missing, too."

"I can't help you there, but like I said on the phone, some gals do go commando-style. And from what the buzz is around about her, it seems to me the late Maxie Connolly might have been a prime candidate for AARP Commando of the Year Award."

"If all that was missing was her panties, it wouldn't bother me as much. I saw surveillance video of her leaving her hotel room with her bag and she went straight from the hotel to the Bluffs."

Tamara asked, "How did she get there?"

"Cab."

"Well, Sherlock, you might want to have a talk with the cabdriver."

"Did that."

"And?"

"And I think I better go have another talk with him," Jesse said. "And you, Doc, I think it's time for you to get going."

"You sure?"

"Positive. We can't do friendly sleepovers every night."

"Tempted?"

He said, "I didn't think there was any question of that."

Tamara stood. "Just checking. You know, I won't hold it against you if you give in to it on occasion."

"But I will."

She wagged a finger at him. "Oh, you're one of those."

"One of those what?" Jesse asked.

"Moralist."

He tilted his head. "I wouldn't say that."

"What would you say?"

219

"That I can usually sense right from wrong."

"I don't know, Jesse. I look at the world and the bodies that come into my morgue and I wonder if I know what's right anymore."

"Let's say I know what's wrong. Easier to know what's wrong."

"You're an interesting man, Jesse Stone, but you're out of place here."

"In Paradise?"

"Yes, but that's not what I mean, exactly," she said. "I mean you were born in the wrong century. You should have been sheriff in a small frontier town."

He didn't say anything to that because he'd had that same thought a thousand times himself. It was one of the reasons he loved Westerns so much. As a kid, he often pictured himself as the sheriff in *High Noon* or as Wild Bill Hickok cleaning up Dodge City. When he thought about it seriously, Jesse realized that right and wrong probably weren't any less complicated back then, but it was easier to pretend they were.

When Tamara had gone, Jesse sat in front of the TV and clicked through the channels, looking for a Western.

40

Jesse tried to reconcile the size of the closed white coffin with the skeleton of the girl inside. He tried to reconcile the images of the girl, of her mugging for the camera with Molly and Ginny, with the dirty bones found in a hole on Trench Alley. He stopped soon after he began. These weren't the kinds of things Jesse focused on. He didn't see the point. The dead were just that, dead. If humans possessed souls and if there was something that came after this world, Mary Kate's had gone there a long time ago. The rest of it, these few hours at the funeral home, were for the less fortunate, the ones left behind to suffer.

Jesse made his appearance at the funeral home before receding into the backdrop. He paid his respects to Tess O'Hara and Mary Kate's sisters and their families. One of the grandkids looked a lot like her late aunt. Mary Kate's father was nowhere in sight. No surprise in that. But Jesse was surprised by the paltry turnout. Then he remembered what Healy had said to him about small towns and shame. They all just wanted to forget, to go to work, come home and have dinner with their families, watch TV, and be left alone. They wanted to forget. It was Jesse's job to remember.

He had given Molly the day off to attend the wake and the service, but she came and sat beside him in one of the empty back rows of folding chairs at the funeral home. Molly's jaw was clenched tightly. Lately, that seemed to be her default expression. The rest of her face was blank, her eyes far, far away.

"Do you think she'll be lonely, Jesse?" Molly said, her voice a brittle whisper.

"How do you mean?"

"She's had Ginny there to hold her all these years. Now . . ."

Jesse turned to stare at Molly. This was a side of her he had never before seen. He understood that she felt guilty about something. Maybe that she had lived happily all these years, had raised a family and built a career, while her friends had been murdered and left to molder in a filthy hole in a forgotten building. But Jesse sensed there were other things at play here. And there was a question he had wanted to ask her from the very start, that in deference to their relationship, he had not asked. He had hoped she would just come to him and explain, but she hadn't. He thought, for both of their sakes, the time had come to ask the question.

"Come with me," he said, standing and walking out back of the funeral home.

Snow was falling in big, lazy flakes. A white dusting covered the few cars that would follow the hearse to Sacred Heart Catholic Church. They stood close to each other under an overhang.

"What?" she asked.

"You know what."

"No, I don't."

"If Mary Kate was your best friend and Ginny was a friend of yours who grew up only two houses away from you, why weren't you there that night?"

Molly looked as uncomfortable as Jesse had ever seen her. He put his hand on her shoulder, friend to friend. Molly's mouth opened and closed. No words came out. She was torn.

He repeated the question. "Why, Molly?"

"Mary Kate and I were fighting over a boy. We hadn't spoken to each other in weeks."

"The boy who you mentioned when we were on Stiles Island, was he who you were fighting over?"

Molly nodded, looking very stoic.

"What was his name?"

"Warren. He went to Sacred Heart Boys."

"Older?"

"I don't want to talk about this, Jesse."

"I know you don't, but you have to talk about it to someone."

"Not now. Not today, of all days."

"Did Mary Kate take Warren away from you, Molly?"

"Please, Jesse, stop. I can't do this now."

Jesse took his hand off her shoulder and watched her head back inside. He had been in therapy long enough to know that Molly would tell him when she was ready and not before. Jesse turned his attention to the weather, looked at his watch, and decided he'd better get over to the church.

41

Sacred Heart Catholic Church was a little out of place in Paradise. It was too large for a small town. It was more suited to Boston or New York. A Gothic Revival structure built from great blocks of light gray stone turned nearly black with a century's worth of coal dust and oil soot, the church was impressive to behold, made even more so by its position atop the highest point in town inland of the Bluffs. When its stone steeple and cross were lit up, they were visible for miles around. The rest of the campus, the school buildings, garages, and other structures, were far more mundane.

Jesse parked his Explorer perpendicular to the church entrance, but down the hill a bit and behind some ivy-covered fencing. It gave him a very good view of things without making his presence obvious to the attendees. He wanted to sit back and observe from a distance. He was hoping to see an unexpected mourner, a face that didn't seem to belong. The turnout at the funeral home had been so small and no one there had seemed out of place. Sacred Heart was something else. It was large enough that you could slip in and out unnoticed. You could be a silhouette in a back pew if you wished. Jesse didn't know that he expected much in the way of results. He had made so little headway so far that he was willing to give it a try.

He called in to the station while he waited for the hearse to show.

"Suit, I'm at the church. The guys in place?"

"They'll keep the media away from the family as best they can."

"Okay. Anything else?"

"Police chief from Helton called. Alexio Dragoa's alibi checks out for the night Maxie Connolly killed herself."

"I figured."

"The roads bad out there?"

"You making small talk with me, Suit?"

"I'm going nuts in here, Jesse."

"So you've said."

"Sorry."

"You'll get back on the street when I'm ready to put you there."

Jesse tapped the end-call button on the

touch screen. The fact was that Jesse didn't know he would ever feel right about putting Suit back on the street. Suit's getting shot the way he did had thrown Jesse a curve he hadn't learned how to hit. He stared at the phone in his palm, thought about finally making that call to Dix.

Somebody rapped their knuckles against the driver's-side window. Jesse, trying very hard not to look startled, turned to see Stu Cromwell lurking. He lowered the window.

"Jesse."

"Stu."

"You here on official business or are you going to the service, Jesse?"

"I could ask you the same thing."

Cromwell said, "Since we're talking, let me ask. You got anything for me?"

"Maybe I do. We can't locate some of Maxie Connolly's personal effects. Items we know she must have had with her when she went up to the Bluffs."

"Like what?"

"Her cell phone, for one," Jesse said.

"Anything else?"

"Yes."

"You're not going to tell me, are you?"

"Not yet, but you should get some mileage out of that."

"Some. I'm sure the missing stuff will turn up."

"That makes one of us," Jesse said.

"How was the turnout at the viewing?"

"Light. The family, Molly and me, but only a few other people."

Cromwell nodded. "Makes sense."

"Not to me."

"It's a black mark against the town. Paints everybody who lives here with a big, broad brush. They all just want it to go away. In a sense, they're punishing the girls for going missing and getting killed. None of them would tell you that, but deep down, that's what's going on."

"Captain Healy said something like that to me," Jesse said.

"Smart man."

Jesse turned to look at the newspaperman.

"You all right, Stu? You don't look like you've slept in a week."

"Rough night with Martha," he said. "Lots of bad nights lately."

"Sorry to hear it."

"I'm going to get up to the church now, Jesse."

Jesse closed the window and watched Cromwell make his way up the hill in the snow. He noticed that people were beginning to show. He recognized most of them.

Saw Molly arrive with her mom. He noticed Bill Marchand's SUV pass by the church and pull into the lot. Jesse was willing to bet Marchand was the only politician who'd show his face today. When the selectman approached the church entrance, he turned and spotted Jesse's Explorer. He smiled, waved, then made his way down the hill.

When Jesse lowered his window, Marchand offered his right hand. Jesse shook it.

"Any progress, Jesse?"

"None."

"I'll keep the mayor off your back as long as I can."

"Appreciate it."

"I don't know how much good it's going to do. The funerals are going to amp up the pressure on your department to get these murders solved."

"You mean the pressure on me."

"I do."

"I'll live with it."

"What are you doing parked down here?" Marchand asked.

"Watching."

"For?"

"For faces that don't fit."

"Sounds like you're grasping at straws."

Jesse shook his head. "Never understood

229

that expression."

"Me, either."

They both laughed.

"It's a sad day, though," Marchand said.

"Did you know the girls?"

"I was older, but I knew who they were. Paradise is a small town, Jesse. It was even smaller back then. As a selectman, I just felt like I had to make an appearance."

Jesse didn't say anything, but he was caught off guard by how closely Bill Marchand's words paralleled what Alexio Dragoa had said on the subject. But he wasn't exactly shocked. Healy and Stu Cromwell were right. Everyone in Paradise had found a way to distance themselves from the girls' disappearance and now the discovery that they had been murdered. It felt to Jesse almost as if they had all rehearsed the same answers. Answers that were meant to insulate them from the horror and the guilt. It wasn't hard to understand. Then he saw a vehicle pull up to the church that got his full attention.

Jesse said, "Isn't that Alexio's Dragoa's pickup?"

Marchand shook his head in disgust. "That's his rusty POS, all right."

"Wonder what he's doing here."

"Got me." Marchand patted Jesse's

shoulder. "I better show my face up there now, Jesse. By the way, I ordered those new softball uniforms."

Jesse nodded, but he was barely conscious of Bill Marchand. All he could think about was Alexio Dragoa and why the fisherman kept turning up in the middle of things.

42

After waiting outside the church for the service to conclude and following the funeral cortege to Saint Paul's Cemetery on the outskirts of town, Jesse had driven over to Paradise Taxi's garage. No one was particularly happy to see him again. Unless you called them, cops showing up at your door usually meant one thing: trouble.

"Yeah, Chief, what can I do for you this time?" said the dispatcher, a heavyset, unshaven man who smelled of cigars and spilled coffee.

"Your driver, Wiethop."

"Jeez, him again? What about him?"

"He have a record?"

The dispatcher made a face and gave a shrug. "Maybe. I don't know. He never stole from us as far as I can tell. We don't do background checks. Most of our guys live in town and have been with us for years. Don't matter anyways, because he ain't my problem no more."

"How's that?"

"He blew off his last few shifts. Didn't even freakin' call in last night. Just didn't show. I called him, but he never answered. When he comes in for his last paycheck, I'm gonna rip it up in front of the bastard. Let him sue me."

"When was the last time you saw him?"

The fat man rubbed his cheeks. "About an hour after you was here the last time. He said he left something in his cab the night before. He went out to the garage and came back in here to say he wasn't gonna be in that night."

Jesse asked, "Did he find what he was looking for?"

"Must've."

"Why's that?"

"He was all happy and smilin' like he hit the lotto or something."

"I'm going to be sending some people over to look at his cab."

The fat man gave Jesse a stained-tooth smile. "Sorry, Chief. That's going to have to wait. It's on the road."

"Get it back in here."

"But it's been vacuumed and washed twice since —"

"Get it back here. Pronto!"

Fifteen minutes later, Jesse and Peter Perkins were standing on the landing half a flight of stairs below Rod Wiethop's apartment. Jesse gave the thumbs-up to Peter. Peter nodded that he was ready. Guns drawn, they took the remaining steps slowly and as quietly as the moaning old stairs allowed. At the threshold, Peter and Jesse stood on opposite sides of the door. Jesse nodded to Peter. Perkins reached over and pounded the door.

"Rod Wiethop," he said, "this is the Paradise Police Department. Open your door."

Nothing.

Jesse spun his index finger for Peter to try it again.

Perkins pounded the door, harder this time.

"Rod Wiethop, c'mon. This is the police. Open up."

This time there was stirring, but not from Wiethop's apartment. The door to the left side of the staircase opened and a white-haired old Yankee with wire-rimmed glasses, a flannel shirt, and jeans worn shiny at the knees stepped out into the hallway.

"Please get back inside your apartment," Jesse said.

"Relax there, pups. That Wiethop fella

ain't been in since near around eleven last evenin'."

Jesse kept his .38 drawn, but turned to the old man.

"How do you know that?"

"I own this buildin', son. Name's Borden, Lyle Borden, and I keep a pretty good eye and ear on the goings-on around here. You don't believe me about Wiethop, I'll show you."

He pulled a fistful of keys from his pocket, found one in particular, and took a step toward Wiethop's door. Jesse blocked his way.

"Peter, try it one more time."

Same results.

"Okay, Mr. Borden. Open her up."

When Borden had opened the lock, Jesse stepped in front of him and asked him to stay in the hall.

Wiethop's apartment was the same charmless place it had been before, and though the cabbie wasn't in, it still stank of cigarette smoke and vodka sweat.

"I'll take this room and the bathroom," Jesse said. "You take the bedroom."

Jesse found pretty much what he expected to find in the medicine chest. Some amphetamines, a little pot, lots of generic painkillers.

"Jesse, you better get in here."

When he walked into the bedroom, he found Peter Perkins on his hands and knees, flashlight aimed under the bed. He got down on the floor next to Peter. In the beam of Peter's flash, Jesse saw Maxie Connolly's missing bag. And draped over the bag, between the handles, was a pair of black panties that shone in the light.

43

"He left first around nine," Borden said, pouring Jesse a cup of coffee. "Then, like I told you before, Rod came back around eleven and left again."

Jesse took a sip.

"Good coffee."

"Thanks."

"You're sure of your times, Lyle?"

"Don't sleep much since the wife died last year. That old woman used to make me nuts, but since she's passed . . ." Lyle Borden shook his head. "Well, anyhoo, I'm sure of my facts, Chief. Old man like me don't have much to fill out his hours, so he holds on to the little things he has."

"Can you tell me anything else about last night? Did you see Wiethop come and go?"

Borden sat down across from Jesse and took a swallow of coffee. "No. Only heard him. That third apartment, the one over on the other side of the stairs, is vacant. Has been for going on two years. So after the sandwich shop downstairs closes, it's just my renter and me moving around up here."

"How long has Wiethop been —"

"Well, Chief, now wait a second," Borden said, interrupting Jesse. "Maybe there was one thing."

"One thing?"

"About last night that I noticed, come to think of it."

"What's that?"

"When Rod come back and left that second time —"

"At eleven."

"That's right, about eleven. He must have had a load on," Borden said.

Jesse took another sip of his coffee. "You mean he was drunk?"

"Sure sounded that way to me. Real heavy footsteps on the stairs. Real deliberate. You know how you get when you've had too much?"

"Uh-huh."

"He sounded like that, and when he got to the door, I could hear him fumbling a lot with his keys. Dropped 'em once or twice. Put the wrong key in the lock a few times. I haven't tied one on like that for many years." The old man smiled, his eyes unfocused.

"How long did Wiethop stay in his apartment before heading out again?"

"Five minutes. Maybe not even that long." Borden made a whistling sound and snapped his fingers. "In and out, just like that."

"And his car is gone?"

"Take a gander for yourself, Chief. If you look out my bedroom window to the right, you'll see his spot in the alleyway is empty."

"Would you know the make and model of Wiethop's car?"

Borden laughed. "Rod must have had a sense of humor."

"How's that?"

"Don't know the year, but his car is an old Ford Crown Victoria like all the police cars on the TV."

"Color?"

Borden nodded. "White."

When Jesse finished his coffee and stood to leave, Perkins knocked and came through.

"It's all been photographed, bagged, and tagged, Jesse," he said. "I'm going to run it to the station. The state forensic guys will be over here after they get done going over Wiethop's cab."

"I'll meet you back at the station."

Jesse shook Borden's hand and left. When he got to the head of the stairs, he about-

239

faced, dipped under the crime scene tape strewn across the threshold of Wiethop's door, and stepped into the apartment. He stood there in the dingy front room trying to figure out what bothered him so much about finally making some progress.

44

Silent tears poured out of Al Franzen's eyes as he stared at the photos. Seeing his late wife's possessions like that had the effect of bringing Maxie back to life for him while once again forcing him to experience the pain of her death.

"Are these her things?" Jesse asked.

Franzen nodded.

"Is that a yes, Mr. Franzen?"

"Yes."

"Please look at the photo of her wallet and the contents. Is anything missing?"

"All of her credit cards are gone," Franzen said, choking down his tears.

"Did she carry cash with her?"

Franzen smiled sadly. "Did she carry cash with her? My God, she didn't go to the bathroom in the middle of the night without bringing cash. She had at least five hundred dollars with her always. She said it was a scar from how she was raised. I grew up poor. I understood. I was glad to give her money. I have enough of it. Why, was there no cash in her wallet?"

"There was only some spare change in the bottom of the bag. See?" Jesse pointed at one of the photos. "But that was it. No bills."

Franzen's mood changed from grief to confusion. "But I don't understand. Where did you get these things from?"

"We found them in the apartment of the cabdriver who took Maxie up to the Bluffs."

"Why would he have them? Are you telling me he killed Maxie?"

"That's not what I'm telling you."

Franzen became agitated, rising up out of his seat, his face turning bright red. "Then what are you telling me, for chrissakes? Why did this man have my wife's underwear? Did he rape her? Oh my God, he raped her and robbed her."

Jesse put a hand on Franzen's shoulder and gently urged him back into his seat. "Relax, Mr. Franzen. He didn't rape her. We know she didn't have intercourse the night she died. It might be that he came back up to the Bluffs after Maxie committed suicide and took the things she left behind. Or he took her up to the Bluffs and robbed her. We don't know."

"But her underthings! How did he get them?"

"We don't know that, either."

Franzen was out of his seat again. "Why don't you know that? Won't he tell you? Let me talk to that bastard. I'll get him —"

"We don't know the answer because the cabbie's gone," Jesse said.

"Gone where?"

Jesse ignored the question. "We'll find him."

"Can I please go now, Chief Stone? I'm not feeling very well."

"Sure. I'll have someone drive you back to the hotel."

He watched Suit walk Franzen slowly to his office door. Jesse thought about how particularly unfair the end of a long life could often be. How to a man like Al Franzen it might feel like punishment. He wondered if Franzen would go to his grave asking himself what he had done to deserve it. Then, as Franzen reached the office door, he stopped. He turned back to Jesse.

"You know what I think, Chief Stone?"

"What's that?"

"Most of the time he loses, but sometimes the devil wins."

Jesse couldn't disagree. He had been a cop for too long, worked too many homicides, seen too much of the pain and damage humans can inflict on one another, often over insignificant things. He had his doubts about the devil, but he had no doubt there was evil in the world. And he didn't have to look beyond the borders of Paradise to find it. There was another thought in Jesse's head, one he didn't want to share yet, certainly not with Al Franzen. After Suit led the old man out of his office, Jesse called Tamara Elkin.

45

He met Tamara at one of those big chain restaurants in a shopping center in the next town over. A cheery hostess greeted them and led them to a booth. They sat silent as they half listened to an even cheerier server ramble on about two-for-one drinks and the sizzling shrimp fajita special. Jesse ordered coffee. Tamara ordered a Diet Coke.

"What's going on, Jesse?"

"I'm not sure, but I figured you'd be the person to talk to."

She said, "I didn't figure you for a fan of these types of restaurants."

"When I was in the minors, a place like this would have been beyond my means. Ate a lot of eggs, canned soup, and hot dogs and beans."

"Sounds dreamy."

"I would trade everything I've ever had to have those days back."

Tamara was skeptical. "Everything?"

"Everything."

His tone left little room for her skepticism.

"Okay, Jesse, come on, why the cloak-and-dagger? Why meet here?" she asked, noticing he wasn't wearing his PPD hat or his ever-present Paradise police jacket.

"I have to talk to you about something and there's still too much press in town. I didn't want to give them anything to speculate about."

She said, "We could have met at your house again."

He shook his head. "We can't do that every night. Not even my liver can take that. And this is kind of official in nature."

"I'm not sure I like the sound of this, Jesse. What is it?"

"Is there any possible way Maxie Connolly's death wasn't a suicide?"

Tamara Elkin looked gut-punched. She wrapped her arms around her midsection. Jesse didn't think she was even aware of it. She opened her mouth to answer, but before she could say a word, the waiter arrived with their drinks.

"Have you had a chance to look at the menu?" the waiter said, cheery as ever. "I'd recommend the corn chowder. It's —"

Tamara cut him off. "Scotch," she said.

"A double, neat."

The waiter looked perplexed even as he kept that practiced smile on his face. He then explained that scotch wasn't part of the two-fers. Jesse shooed him away with a promise of a big tip and kept quiet until the waiter was out of earshot.

"What's wrong, Doc?"

"How did you know, Jesse?"

He was confused. "Know what?"

She got that gut-punched look again. "About what happened to me in New York."

"I don't know anything about what happened to you in New York."

She smiled, but it quickly vanished. "Remember when I told you that it would take some twisted logic for me to explain how taking the medical examiner's job here was career advancement?"

"A long story for another time," he said.

She nodded. "Exactly."

"Let me guess," he said. "Now's the time."

She smiled without joy. "It would seem to be."

The server returned with the scotch and started to ask about a food order. When he saw the scowl on Jesse's face, the server disappeared.

"Perfect timing," she said. She gulped her scotch and took a second to compose herself. "Two years ago, I was working a night rotation and I signed off on an autopsy done by a more junior colleague on a nineteen-year-old female suicide. The deceased had been found unresponsive in the bathroom at a friend's party in Greenwich Village. It all seemed like a pretty straightforward opioid overdose. There were no signs of violence, no physical trauma. The victim had ready access to the drugs. Grandma had terminal cancer. The girl also apparently had a history of chronic depression. But the family refused to accept our findings."

"Parents never want to hear that their kid's killed herself. Means they failed."

"Especially politically connected parents with money."

"Lots of those in New York City," he said.

"They brought in their own expert and had a second autopsy done."

"And?"

"And their expert found something we missed, some very slight swelling around a tiny puncture wound that he claimed was an injection site. With this one fact, he fabricated a ludicrous scenario involving forced ingestion of pills and a lethal injection. It was absurd."

"But."

"But the doctor who performed the original autopsy had missed the swelling and I missed that he missed it."

"That couldn't be enough to get you fired," Jesse said.

"It could be if you were having an affair with the person who screwed up the autopsy and if a jealous, backstabbing son-of-a-bitch coworker whispered in your boss's ear."

"Uh-oh."

"I didn't get fired, exactly," she said. "None of this was leaked to the media, but it was made pretty clear to me that if I pushed back, there would be consequences. So I got pointed to the exit door and got a kick in the ass for a good-bye present. I took a year off and traveled to let things settle out before I began applying for jobs. Not too many takers, though. I guess not many folks believed I just wanted a more quiet life than New York City offered."

"Or just maybe there were carefully directed whispers."

"Maybe. So you can see why I thought that your questioning my findings about Maxie Connolly's COD would make me think you knew," she said, her voice brittle.

He nodded. "But that doesn't answer my question."

"I suppose what happened to Maxie Connolly might've been the result of foul play, but I didn't find any evidence indicating that it was."

No one needed to teach Jesse Stone a lesson on following the evidence.

"Do you really think it was a homicide?" she asked.

He explained about the missing cell phone and about what they had so conveniently discovered under Wiethop's bed.

"It was like it was left there for us to find. It should have been gift wrapped with a bow on it."

"Or maybe the guy wasn't exactly a criminal genius."

"He was a con, Doc. I could tell. He reeked of jail time. He might not have been a genius, but he was a criminal and he wasn't a kid. He'd know not to leave evidence around like that even if he was taking off for good. Without that stuff there, no one would have even cared that he left. Leaving that stuff under his bed was like leaving a sign that said *Come and get me.*"

"What's that expression cops always use? If criminals had half a brain —"

"We'd be in trouble." Jesse nodded. "If we had only found the phone or a suicide note by where Maxie went over the Bluffs, I would feel better about it being a suicide."

"It was pretty windy the night she died, Jesse. The note might've blown out to sea from up there for all you know and the cabbie might've taken the cell phone with him when he split."

"Maybe." He didn't sound convinced.

"Look, Jesse . . ." Tamara stared into her empty glass.

He understood. "Don't worry about it. No one will hear about what happened in New York from me, not even if my hunch turns out to be right. I don't throw my friends under the bus."

"Good to know."

"Can't afford to," he said.

"Why's that?"

"Don't have many friends."

Tamara Elkin smiled again and let out a big sigh of relief.

Jesse said, "Can we order now? I'm pretty hungry."

She nodded and Jesse waved to the waiter.

46

After his rendezvous with Tamara Elkin, Jesse went back to his house and poured himself a few fingers of Johnnie Walker Black. Somehow he couldn't bring himself to drink it. He just turned the glass around and around in his fingers, staring at it. He had struggled with drinking for most of his adult life and had, with Dix's help, come to a sort of peace about it with himself. It was the same kind of uneasy Zen he'd reached about his shoulder injury: He wasn't ever going to play shortstop in the major leagues and he was never going to stop drinking. When he finally accepted the reality of his drinking, it ceased filling in every crease and crack in his life. The struggle no longer took up so much of his energy.

The strange thing is that he could stop the physical act of drinking. Had stopped for weeks at a time. For months at a time. But the thirst, the desire, never left him. So even when he wasn't drinking, he never stopped wanting to. He played out the rituals of it with club soda and lime. He still came home and discussed his woes with his poster of Ozzie Smith, glass in hand. It was folly and somewhere he knew it. Like many things drinkers do, he told himself he was doing it to prove a point to the world when, in fact, the world didn't care and it proved very little. As was often the case, it was Dix who'd held the mirror up to Jesse's version of the emperor's new clothes.

One day he got fed up with Dix and told him so.

"You know I come in here every week and tell you I haven't had a drink in months and you can't be bothered to say a word about it."

"Dickens got paid by the word, Jesse, not me."

"What's that supposed to mean?"

"It means that you don't pay me to pat you on the back for being a good boy."

"An occasional attaboy would be nice."

"If I thought it was called for, I'd give it."

"And not drinking for nearly a year doesn't call for it?"

"Look, Jesse, like I said, I'm not here to pat you on the back and you're not here to be a good patient. You drinking or not drinking doesn't change the nature of my job. Other than not actually ingesting alcohol, have you changed?"

"I guess not."

"I never fooled you that talk therapy was going to do much to stop your drinking. If you want to stop, you'll stop. But if you do, when you do, do it for yourself because it's what you want, not to prove something to me or Jenn or anyone else. What you're doing now, it's like someone proving he can hold his breath for a long time. No matter how long he holds his breath, it doesn't mean he's going to actually stop breathing. Eventually, he's going to take another breath."

That night Jesse went home and stopped holding his breath. And when he drank again it was as if he had lost the weight of the baggage he'd been toting around with him since he'd left L.A.

This was different. He kept staring at the scotch in his glass. It was just as pretty to him as it had always been. He knew that even non-drinkers, or beer and wine drinkers, often wished they liked scotch because it was so damned beautiful. Yet he just didn't feel like drinking. He kept seeing the look on Tamara's face and how she gulped down the scotch when the waiter brought it to the table. She hadn't said it outright, but she and Jesse *were* a lot alike. He had been where she was now. He imagined he hadn't looked too dissimilar from her in the wake of his dismissal from the LAPD. It haunted him still. Maybe, he thought, this was the moment he and Dix had talked about. The moment when he decided for himself that he wanted to stop and would stop drinking. He knew better than to delve too deeply into it, that if it was the moment, he would know it only in retrospect.

Jesse turned on his TV and tuned it to the news. He realized it was a mistake almost as soon as he had done it, but it was already too late. There on the screen before him was a reporter he recognized from one of the big Boston stations. She was an older, handsome woman with perfectly cut, shoulder-length graying hair and striking blue eyes. She and Jesse had crossed paths a few times in the past and they had a kind of grudging respect for each other. She believed in what presenting the news used to mean and Jesse believed in being a good cop, no matter what. But Jesse realized that as fair as the reporter was and as disinterested in salacious speculation as she might be, there was no good way to spin what was going on in his town. He had three homicides — four, if his hunch was right — on his hands and he wasn't any closer to solving them than he was the morning they removed the debris of the collapsed building. If anything, he had more questions and was further away.

The reporter might have had a Cronkite-era ethic, but she also had an eye for the dramatic. She did her report from Trench Alley, the wind whipping the remnants of the crime scene tape so fiercely that it made snapping noises. The overcast skies and Sawtooth Creek as a backdrop only enhanced the drama. As she spoke, old photographs of Ginny and Mary Kate flashed over her shoulder. Basically, she rehashed what was already on the public record. She discussed Maxie Connolly's "suicide" and the discovery of the body in the tarp. Images of Maxie and of the dead man's tattoo replaced those of the girls. Although she took no visible delight in it, the reporter reminded her audience that neither the state police nor the Paradise PD had made any progress in solving the crimes nor in identifying the mysterious victim in the blue tarp.

Then, as a closing shot, the reporter had her cameraman move the focus away from her face. He zoomed in on the floor of the old factory building, specifically at the police barricades surrounding the two holes in the concrete slab where the bodies had been found. Piles of flowers, wreathes, dolls, notes, and crucifixes had been laid around the barriers to create a makeshift memorial to the dead girls. Wisely, the reporter remained silent for several seconds before signing off.

When Jesse looked back down at the glass in his hand, he noticed it was empty.

47

Suit, Molly, Peter Perkins, and Captain Healy were seated around the table in the conference room. Jesse stood by the whiteboard. With the exception of Healy, Jesse had called them all into his office that morning. He'd invited the captain to the meeting the previous evening between drinks in the wake of the news report from Trench Alley. Jesse had a good laugh at himself for thinking that he was on the verge of leaving alcohol behind him. Then he passed out on his couch, woke up at three in the morning, and couldn't get back to sleep.

Everyone was finished with their coffee and donuts when Molly asked the question they were all thinking about.

"What are we doing here, Jesse?"

"We're going to shake things up."

Molly kept after him. "Shake things up how?"

"I'll get to that," he said. "First I want to talk about what we're dealing with, one case at a time. Any progress on John Doe? Anybody?"

Suit raised his hand. "Nothing on this end, Jesse. We haven't even gotten any calls since that weirdo from Arizona called."

"Nothing on our end, either, afraid to say," Healy said. "John Doe's prints don't seem to be on file anywhere and no one's come forward about that tattoo. If we're going to get an ID on the vic, we may have to try and wrangle up some funds to do a forensic facial reconstruction."

"We might just have to, but today's not going to be the day to ask." Jesse looked at his watch. "My guess is that Bill Marchand or one of the other selectmen will be in here sometime this morning to deliver a warning to me. Not exactly the time to ask for favors."

"A warning about what?" Suit asked.

Molly gave Suit a cold stare. "About his job."

"They wouldn't fire you, Jesse," Suit said. "Where would this town be without you?"

"Thanks, Suit, but I wouldn't blame them. We've got three unsolved homicides and a questionable suicide on our hands. You played ball. You know how it works.

259

When a team is losing, you can't fire the whole team, so you fire the coach. It makes you look like you're doing something. If they fire me, it will take the pressure off them for a little while. But we'll worry about that later. Where are we on the cabdriver?"

Suit spoke again. "Just like you thought, Jesse, Wiethop's got a record. Kiting checks, shoplifting, stuff like that. Nothing violent."

"No sex offenses?" Perkins asked.

Suit shook his head. "Nothing like that."

Jesse said. "You put it all out on the wire?"

"I did, but he's not exactly public enemy number one. All we got him for is suspicion of possessing stolen property. If he ditches his car and keeps his head down, it's not going to be easy to find him."

Molly said, "Wait a second. Am I the only one in the room who heard you call Maxie Connolly's suicide questionable? You think Wiethop killed her?"

"I'm not sure what I think about what happened to Maxie, but there's a lot not to like about it."

"I agree," Healy said. "First we can't find any of her possessions, then most of her stuff turns up under the cabbie's bed like that." He snapped his fingers. "No, sir, it feels like amateur hour to me. A guy like this Wiethop fella, he's done time. He wouldn't keep her stuff. He'd take her cash and cards and dump the rest in a garbage can or toss it in the ocean. Never mind the panties. Suit says he's not a perv, so that really doesn't make sense. It's like maybe someone wanted your department to find it all there."

Jesse took some quiet pride in Healy's confirmation of everything he'd said to Tamara Elkin the night before.

Perkins said, "The funerals for the Connolly woman and her daughter are tomorrow, Jesse. Are you going to get a court order to stop the mother's burial?"

"No. The forensics report from the state came up with nothing and I spoke to the ME about it this morning. She went over her autopsy results again last night. The cause of death hasn't changed, and without evidence to the contrary, it still looks like a probable suicide. I can't go to a judge and ask him to stop the interment because I have a gut feeling. For now, we're going to keep any doubts about the suicide to ourselves," Jesse said. "But when it comes to the girls, I'm going to start being very cooperative with the press."

Suit made a face. "But we don't have anything."

Jesse smiled. "They don't know that. As a

261

matter of fact, we now have a prime suspect and a report from the lab that says they might be able to salvage some DNA from the blanket found near the girls' remains. We also might have some hairs and fibers that aren't a match to either of the girls. First thing you're going to do, Suit, is release the girls' autopsy results, but without the photographs."

Suit opened his mouth to speak, then thought better of it.

48

Only Jesse and Healy were left in the conference room, both of them looking at the whiteboard. Jesse hadn't written on it. Healy wondered if Jesse ever meant to write anything on it and asked about it.

"So was all of that smoke or just mostly?"

"Mostly," Jesse said.

"I know I'm only the head of the state homicide bureau, but do you think you might manage to sort out the smoke from the facts for me? I get cranky when smoke gets blown into the wrong places. Gives me a rash. Is there a suspect or isn't there?"

"Sort of."

"We going to play twenty questions?"

"Alexio Dragoa. You know the name?" Jesse asked.

"Sounds Portuguese to these old ears."

"Uh-huh. Fishing family. Father died a few years ago and the son's taken over the trade. Both of them ornery SOBs. The son's

263

not quite as bad as the father, but bad enough. Good-looking bastard. Likes to drink and gets into the occasional bar fight."

"Yeah, well, fishermen are a tough breed. Not the kind of guys you want dating your only daughter. What about this Alexio?"

"A little while before Maxie Connolly went over the Bluffs, I got him on hotel security video having a confrontation with her in the bar."

Healy raised his eyebrows. "Confrontation?"

"He says he was drunk and horny and he used to have a thing for her when he was a kid. When she tried to blow him off, he says he had a sudden attack of conscience and apologized to her and gave his sympathies about Ginny."

"Wait a second here, Jesse. Maxie Connolly left this town, what, twenty-four, twenty-five years ago? She had to be sixty if not older when she went off the bluff. How old is the fisherman?"

"Few years older than Molly."

"The fisherman must've been carrying that old crush around a long time."

Jesse shrugged.

Healy asked, "So you've spoken to him?"

"Uh-huh."

"You think he killed Maxie?"

"No, he has an alibi that totally checks out. Airtight."

"You think the cabbie did it?"

Jesse shook his head. "Maybe, but I doubt it."

Healy was confused. "You don't think the cabbie killed her. You *know* Dragoa didn't kill her, but you don't think she killed herself."

Jesse nodded. "That's about it."

"Then who, Colonel Mustard?"

"When I catch the killer, I'll let you know."

"Okay, wait . . . you know Dragoa didn't kill Maxie Connolly. But is he the suspect in the girls' murders or am I missing something here?"

"What I can tell you is that something's up with Dragoa."

"But I thought you just said —"

Jesse held up his palm. "First he hit on a woman who winds up dead a few hours later. Then he shows up at Mary Kate O'Hara's funeral. Unexpectedly, too."

"He does seem to be showing up in interesting places," Healy said, scratching his chin.

"Can you spare a man? With Gabe still in rehab and Suit on light duty, I can't afford to dedicate anyone to Dragoa. When I start putting all this stuff on the street over the next day or two, I'm thinking maybe he'll get spooked and show his hand."

"If he has a hand to show."

Jesse made a face. "I know it's flimsy, but when flimsy's what you've got, you go with it."

"Your instincts are good enough for me. For a few days, sure, I can give you somebody to tail the fisherman."

"Not just somebody."

"Don't sweat the details, Jesse. Dragoa eats half his pickle at lunch, you'll know it and you'll know whether it was a kosher dill or a sweet gherkin. But once he takes his boat out . . ." Healy shrugged. "Well, I can't help you there. Black helicopters and drones aren't in this year's budget."

"Understood."

"When should I have my man start?" Healy asked.

"Tomorrow, early, before sunup. Alexio's been known to head straight from the bar or the drunk tank to his boat. Here's Dragoa's address and where he docks his boat," Jesse said, pulling a slip of paper out of his back pocket. "Let's give my lies a couple of hours to percolate."

Healy took the paper, waved it in the air. "Pretty confident I was going to agree to lend you a man."

"Let's just say I was hopeful and leave it at that."

"You owe me a drink."

"Several."

Healy extended his right hand. "You got it."

There was an insistent knocking on the conference room door and an impatient person on the other side.

49

Jesse had never seen Bill Marchand look beat-up and disheveled. That was no longer the case. Men like Marchand had an image to maintain and usually went to great lengths to protect it. It wasn't so much out of vanity or ego, as people often assumed. Defending their images was something Jesse understood about politicos that most people got wrong. The person beneath the image, rotten or pure, beau or bully, was almost beside the point. The electorate voted for the image, not the person behind it. Jesse thanked his lucky stars that his job was by appointment because he didn't think he could win an election, nor would he ever want to.

Although Marchand had been impatient to get into the room, he seemed to be fumbling for his words. This, too, was a phenomenon Jesse had never before witnessed. Marchand, even when bearing bad news, usually delivered it calmly and without hesitation. Just when Jesse was about to come to the selectman's rescue, Marchand found his footing and his words.

"Can a friend get a drink around here?"

This is going to be bad, Jesse thought. Maybe worse than he'd anticipated.

Jesse threw a thumb over his shoulder. "Sure, Bill. Let's go into my office."

Jesse got a funny feeling in his stomach, a feeling he had had only twice in his life. The first time had been when he was in A ball and got called into his manager's office after going hitless in three consecutive games. He knew then as he knew now that it was trouble. The other time was when he found out Jenn was cheating on him. Both times it signaled the end of things. One ending was temporary. He earned his starting job back the next week. One ending wasn't, though it took a decade for him and Jenn to realize it.

It was strange how things worked. Jesse's job had been threatened before, more than once, and he'd taken it in stride. Jesse always took life in its stride, sometimes with an assist from Johnnie Walker. It was his way. He was tough, a man unto himself. Molly had summed him up best when she compared him to Crow. She said they were both self-contained men, immune from the petty vanities and forces that swayed weaker men. He wasn't feeling immune presently. Just at the moment he had finally accepted that Paradise would be his life's work, he was going down.

When they were settled in at his desk, Jesse poured some of the same Irish he had poured for Maxie Connolly only a few days earlier.

"You sure you won't drink with me?" Marchand asked, his hand a bit unsteady.

"Too early even for me." Jesse managed a laugh.

"You sure?"

"Bill, say what you've got to say. We keep on like this, you're going to offer me a cigarette, a blindfold, and ask if I have any last words."

Marchand didn't guzzle his drink, but he didn't sip it, either. He stretched his neck. Spoke.

"Jesse, you've got a week."

Although he felt a warm sense of relief, Jesse sat stony-faced. A week could be an eternity or it could be over in the blink of an eye, but at least he still had his job and a chance to do right by the dead girls.

"Did you hear me, Jesse?"

"I've got a bad shoulder, not bad ears."

270

"The mayor wanted your ass on a silver platter and she wanted it right now. My other colleagues were pretty tepid in their support of you. I bought you a week."

"A week to solve three homicides, two of which happened twenty-five years ago. Should I find the killers of Judge Crater in my spare time?"

"Jesse, you can be an ungrateful SOB and a hard man to like sometimes."

"Sorry, Bill. I know that most of the time you are my sole backer in town."

Marchand grabbed at his chest to feign a heart attack. "I think I need another drink and some CPR. Was that an apology I just heard coming out of your mouth?"

"Giving me a time limit isn't going to solve these cases for you or for anyone you bring in to sit in this chair."

"I know that, Jesse. I told them all that. I told them that till I was blue in the face." Marchand stood, looking worse than he had when Jesse had laid eyes on him earlier. He walked to the office door and turned back to Jesse and in a voice as cool as a crocodile's said, "You've got a week."

50

Stu Cromwell was happy to see Jesse walk into his office. It was easy for Jesse to read Stu's smile. Murder sells papers, and just recently Paradise had plenty to sell. And Jesse knew that the few crumbs he'd thrown Cromwell's way had let the newspaperman sell some stories to larger news services and earn a little money beyond the sales of his own paper, the circulation of which was forever dwindling. Until their last visit together, Jesse hadn't realized just how dire the paper's situation was. If the current events kept the paper going a little longer, so be it.

Cromwell nodded, gestured to the empty seat across from him, but didn't get up.

"Jesse."

"Stu."

Cromwell reached into his drawer, pulled out a fresh bottle of Canadian Club and two glasses. "Drink?"

"Everybody's starting early today."

"How's that?"

"Forget it, Stu. None for me, but go right ahead."

"Don't mind if I do," he said, twisting the cap and breaking the seal. "You sure?"

Jesse nodded. Cromwell poured and sipped.

"You've been hitting it mighty hard lately, Stu. Last time I was in here, the bottle was still pretty full."

Cromwell looked confused, then recovered. "Yeah. Between Martha and the long hours since the bodies have been discovered. You know how it is."

"I do."

"So what can I do you for, Jesse? You have something for me?"

"I might, but first I'd like to talk about Paradise."

"What about it?"

"When the girls went missing, what was the town like? I haven't been able to get a grip on that, no matter how many old files I read or pictures I look at. Everyone tells me it was smaller then. I get that much."

Cromwell poured himself some more rye, then put away the bottle and the extra glass he'd taken out for Jesse. He sat back in his seat.

"It was a different place back then," he said, a wistful look on his face. "Obviously we were just as close to Boston, but it might as well have been a different world. It was a smaller town with a small-town feel. But for the ocean and the whaling nonsense, it was more like northern New England, more Maine or New Hampshire than a secondary suburb of Boston. Does that make any sense?"

"Some."

"It was less affluent. The old families that had established the town were either dying off, moving out, or running out of funds. Stiles Island wasn't very developed yet. The people who lived here then were, for the most part, people born and raised here. We'd had a few 'white flight' refugees from Boston, but not many to speak of. There wasn't a whole lot of crime."

"Sounds a little too good to be true."

Cromwell sipped some more of his drink. "Don't misunderstand. It wasn't nirvana. We had our issues. The Swap was getting pretty bad and there weren't a whole lot of jobs being created in the area. We had our share of abusive parents, wife beaters, drunks, and thieves, but until the girls went missing, most people left their cars and houses unlocked."

Jesse asked, "Are you saying that the town changed when Mary Kate and Ginny went missing?"

"No. It had already started to change, but that July fourth is a convenient line of demarcation. By the time the girls disappeared, the whole world had changed. It had begun to contract, and as the world seemed to get smaller, Paradise seemed to lose its small town–ness. Maybe it was AIDS or MTV or the first computers, I don't know. It just became harder to be apart from the rest of the world. Stiles Island was slated for development. The yacht club was expanding and people with money had begun to move in from Boston and New York City. But when the girls went missing, it became an easy dividing line with which to view Paradise's history. And here's the hardest part to believe. Paradise supported two daily newspapers. Amazing."

Jesse took it all in, thinking if he had any other questions. Cromwell got impatient.

"Anything else, Jesse? You mentioned you had something for me."

"I said I might have something for you."

"Do you?" He finished his drink.

"Remember I told you about Maxie Connolly's missing items?"

"Was on this morning's front page." He

held up a copy of the paper for Jesse to see, his index finger pointing at the headline:

NO PEACE EVEN IN DEATH
MAXIE CONNOLLY'S GOODS GONE

"I take it you haven't seen this until now," Cromwell said.

"I've been a little busy today, Stu."

"Sorry, but what about Maxie's missing items?"

"They're not missing anymore. We found them in the apartment of a cabdriver, a man with a record named Rod Wiethop. W-i-e-t-h-o-p." Jesse spelled it out and slid a file across Cromwell's desk. "Here's his driver's license photo, his license plate number, and a description of his car. As far as we know, he was the last person to see Maxie alive."

"I take it Mr. Wiethop isn't in police custody?"

Jesse nodded.

"Do you think he robbed her?"

"Possibly."

Cromwell smiled. "Possibly?"

"That's what I said."

"Are you now questioning whether or not Maxie committed suicide?"

"Draw your own conclusions. That's what newspaper people do, isn't it?"

Cromwell's smile got bigger. "Can we go off the record?"

"Okay," Jesse agreed. "Off the record."

"Do you think Wiethop killed her?"

"No."

"But you think somebody did?"

"Maybe."

Cromwell was silent.

"You have my permission to attribute all the on-the-record stuff to me. You print any of that off-the-record stuff and attribute it to me, Stu, we'll have a major problem. It'll be personal, not official." Jesse walked to the door. "By the way, I'm about to call a press conference for . . ." He looked at his watch. "For one p.m. You'll want to be there."

"About Maxie?" Cromwell asked.

"Everything but. Maxie's your exclusive."

"Anything else, Jesse?"

"Uh-huh."

"What?"

"Bring a big notepad. You'll need it."

51

That was the odd thing, that it should have been the three of them to have killed the girls. It wasn't like they were that close, not then and certainly not now. Of all the many things haunting him about that long-ago Fourth of July, it was that it should have been the three of them. There were a thousand what-ifs that might have changed all their destinies, but it was his curse that he should be bound to these two morons for eternity. They had been teammates. Friendly enough, but not really friends. John and Alexio were buds. He and Zevon were close, but it wasn't like they all hung out together. Before that night, he couldn't recall a single time when he'd hung out with Millner and Dragoa without the other guys around.

That wasn't how it was supposed to be. For the weeks leading up to that Fourth, the plan was for him and Zevon to meet

Ginny Connolly and Mary Kate O'Hara at the park and for the four of them to head out to Humpback Point. Just the four of them and no one pretended they were headed out there to watch the fireworks from Stiles. They'd kept it pretty quiet. The girls were sixteen, and though no one in Paradise made a big deal about statutory rape back then, they all agreed it was best not to advertise. He'd scored half an ounce of good weed and taken bottles of Southern Comfort and Jack Daniel's from his dad's liquor cabinet. He'd even paid Dragoa twenty bucks to use his rowboat. It was all perfect until Zevon backed out that morning. Fucking Zevon had ruined everything and paid for it with his life. But not even that sacrifice could undo the old blood. Now, as he walked to the maintenance shed, he knew there would be more blood. There would have to be.

And here they were again, the three of them. They had tried very hard not to ever be seen in public together for fear of anyone in town piecing together the events of that night. In spite of the fact that it was pretty clear early on, after the police interviews, that both girls had kept the secret, they could never be one hundred percent certain. They had worried most about Molly Burke.

Although they were seniors and didn't know any of the girls very well, they'd heard that Molly Burke and Mary Kate were best friends. Dragoa, the stupid hothead, had suggested killing Molly, but had been voted down. They had another way of keeping tabs on Molly. He convinced John and Alexio that if Molly knew anything, she would tell Zevon and that Zevon would tell him. Of course, in the end, the joke was on him. He was the one to confess their sins to Zevon.

"Did you hear what Stone said on the TV today?" Dragoa said almost before he'd stepped fully into the maintenance shed. "They got our DNA, maybe."

"I heard."

"They found hair and fiber samples from that goddamned picnic blanket you made us wrap them in," Millner said. "I told you to just chuck 'em in the freakin' hole. I mean, jeez, they was already dead. What the hell did it matter?"

"It's twenty-five years too late for second-guessing, guys. Besides, we would have had to get rid of the blanket anyway. If we burned it, we would have attracted attention. If we tossed it in Sawtooth Creek, we risked having it traced back to the building we buried them in. And don't forget, that blanket is the thing that helped us carry their bodies without getting covered in their blood. Sometimes there aren't good choices, just less bad ones."

"They know there was more than one of us," Millner said.

"They don't know. They think it's a possibility. Very different things."

"Cut it out, man," Dragoa said. "You heard that reporter from Boston. She said that because one of the girls was stabbed and that the other had a fractured skull that it meant there had to be more than one killer."

"She said it suggested there might be, not that there was. Jesse didn't confirm it. He said he will follow the evidence."

Millner laughed. "Stone always says that crap. Do you think they really found all that evidence like Stone is saying?"

"Well, maybe if Alexio had been able to control his appetites better. Maybe if he didn't stab Mary Kate so many times, there wouldn't have been so much blood and a need for —"

"I was drunk."

"You're always drunk."

"Shut up! Shut up!" Dragoa said, charging at him. "I'll kill you, you mother —"

Millner grabbed him, clamping his arms around the fisherman. "Relax, buddy. Relax.

It don't matter now."

"Johnny's right. I'm sorry. None of that matters now. The only thing we can do is wait it out."

"We been waiting it out for twenty-five years," Millner said.

"Then a few more days won't matter."

Dragoa didn't like it. "Easy enough for you to say."

"You're wrong, Alexio. It's not any easier for me. I'll see what I can find out and I'll keep in touch same way as always."

There was no handshaking when he left. There never was. As he walked quickly back to his vehicle under cover of darkness, his mind was churning as it had on that beautiful summer night all those years ago.

52

Jesse was angry to see how few people came to the wake for Ginny and Maxie. It was held at the same funeral home where Mary Kate O'Hara had been laid out. Along with Jesse and Molly, only Al Franzen, Stu Cromwell, Bill Marchand, and an old priest from Sacred Heart had turned out. Jesse could hear the excuses in his head, the stuff about how small towns dealt with their shame and their secrets. But today he wasn't in the mood for excuses or for rationalizations. There was one person's absence in particular that bothered him: Alexio Dragoa. He was nowhere in sight. Given Jesse's suspicions about the fisherman and Dragoa's confrontation with Maxie at the bar, he was sure Dragoa would turn up. Maybe at the church, Jesse thought, like with Mary Kate.

Molly elbowed Jesse. "That's so Maxie."

"What is?"

"Her coffin . . . the lid is open. God, even in death the woman is vain."

"Don't blame her. Check out Franzen. It's his doing. I'm sure of it."

Al Franzen, looking frail and distraught, had moved a chair to within a foot or two of the coffin.

"He really loved her," Jesse said. "He fed off her energy. No matter what you thought of Maxie, she was full of life."

Molly resisted the urge to argue with him.

Marchand leaned over to Jesse, said, "Sorry about yesterday. I don't enjoy playing the heavy."

"I figured the warning was coming. Might as well have heard it from you."

"You going over to the church?"

"Uh-huh. You?"

"Can't," Marchand said. "Business. Sometimes that earning your daily bread gets in the way."

"Tell me about it."

Marchand patted Jesse on the shoulder. "Again, sorry about yesterday."

About five minutes later, the insurance broker knelt down by both coffins, mouthed silent prayers, crossed himself, and slipped out.

With all eyes on Marchand, Jesse walked over to the back row, where Stu Cromwell

284

was seated. Cromwell looked in worse shape than Al Franzen. Cromwell was in his sixties, but he was one of those people who, because of their energy, was kind of ageless. But the newspaperman looked every bit his age that morning.

"Another rough night with Martha?" Jesse said.

"What? Huh?" Cromwell sounded as if he had been very far away. "Yeah, it's rough. She's in so much pain."

"Then what are you doing here?"

"Following up. The missing cabbie is front-page news today, or haven't you seen the paper?"

Jesse nodded. "I've seen it."

"You seem POed, Chief."

"There's no one here."

Cromwell said, "After our talks, that surprises you?"

"Disappoints me."

"I'm a newspaperman, so I'm cynical by nature. My view is that if you give anyone ample opportunity, they will disappoint you. The people of Paradise are no better or worse than anywhere else."

Jesse was willing to leave it at that, but Cromwell seemed to be in a particularly philosophical mood that morning. And Jesse could smell the alcohol on the newspaperman's breath.

"They're not monsters," Cromwell said. "I had a writing professor who once told me that everyone is the hero of his or her own story. I'm sure most folks got up this morning and were more concerned about the dramas in their own lives than whether or not they should come to this. Even monsters don't see a monster reflected in the mirror. I always try to remember that when I do my work."

Jesse found that last bit of Stu's ramblings out of place and out of character, but he let it go.

He sat back next to Molly. The old priest stood up. He said a few words about the church service and about the burials. Then led the assembled in a prayer. Al Franzen willed himself to lean over the open coffin and to kiss his wife on her cold, lifeless lips. Jesse and Molly headed out to where Molly's cruiser was parked.

"I know you wanted the day off," Jesse said, settling into the cruiser next to Molly. "But you know how short we are."

"Forget it, Jesse. My big sister's taking my mom to the church. And it's about time I started pulling my weight again."

53

Molly chatted through most of the drive to the church. Jesse didn't know what got Molly going, whether it was how the planets aligned or if it was that her friend Ginny was finally being laid to rest. Whatever it was, Jesse was glad for the chatter. Though no one who knew Jesse now would have believed it, one of the things he missed about his old job in Robbery-Homicide was the camaraderie with his partners. That job entailed long hours during stakeouts, waiting around the courthouse, hours filled up with chatter.

It was a holdover from his ball-playing days. Even loners and self-contained men like Jesse Stone missed being part of a team. Anyone who'd been in the military, inside a locker room, or on an endless road-trip bus ride would understand it. You didn't have to like all the guys on the team or in your unit. Jesse certainly didn't, but it was an us-against-the-world type of deal. You did battle together and that bred a closeness unlike any other.

Things were different for him now that he was the boss. And when you're the boss, the dynamics change. There was no longer talk among equals. He missed talking baseball. He remembered arguing over which was the best East L.A. taqueria or which restaurant served the best barbecue in Koreatown. In the end, it was his last two partners that got him fired. When they went to Cronjager, Jesse's boss, and told him they wouldn't ride with Jesse because he was so drunk that they couldn't trust him to back them up. That still stung. Not because he blamed them. He blamed himself and he guessed he blamed Jenn a little bit, too.

His time at the station with Molly and his occasional forays into the field with Suit were as close as he came to his days in L.A. So when Molly started talking about being a kid in Paradise, Jesse wasn't about to stop her.

"Mary Kate and I were closer than my sisters and me. In a family, there are resentments, you know. My sisters and I competed for things, everything. Everything from my dad's affection to who got the biggest piece of my mom's strawberry-rhubarb pie for dessert. I loved that pie, how it smelled so sweet from the berries, but that when you bit into it it tasted tart, too. That was the best part. My mom doesn't make it anymore, not since Dad passed. I try to make it for my kids sometimes, but it's not as good as Mom's. The competition, it wasn't like that with Mary Kate. We shared stuff. We didn't fight over things. We were always on each other's side."

"What about Ginny?"

Molly looked over at Jesse. "Ginny lived near us, spent a lot of time in our house, but we weren't nearly as close as me and Mary Kate. I guess because she was around so much, she was competing for some of the same stuff as me and my sisters were."

"I can see that."

"It didn't mean I didn't like Ginny. I did. A lot. It's just the difference between good friends and best friends. Like that," Molly said, turning the cruiser onto the road leading up to Sacred Heart Church.

Jesse nodded.

"And Ginny was quieter than Mary Kate. I also think I was a little jealous of Ginny. You could see that she was going to be beautiful, even better-looking than Maxie. I think Maxie saw that, too. Probably resented her for it. Mary Kate and I used to talk about how easy it was going to be for Ginny to have all the boys she wanted, but Mary Kate felt sorrier for Ginny than I did. She was protective of Ginny, too. I guess that was because she didn't live on my block and didn't have to deal with Ginny and Maxie like my family did."

Jesse said, "You and Mary Kate didn't fight over things until Warren."

Molly came to a stop at a light, checking her rearview to make sure the small procession was intact behind her.

"That's why it hurt so much, I guess," she said. "We had always been able to work things out between us without fighting until then."

When the light went green, Molly eased off the brake and drove slowly ahead, the hearse close behind the cruiser.

"What happened?"

"I — I, um . . ." Molly faltered for the first time since she'd started talking.

Jesse let it go. He was glad for the chatter while it lasted and he loved seeing the young Molly make another appearance.

"You know, Jesse, it was me, not Mary Kate," Molly said, seeming to have regained her voice.

"It was you what?"

"I was the one who tried stealing Warren

away from Mary Kate, not the other way around." Molly's face reddened. "I gave him the one thing Mary Kate wouldn't."

"Oh."

" 'Oh' is right."

"I can see how she might not want to talk to you after that," Jesse said.

"She never forgave me. How could she?"

"She would have . . . eventually."

"Thanks for saying that, Jesse. But I'll never know that."

"It might not have been right away, but when you both realized that this Warren guy wasn't going to be either your prince or Mary Kate's, she would have come back to you."

"It wouldn't have been the same," Molly said.

He shrugged. "Whatever happened to Warren?"

"He got a full ride for basketball at some small school in the Midwest. Butler, maybe, or Davidson. Didn't matter, because he was gone. He played one year, the year after Mary Kate and Ginny went missing. Then . . . then . . ."

"Then what?"

"We're here," Molly said, pulling onto the grounds of Sacred Heart, the huge church looming at the top of the hill.

Jesse was happier to see more people had turned out for the church services than had been at the funeral home. Molly's big sister and her mom were there. Robbie Wilson, the fire chief, and a few of his men showed with their wives. Jesse saw the faces of some men who seemed familiar to him, though he couldn't place them.

"From the demolition crew," Molly said. "The guys who found the bodies. They came to Mary Kate's service, too."

Now Jesse could place their faces and it explained what Robbie Wilson and his men were doing there. Jesse remembered that he, too, sometimes would attend victims' funerals, and not always to hunt for suspects.

Molly pointed out some of her old classmates to Jesse as well, but Alexio Dragoa was still nowhere to be found. Jesse considered stepping outside and making a call to see if he could get an update on the fisherman's whereabouts. With everything that had gone on since yesterday afternoon, Jesse hadn't bothered to check with Healy to see if he had followed through and arranged for someone to tail Dragoa. He resisted the urge to call. Either there was a man on Dragoa or there wasn't. Nothing he could do now was going to change that.

Then suddenly, during a moment of silent prayer, the sound of ringing cell phones echoed through the cavernous stone church. Jesse, Molly, Robbie Wilson, and his men all grabbed for their phones, put them to their ears, and headed for the exit doors, many muttering, "Sorry." Even before they made it outside, the insistent droning of the town fire alarm filled up the air. Wilson and his men ran for their vehicles. Many in the crowd looked to Jesse for an answer, but Jesse had no answer to give them as he and Molly headed for the cruiser.

"Suit, what's going on?" Jesse said as Molly hit the lights and siren.

"We've got two big house fires in progress."

"Maybe you have spent too much time at that desk. Last time I checked, Robbie Wilson was fire chief. Why call me and Molly? Dispatch two units for crowd con—"

"It's where the fires are, Jesse."

"Is this *Jeopardy!*? Do I need to ask you in the form of a question or are you going to tell me?"

"Sorry. It's the dead girls' houses."

"The O'Hara house and —"

"The Connollys' old place two doors down from Molly's mom's house," Suit said. "I thought you'd want to know."

"You were right to call. Thanks, Suit."

54

Tess O'Hara stood on the sidewalk, wrapped in two fire department blankets. She just stood there, staring, immobile, her face empty. When Jesse and Molly approached her, all she could say was "Mary Kate's all gone now. She's all gone, forever."

The sad and sagging house Jesse recalled from the day he and Molly had come to notify Tess that Mary Kate's remains had been found was totally engulfed in fire, the flames snapping in the breeze in seeming defiance of the endless water spray shot into their midst. The firemen did what they could, but Jesse had been around long enough to know a lost cause when he saw one. All the water and foam in the world wasn't going to save Tess O'Hara's house.

The firemen were trying to contain the blaze so that none of the burning embers could ride the cold winds and spread the fire to the houses on either side, or worse.

Pictures, Jesse thought, never did fires justice. For as dramatic as pictures were, they failed to capture the intensity of the heat or the smells. The acrid chemical stench of melting plastic and burning rubber. The choking stink of steam from floor joists and wall studs turned into charcoal and ash.

Jesse spoke to Stan Dolan, Robbie Wilson's deputy.

"What do you think?" Jesse asked.

"Arson. There was definitely an accelerant used. You could smell it in the air when we arrived on scene. The place went up like that." Dolan snapped his fingers. "Wouldn't have happened that fast without a chemical assist. And the garage was involved, too. No reason for a detached garage to be burning like that before the fire could spread. Nope, someone made this happen. The old lady was lucky to get out."

Jesse wondered if Tess O'Hara thought she was lucky to get out.

He asked, "Have you talked to Robbie? What about the other house?"

"Same deal," Dolan said. "Went up like the sun."

"Thanks."

Jesse stood next to Dolan for another minute, watching as the O'Hara house crumpled into a pile of burning sticks and memories. Unlike the building that collapsed on Trench Alley, there was no groan or shudder. It just collapsed, as much from grief and mourning as from fire.

"What do you think it means, Jesse, these two fires at once?" Molly asked when he got back to the cruiser.

"It means my plan's working and that someone's scared."

"Who?"

Jesse just smiled, sure that he knew the answer. The smile lasted only the time it took to call Healy. According to him, Jesse was wrong.

"Dragoa's been working on his boat all day," Healy said. "My man's been on him from before five this morning. He's still with him."

"Are you sure?"

"Jesse, this is one of my best men. He's got photos of Dragoa taken every quarter-hour. You want to see them?"

"Forget it," Jesse said, watching the firemen roll up their hoses.

Healy asked what the fuss was and Jesse explained about the fires.

"Anybody hurt?"

"No. Tess O'Hara made it out of the house and the family that lives in the old Connolly house wasn't home."

"Could they salvage the houses?"

"Both are total losses."

"Well, you scared somebody into covering all his bases," Healy said. "Didn't want you poking around in the girls' old rooms looking for stray hairs or fibers that might be matches for him."

"Problem is I think it's more than one somebody and the one somebody I thought I had is the wrong one."

"We all get it wrong. In baseball you get it right only three times out of ten and you're the batting champ."

"Batting three hundred in homicide gets you fired, not the batting title. And I've been guessing wrong a lot lately."

"Hey, look at it this way, you may be wrong about who, but the misinformation is working and that's what counts, no? The press stirred the pot for you. You catch the firestarter and maybe we'll finally have the murderer or murderers."

"Maybe. These fires do confirm at least one thing. One of the killers is still here."

"Your John Doe turning up where he did told you as much," Healy said.

"Now there's no doubt about it. Coincidence is totally off the board."

"About your John Doe, any progress there?"

"None. We're not even getting any crazies calling in."

Jesse looked back at the pitiful remnants of the O'Hara house and clicked off.

"You hungry, Crane?"

"Sure, Jesse."

"Daisy's? We haven't been there for a while."

"Good idea," Molly said. "You don't want her to think you don't like lesbians."

"I never met a person less insecure about their sexuality than Daisy. I'm more worried she'll think I don't like her food."

"Good point." Molly put the cruiser in gear.

55

After he got back from lunch at Daisy's, Jesse called Suit into his office. As he walked in, the big man seemed to be moving with a little more ease than he had in recent weeks. Jesse wondered if he wasn't seeing Suit more with his heart than his eyes. He took a long look at Suit's face. The goofiness and boyish good looks were still there, but some of the joy had been drained out of him. His reddish hair had taken on darker tones and gray threads were showing through. Getting gut-shot will do that to you, Jesse thought. It was more than that, though. Suit wasn't a man made for light duty. Jesse guessed he'd always known Suit would detest working the desk, and Suit had certainly made no secret of his displeasure.

When Suit was shot, Jesse had been only a hundred yards away. Jesse didn't like thinking about that day last spring when it had happened. A thousand things had gone through Jesse's head when he reached Suit and saw the wounds. Not least among them was rage. Rage not at the man who had shot Suit, but at Suit for getting himself in a position to get shot. He thought he'd done a good job of keeping that to himself.

"What is it, Jesse? Did I screw something up?"

"Why would you say that?"

"Because you mostly seem pissed off at me all the time."

"No, I don't."

"If you say so, Jesse. You're chief."

"I didn't call you in here because you screwed something up, and I'm not mad at you."

"Okay. Then what?"

"You up for a little overtime tonight?"

Suit couldn't hide his unhappiness at the thought of more hours answering phones and brewing coffee. On the other hand, he didn't want to ruin his chances of getting back on the street by whining.

"Sure, Jesse, if that's what you need."

Jesse laughed.

Suit was confused. "I say something funny?"

"You got it wrong. I don't want you in here."

Suit's confused expression turned to joy

301

before Jesse's eyes.

"Relax, Suit, it's not full duty, either."

"But —"

"Go home and throw on some civilian clothes. Then I want you to help canvass the blocks around the two fires. Peter and Ed are out there now, but you're better with people than either of them. Somebody must have seen something. Those two fires didn't start themselves and they're miles apart."

"You're thinking somebody must have seen a vehicle, otherwise how could the arsonist have gotten from one place to the other."

Jesse smiled. "That or there were two firebugs at work. Go find me something."

Suit asked, "Should I carry?"

"Not your service weapon. This is officially unofficial. Remember, you're on light duty. If anyone asks, you volunteered to help after your shift. I'll take care of your overtime."

"Thanks, Jesse."

Don't get yourself shot. "You're welcome" is what Jesse said. "Now get out of here."

It seemed to Jesse that Suit was moving even better than he was when he walked into his office. After Suit closed the door behind him, Jesse made two calls. One was to Tamara Elkin. The other was to Dix.

56

Tamara Elkin reached over Jesse to fill his wineglass. Jesse was glad he had a friend like Tamara, someone to talk to if he wanted to talk. It wasn't all roses. He knew that at least for a little while yet there would be tension between them, that Tamara would want to move beyond friends and that he, too, would have to fight the temptation to move in that direction. If she kept coming over and they kept hanging out and drinking together, that temptation was bound to get stronger.

Tamara liked a lot about Jesse. For one thing, he was sure of himself. He didn't need the constant reassurance that most men seemed to require. So many men she had known were still little boys who were interested either in themselves or in trying to re-create that one someone they had lost in high school. Jesse was in the moment. She cringed at thinking those words, but there it was. Another thing she liked about him was that he wasn't a talker. No fishing for compliments for him. But the truth was she was attracted to him and didn't know how much longer she could play the role of Tonto to his Lone Ranger.

"Cheers," she said, lifting her glass.

"Cheers."

He sipped, staring out into space and seeming to lose himself in the music playing on his stereo. She wasn't much for jazz, but she understood how someone who liked it could get lost in it. She sat down on the couch, staring at him staring into space. She ascribed it to him zoning out to escape from the pressure he'd been under and wondered if now was the right moment to revisit a discussion of their friendship. She opened her mouth to say it, but those weren't the words that came out.

"I heard about the fires in Paradise today."

"Uh-huh."

"What do you think it means, both of the dead girls' houses being torched like that?"

That got Jesse's attention. "Torched? Who said anything about arson?"

"Come on, Jesse. I am the ME. I hear things."

He nodded. "They were torched, all right. What does it mean? Means my misinformation's got someone worried."

"You might say you lit a fire under someone's ass."

He laughed. "No, *you* might say that. I never would."

"Puns beneath you?"

"No, Doc, just bad ones."

Tamara said, "You have an idea who you upset?"

"I thought I did, but the suspect had an alibi. Guy always seems to have an alibi."

"Can't you shoot holes in it?"

"The alibi? Not this one," he said. "He was under police surveillance while the fires were being lit."

"Bummer." Fortified by her wine, Tamara decided now was as good a time as any to broach the subject of the nature of their friendship. "Listen, Jesse, I —"

He raised his hand to cut her off and reached into his pocket for his phone. He waved the phone at her. "I better get this. Jesse Stone," he said without checking the screen.

"Jesse, are you all right?" It was Jenn.

He sat up straight, tensed.

Tamara mouthed, "Who is it?" He shook his head.

Jenn asked, "Jesse, is something wrong? You're breathing funny."

"I was just relaxing. I'm fine, Jenn." He emphasized the name so Tamara would understand. He stood up and lowered the stereo.

"No you're not," Jenn said. "I've seen all the stuff on TV. I read the papers."

"You know me. I'll be okay."

"You say that."

Tamara Elkin walked out of Jesse's living room and began clearing the dishes off the dining room table and tossing the cartons away from their takeout dinner.

"Why are you calling, Jenn?"

"Because of what you're going through. Just because we're not together anymore doesn't mean —"

"Cut it out," he said. "We haven't spoken since last spring and then you call in the middle of the evening out of the blue."

"What time is it there?" she said, innocent as a lamb. "It's not that late, and why shouldn't I call to see how you are?"

Jesse recognized the pattern. When Jenn called him like this, it meant she was in trouble or was feeling needy.

"I'm not doing this anymore, Jenn. I thought we had an understanding."

The dishwasher came on in Jesse's kitchen and Tamara came back into the living room. She poured herself another glass of wine.

Jesse shrugged his shoulders at her as Jenn talked into his ear about how he was wrong about her and how it was different now. He held up his left hand to Tamara and showed her two fingers. He mouthed, "Two minutes." But she made a face at him and left the room. Ten minutes later, he heard the front door slam. Twenty minutes after that he realized he was still on the phone with Jenn.

57

He had lost track of the last few days as he had lost his sense of self since his third tour in Afghanistan. He thought he'd been solid until then, but it was impossible to hold on to things these days. Facts moved around on him like water bugs behind a kitchen wall. They were oily things for him, facts. Even when he had a grasp of one, it would slip away. He remembered people calling him a good soldier, a good man, and a good friend. He didn't have friends anymore. His life was too scattered for that. There just didn't seem to be enough of him left to spare for friendship. Sometimes late at night in the desert, he'd look up and see all the millions of stars and he'd think he still had a soul. They couldn't take that from him. Not that, too.

He panicked for a second. *Where is that ticket to Boston?* He clutched at the back left pocket of his filthy jeans, relaxing only after he felt the paper in his fingers. The ticket was still there. He'd spent his last money on it and he meant to make it to Boston no matter what. He tried to remember if he had ever been to Boston, but that was another one of those things he had lost in Helmand Province. He figured he'd hitch from Boston to Paradise. He'd tried to buy a ticket from New York to Paradise, but the lady at the counter stared at him funny and kind of laughed. *No tickets to Paradise.*

"Like the song," she'd said. "You know, 'Two tickets to Paradise . . .' "

But he didn't know. Maybe he did, once.

She said you can't get there from here. He wondered what that meant. It kept going around and around in his head until he wanted to tear the words out of his brain. That's when he ran outside, out of the bus terminal and into the New York City night.

It was good that he ran. All the headlights, neon lights, traffic lights, all the blaring horns, all the people pushing, the aroma of chestnuts burning on hot charcoals, all of it took the words out of his head and the panic out of him. It was like that. One minute his head was full to exploding and the next it was empty. One minute he was back in country. The next he wasn't. He even managed a smile at a little brown girl who stared at him with happy eyes. The smile didn't last. Nothing lasted. He caught a whiff of something heartbreaking and familiar, the scent of grilling lamb. It sent him running again, this time far away as fast as his wrecked legs would move him.

To calm himself as he ran, he tried to count how many buses he'd taken, how many rides he'd hitched just to get this far. A guy at the motel had let him catch a ride from Diablito to Tucson. From Tucson, he'd taken a bus to El Paso. He'd hitched a few rides from El Paso to San Antonio. Then there was that blackout period where he couldn't remember anything, but somehow he'd woken up on a sewer grate in a little town in the Missouri Ozarks. He'd hitched from there to Saint Louis. In Saint Louis, he spent a day begging for money on the street and bought a bus ticket for New York City. He couldn't recall why he hadn't just bought a through ticket to Boston. But all that was in a jumble of yesterdays. By the time his legs hurt so much they wouldn't move anymore, he found himself at a river. He sat down on a bench, gazing out at the lights across the way and letting their broken reflections on the black water hypnotize him. He felt his eyes close.

He was so very cold and felt something hard against his face. Then he felt something else: a hand on him, more than one hand. Hands were pulling at him. One reached into his back pocket and pulled at the bus ticket to Boston. The last thing he remembered was reaching his own hand back and grabbing hold of the wrist of the hand in his pocket. When he came back into his body he was on his back on the concrete. He had a man's forearm clamped between his. His legs were draped across the man's chest and the man was screaming in pain, writhing in pain. *An arm bar.* He released the man's forearm, but the damage had been done. When he let go he could feel the broken bones. He jumped to his feet, alive with adrenaline, and assumed fighting position. There was no need. The fight was over. Three men, including the man with the broken arm, were on the ground near the bench. One was unconscious. The other one's face was a mess of blood. He was holding his hand on his broken nose and choking for air.

Then he noticed the flashing lights. Heard the low, electronic *whoop whoop* of the siren, the screech of tires and brakes. More important, he heard the slide of a nine-millimeter as someone at his back racked a

311

bullet into the chamber.

"On your knees, motherfucker. Hands above your head. On your knees now!"

He did as he was told. *At least,* he thought, *I won't be cold anymore tonight.*

58

Dix stared at Jesse not unlike the way Tamara Elkin had stared at him the night before.

"Jenn called last night."

Dix asked, "Before or after you called to make this appointment?"

"After."

"Then she's not why you're here."

"What does that matter? She called."

"And?"

"And it was the same old thing. She called pretending she was concerned about me, with what's going on in Paradise with the murders."

"Don't you believe her?"

"Do I think she's concerned? Maybe. Sure. But is that why she called? No, probably not."

"Then why did she call?"

"I don't know. Her job isn't working out or her most recent boyfriend is about to dump her or she saw a line on her face that wasn't there the day before. Take your pick," Jesse said.

"Not my job. But you apparently understand Jenn very well."

"We worked it out in here. You know how she is. She needs me when things are broken. Then when things get fixed, she doesn't."

"Were you tempted to fix whatever was broken this time?" Dix asked.

"Not really, but I did stay on the phone with her for twenty minutes without getting anywhere."

"You sound angry about that."

"There was another woman with me when Jenn called."

Dix nodded.

"I hate when you do that," Jesse said.

Dix kept nodding. "What happened?"

"First she retreated, then she basically left without saying a word."

"Who's responsible for that?"

"Me."

"Is the damage irreparable, do you think?"

"Probably not."

"Then why are we talking about this?" Dix said.

"Weren't you listening?"

"Look, Jesse, your ex called. It took a lot

of hard work on your part to figure out the patterns that kept you and Jenn locked together in a very unhealthy emotional pas de deux. You parted ways, but none of that means either of you stopped caring or that parts of you still don't hunger for the old comfort you found with each other. It seems to me you get it. You see Jenn for who she is and for what she wants. You say the damage between you and this other woman is fixable. So let me ask you again, why are we talking about this?"

"Because I don't want to talk about Suit."

"The cop who got shot last spring."

Jesse nodded. Then sat silently, staring at anything but at Dix. After a few minutes of that, he said, "It's almost time for him to get back on the street."

"And?"

"And I'm scared for him."

"Why?"

"Because the last time he was on the street he was two inches away from being killed. And I'm not joking about the two inches. An inch this way or that and he'd be dead."

"I point this out only as a matter of discussion, Jesse, but you've had other cops die under your command previous to this and I don't recall you reacting this way. What do you think that means?"

"Those other cops weren't Suit."

Dix nodded. "What's special about Suit?"

"I don't know."

"Of course you do. You've spoken about him in here many times."

"I have? I guess I must have mentioned him."

Dix smiled. "I can tell you a lot about Luther 'Suitcase' Simpson, Jesse, but it will do you no good for me to tell you. What's special about Suit?"

"He wants to be a good cop so bad."

"Is he bad at his job?"

"He's fine for where he is."

"For Paradise, you mean?"

"He's good with people and he can handle himself in a fight."

"But . . ."

"He couldn't make it on a big-city force. He'd get eaten alive. You know what it's like. What you have to deal with."

"I do. Not everybody can handle it. But it's more than that."

"I've tried to coach him up. I've encouraged him. Tried to get him to take the initiative."

Dix said, "And has he taken the initiative?"

"It's what nearly got him killed."

"Do you blame yourself?"

316

Silence, a long silence. Then, "He was trying to impress me."

"Why would he want to impress you?"

"Because I'm his boss," Jesse said, unable to look Dix in the eye.

"You're fighting yourself pretty hard not to say what you've come here to say."

"When he was shot, I got madder at Suit than at the shooter."

Dix smiled, or what passed for a smile. "Why?"

"Because he shouldn't have been there."

"If it was another one of your cops, would you have felt that way?"

"Maybe." He shook his head. "No."

"Why?"

Jesse said, "Because Suit was in way over his head. He wasn't equipped for the situation."

"Who was responsible for that?"

Silence. Jesse checked his watch.

"Do you ever regret not having children, Jesse?"

"What's that got to do with anything?"

"You tell me."

"Jenn and I would have made terrible parents."

"I didn't ask about Jenn. I asked about you. Think about that. It's time. We have to stop."

Jesse checked his watch again and looked more than a little relieved.

"I can't force you to come here, Jesse," Dix said, "but I would urge you to come in next week."

Jesse grunted something about trying and was gone.

59

Robbie Wilson was waiting for Jesse when he got back from Dix's. Robbie, built like a lumpy bowling ball, was in a fresh set of his fire-chief blues, his little white legionnaire-style cap looking silly on his balding head. Jesse waved to him that he'd be with him in a minute and stopped to talk to Suit at the desk.

"You come up with anything yesterday?"

Suit stood and motioned for Jesse to come into the conference room.

"What's up?" Jesse asked when Suit closed the conference room door.

Suit smiled that big goofy smile of his. "I got two witnesses said they spotted a white van in the area. One witness at each location. Their statements are on your desk."

"We get a description of the van beyond it being white?"

"We did. Both witnesses say the van was pretty banged up. One says he thinks it was a Chevy."

"Thinks or is pretty sure?" Jesse wanted to know.

"Pretty sure."

"Beat-up white van sound familiar to you, Suit?"

"John Millner."

Jesse said, "Great minds think alike." He clapped Suit on the shoulder. "Good work."

"It gets better. Last night Millner called in after we were both gone and —"

"Reported his van was stolen."

Suit's smile got even broader. "Some coincidence, huh?"

"Remarkable."

"Sounds like somebody's covering his ass to me."

"To me, too," Jesse said. "We get a description of the driver from either witness?"

Suit shook his head. "Nothing solid. Sorry. One witness thought he saw a tall man in blue work clothes by the O'Hara garage, but wouldn't swear to it."

"Could be Millner," Jesse said.

Suit agreed. "Sounds like him. Should I send somebody around to pick John up for questioning?"

"Not yet. Maybe later the two of us will go have a little talk with him. Give me a few minutes in my office and then send Robbie in."

"It felt good to be on the street again, Jesse."

"I know." He patted Suit's biceps. "We'll talk about it later."

Jesse sat down at his desk and picked up the phone to call Tamara Elkin to apologize for his behavior. He put the phone down. He thought he should get a better sense of what was going on with him before he called. It was his experience that a call too soon was worse than no call at all. He pulled out his bottom drawer and looked at his office bottle. He thought about it for a few seconds, then closed the drawer.

Robbie Wilson knocked on the door and stepped into the office without waiting for the come-ahead. That was Robbie Wilson to a T. Jesse could only imagine the fit Robbie would have thrown if Jesse just strolled into Robbie's office without permission.

"Chief Stone."

"Robbie." Jesse nodded toward the chair in front of his desk.

"No, thanks. I'm just here to give you these." He placed two folders on Jesse's desk. "They're the preliminary reports on yesterday's fires. I knew you'd want them. We're declaring them both arson. An ac-

321

celerant was used in both fires, probably the same one. My guess, it was gasoline, but we won't know until we get the full analysis back from the lab. The idiot didn't even use a lighter. We found matches at both scenes."

Jesse laughed, remembering that Tamara had brought up the old saying about criminals having half a brain.

"I say something funny, Chief?"

Jesse shook his head.

"I heard Marchand bought your boys new uniforms for the softball season. I didn't ask our sponsor yet. I guess you beat me to the punch on that one, Stone."

"Not everything is a competition, Robbie."

"Yes it is. Everything's competition. That's what Coach Feller used to say. Used to tell us that anyone who doesn't realize everything's a competition is a loser and will always finish second."

"Coach Feller?"

"He was a legend around here. Coached basketball at Sacred Heart Boys Catholic for thirty years."

"No offense, Robbie, but you don't look like much of a b-ball player," Jesse said as diplomatically as he could manage.

"Wasn't. Football was my game. But I was team manager for the basketball team. It was an honor just to be around Coach."

"Were you manager when a guy named Warren played?"

"Zevon? Sure."

Jesse made a face. "Warren Zevon, like the rock star?"

"His name was Warren Zebriski, but everybody called him Zevon. Small forward. Stupid asshole had a full scholarship and just pissed it away." Wilson shook his head in disgust. "Came home after his first year and never went back to school."

Jesse was curious. "What happened to him?"

Robbie shrugged. "I don't really know. Heard he just left town that summer. Why do you ask?"

"Forget it. Thanks for these." Jesse held up the files. "Let me know when you get the full lab report back."

Wilson turned on his heel and left. Jesse suddenly had a much better understanding of Robbie Wilson. Some people, he thought, never do graduate from high school.

60

Jesse let Suit drive the cruiser over to Sacred Heart. He knew it would please Suit to be in control. Jesse sat quietly looking out at the streets of Paradise. He still couldn't get past how that nor'easter had blown through town and, in a few short hours, blown up his illusions all at once. He had thought that after a decade-plus as police chief Paradise was finally his town, that he had its measure, knew its rhythms. But it seemed to him now that illusion, not knowledge, was exactly what he had until the night of the storm.

Suit broke the silence. "So why would a guy like Millner set fire to those houses?"

"He's a punk. Somebody probably hired him to do it."

"But who?"

Jesse smiled. "That's the big question. We find out who hired him, we're one step closer to our killer."

"You think there was only one killer?"

Jesse shrugged. "Let's start with one and work our way up. If there's more than one, when the first one falls, they'll all fall. It's one thing for a guy to take a burglary rap for someone else. Do your bit, keep your mouth shut. I haven't met too many people willing to take the fall to protect someone else from a murder rap. Not many people worth doing twenty-five to life for."

"But some do?"

"Gang members do it."

Suit made a face. "Why?"

"Sociologists will tell you it's part of the gang mentality, part of the macho culture and the brotherhood code."

"You don't buy that, do you, Jesse?"

"Makes for good textbooks. The truth is uglier."

"Uglier?"

Jesse said, "Roll over on your gang brothers and there's a big price to pay. Even if you snitch, you're still going to do time. Prison is the loneliest place in the world without protection, and about the most dangerous. If you think gangs are bad news on the street, they're worse in close quarters. You got black gangs, Muslim gangs, white supremacist gangs, Hispanic gangs, Asian gangs. The list is long and you don't want to be in that shitstorm without an umbrella.

You keep your mouth shut and your head down, you've got protection. Maybe your family on the outside gets taken care of. You snitch and maybe it's not only you who pays the price."

Jesse could see that Suit was thinking about that. Then Suit's expression changed.

"You know, Jesse, we never talked about what happened after I got out of the hospital. Not really."

"Forget it."

"I wish I could."

"You're going for your sessions, right?"

"I told you I was," Suit said, his voice tinged with anger and impatience. "You know, Jesse, it's not like I was trying to get shot."

Jesse felt the pressure building, but kept it in.

Suit wasn't through. "I was only doing what you are always at me to do. I thought you would need help, and you're not the kind of man to ask for help. I was just trying to help, is all."

Jesse's jaw was clamped so tight his teeth ached.

"I'm not stupid, Jesse. I know what you think of me as a cop."

"What's that supposed to mean?" Jesse asked, knowing exactly what it meant.

"Nothing. Just forget it."

"We'll talk about this later."

"Sure, Jesse."

As they walked to the door of the maintenance shed, it seemed to Jesse that Suit's steps were once again slow and labored.

61

John Millner, his unkempt black hair hanging limp around his shoulders, was busy sharpening a mower blade when Jesse and Suit walked into the maintenance shed on the grounds of Sacred Heart. Millner barely acknowledged their presence, choosing instead to continue scraping a metal rasp along the edge of the blade clamped in the jaws of an old bench vise. Dressed in blue, oil-stained coveralls and scuffed black work boots, Millner wore a pair of protective goggles that, like all the equipment in the shed, had seen better days. The plastic of the goggles was scratched and pitted, the lenses grown foggy with age. A silver-colored space heater shaped like a radar dish sat on the concrete floor a few paces to Millner's right, its caged element glowing a fierce orange-red. As fierce as it was, it did little to warm the drafty old building. The winds outside rattled the corrugated bay door.

Millner took off his right work glove and ran his index finger along the edge of the freshly sharpened blade. Satisfied, he twisted the vise handle, releasing the blade from the vise's wood-covered jaws. He slipped his glove back on and took the blade fully into his hand. He turned to face Suit and Jesse, showing them his handiwork.

"Little snowy outside to be mowing lawns, isn't it?" Suit asked.

Millner sneered at him. "Shows what you know. You do your prep and maintenance work for the spring now. You don't wait till the grass is up to your balls to sharpen the blades."

Suit wasn't having it. "They teach you that in the joint between soap swapping with the boys in the shower?"

"Nah, I learned watching the movie about that tall retard, *Sling Blade.* Tall retard, kinda reminds me of some cops I know. No offense, Officer Simpson." Millner smiled a crooked smile full of nasty teeth.

Jesse didn't like it. He didn't like the way Millner was acting. There was a little too much cockiness in him. Then again, he didn't like Millner from the get-go. Still, he didn't say a word.

"You boys find my van? That why you're here? Did you deliver it to me?" Millner asked, placing the sharpened blade on the bench and removing the goggles. "That's pretty good service. You boys have it washed and detailed for me?"

It took a lot to push Suit to lose his temper, but Millner had done a pretty good job of it.

"Listen to me, you piece of —"

"That's right, John, we're here to talk about your van," Jesse said, cutting Suit off. "But we haven't found it."

"Then what, you here to give me a status report or something?"

Jesse nodded. "Or something."

"You mind hurrying up, then? I've got another blade to get to and a ton of other work to do."

"We don't mind, do we, Suit?" He didn't wait for an answer. "John, what took you so long to report your van as stolen?" Jesse asked.

" 'Cause I didn't know it was gone till I got back home last night."

Suit said, "So you didn't drive it to work?"

Millner shook his head. "Nah. The tranny's been giving me a little trouble lately, so I got a lift in and a ride to the bar after work."

330

Suit made a sad face. "That's too bad, about your transmission, I mean. So who gave you the rides? If you don't mind me asking."

"Sure, Officer Simpson, anything to help the cause of justice," Millner said, putting the next mower blade into the bench vise. "I got a ride in from Sister Marie Frances and Father Bogan took me to the Scupper after work. He let me buy him a beer, as a matter of fact. I walked home from there. That's when I called in that my van was stolen."

"Did you leave the grounds during your shift?" Jesse asked.

Millner placed the goggles back on top of his head. "Yesterday? I don't think so, Chief. Nah. I spent most of the day in the rectory, fixing a leak in the kitchen. You can go on over and see the patch on the wall yourself. I had to remove tiles to get at the pipe." He plopped the goggles down on his nose, slipped on his gloves again, and started working on the second blade.

Between the glowing steel of the space heater and the grinding of the file against the blade, the air in the shed had taken on a distinctly metallic scent. Suit looked at Jesse for their next move.

"Okay, John," Jesse said, "we'll leave you

to your work."

Millner kept his focus on his sharpening. "That's real good of you, Chief. You'll find Sister Marie Frances in the main office. Father Bogan is in the gym at the boys' high school. And do me a favor, huh? Let me know when you find my van. I sure do love that old truck."

Jesse and Suit were both thankful for the cold, bracing air outside the shed. Suit reached into the cruiser and came out with two bottled waters. They both tried to rinse away that raw, metallic tang.

"You go talk to the nun," Jesse said. "I'll take the priest. Let's meet back here in fifteen minutes."

"You see all the chemicals and stuff in there. Like a department store of accelerants."

"Uh-huh."

"So what do you think, Jesse?"

"I think someone was trying really hard to establish an alibi for himself for yesterday."

"Almost like he knew he would have to account for his whereabouts."

"Yeah, Suit. Just like that. Makes you wonder about things."

"What things?"

"Everything, Suit," he said, walking toward the boys' high school. "Everything."

62

Jesse was back in his office, pounding a hardball into the pocket of his old Rawlings glove. The leather in the pocket of the glove was nearly a memory. Any padding in the glove had long since been beaten into dust and disappeared. He stared at the glove as he pounded the ball, each impact making a loud *thwack* that echoed through the station, each impact stinging his left palm. He remembered back to when his left hand, his glove hand, was so accustomed to rocket line drives and relay throws from the outfield that came in like shotgun slugs that he barely noticed them. That had been a long time ago now, longer with each passing breath. But he didn't mind the stinging. It helped him think and he had a lot to think about. What he was thinking about in particular at that moment was John Millner and his alibi.

Although the maintenance man's alibi

held up to scrutiny, Jesse didn't doubt for a second that John Millner was somehow involved in the arson from the tips of his steel-toed boots to the tip of his fist-flattened nose. Mutts like Millner knew a hundred other lowlifes who would do dirty work for pay, who would set their own grannies' houses afire for a few six-packs and a hundred-dollar bill. But why had Millner made himself so conspicuous? The answer was unsettling and simple: He was giving cover to someone else.

It didn't remind Jesse of anything so much as a magic trick. The magician is waving one hand with a flourish to get your attention while doing the real business with his other hand. The thing was, John Millner was no magician. The guy could barely keep himself out of prison, let alone pull a rabbit out of a hat. That was the unsettling part. If it wasn't Millner pulling the strings, who was pulling Millner's? And what was the endgame? What was the trick? That's what he was asking himself when there was a knock on the pebbled glass of his office door.

"Come," he said, folding the ball into the glove and placing the glove in its spot of honor on his desk.

Bill Marchand stuck his head through the

334

door. "You sure this is a good time?"

Jesse laughed. "No, but come in anyway."

Marchand sat across from Jesse, dispensing with the usual handshake.

"My week's not up," Jesse said.

"It's not, but the fires yesterday aren't helping me help your cause any."

"You're just pissed off because you've probably got to pay on those policies."

"Only one of them." Marchand winked. "Can a man get something to drink in here?"

Jesse didn't answer. He just reached into his desk drawer, pulled out the bottle, and poured a few fingers for the selectman. As he poured, Jesse studied Marchand out of the corner of his eye. He was back in form, looking his usual well-put-together self. Jesse was glad he hadn't been a party to the meetings where his fate was being discussed. He suspected that Bill had fought the good fight, but in the end Marchand was a politician and politicians did a strange kind of calculus. Deal-making is like sausage-making, not usually a pretty sight to behold. Jesse was fairly sure that when push came to shove, Bill Marchand held his nose and threw Jesse to the wolves. He didn't blame Marchand, nor had it changed his opinion of the man.

"Nothing for you?" Marchand asked when Jesse slid the drink across his desk.

"That's all I need, to drink on the job in front of a selectman. No, thanks, Bill. I want the rest of my seven days."

"Come on, Jesse, I would never report that. You know me."

"I don't think you'd report me, Bill. But that second thing you said, that's wrong. Nobody knows anybody else. Not really. Cops learn that early on or they don't stay cops for long. Go ahead, drink up. *Cheers.*"

Marchand nodded, raised his glass, and drank. "So, any progress on any fronts?"

"Some."

"Some?"

"That's what I said."

"Care to elaborate?"

Jesse shook his head.

Now Marchand shook his head, too, only in a more exaggerated manner. "I don't get you, Jesse. I'm trying to help."

"See, Bill, that proves my point. Nobody knows anybody else." He held the bottle up. "A little more?"

"I haven't finished this one yet."

There was another knock at the office door. This time Suit stuck his head in.

"What's up, Suit?"

"You got a Captain Giulio from the

NYPD on line two."

"About?"

"He wouldn't say, but he asked for the chief. Last time I checked, that was you, Jesse."

"Thanks, Suit."

Marchand stood and pantomimed leaving, but Jesse waved at him to stay and finish his drink. Marchand sat back down and Jesse picked up the phone.

"Captain Giulio, Chief Stone here." Jesse didn't speak for the next two minutes. He made a few noises in the right places to indicate that he was listening and that he understood what the captain was saying on the other end of the line. He jotted a few notes, then said, "Okay, Captain, if you think so, sure. Fax his photo over and I'll have someone meet him at the bus station in Boston. I appreciate the help. If I can ever return the courtesy, let me know. Thank you. Bye."

"What was that about?" Marchand asked.

"Probably nothing. Some wounded Afghanistan war vet named Jameson with PTSD got into a fight in Manhattan last night. He was picked up by the NYPD."

"That's too bad, but what's it got to do with Paradise?"

"This Jameson guy says he can identify

our John Doe, and this Captain Giulio believes him."

"Do you?"

"We'll see. He's scheduled to arrive in Boston tomorrow morning around eleven."

Marchand finished his drink. "Thanks for that. I've got to get going."

"All right."

"Listen, Jesse, I'm sorry about how all of this is turning out. You know how highly I think of you."

"That's fine. I've still got a few more days."

Marchand said, "That's true. Things could turn around."

"Bill, you never did tell me why you came here today."

"It was nothing, forget it."

With that, the selectman was gone. And Jesse went back to thinking about John Millner and trick rabbits.

63

Jesse took Marchand's visit as a sign that the clock was ticking on him faster than he had been led to believe. Although Marchand had promised him seven days, what did that matter? One more bad turn in any of the cases and the mayor and/or the selectmen could decide to cut him loose and name an acting chief. He also realized that the arson and Millner's smug attitude meant he had finally gotten some traction. So he decided he would push the envelope of lies and half-truths even further than he'd already dared to. He had no clue whether this war vet could identify his John Doe or not, but that's not what he planned to tell people.

On his way out of the station, he was mobbed by the usual throng of reporters.

"Chief Stone," a faceless voice called out to him from the crowd, "any word on the DNA results?"

He lied. "Yes, as we stand here now, the

state police are checking the results against existing databases."

"What do they hope to accomplish by that?" the same reporter asked.

"To find a killer."

Someone else called to him, "What's your reaction to the situation in Framingham?"

Jesse didn't know what the reporter was referring to, but he didn't let on. "It would be improper for me to comment on other jurisdictions."

There was another question. "Are there any other developments?"

"Yes. Someone will be here tomorrow who has come forward who can help us identify our John Doe."

"You're referring to the man in the blue tarp?" a fourth reporter asked.

"Exactly," Jesse said. "Once we have his identity, the rest of the case should fall into place. Now, if you'll excuse me."

Jesse pushed through the crowd and made his way to his Explorer. Healy called as Jesse pulled out of his spot.

"What's going on in Framingham, Healy? I just got ambushed by a reporter outside the station asking me about it."

"It's a mess. A triple homicide in the tony part of town. Three DBs and not a stitch of

340

clothing between them. All done execution-style."

Jesse asked, "Why are the staties involved?"

"One of the victims is a congressman's brother and neither of the two murdered women found with him was his wife. You know how that goes."

"Uh-huh."

"Three vics, one man and two women. Kind of like what you're dealing with in Paradise."

"At least your victims were all killed in the same century."

"Good point. Listen, Jesse, I'm sorry to have to do this, but I gotta pull my man off Dragoa. He's too good a man for surveillance duty with this triple dumped in my lap. Framingham is an all-hands-on-deck situation," Healy said. "If this thing gets cleared up soon, I'll give him back to you."

"Don't sweat it. Stuff happens."

"Bad stuff, yeah, and a lot of it all at once."

"Tell me about it," Jesse said. "Let me give you a heads-up. I lied to the press again. Told them you guys were comparing my DNA results to the state database."

"I'll cover for you. It's the least I can do since I've got to pull my man."

Healy clicked off and Jesse headed to the morgue.

64

Jesse didn't usually associate the morgue with friendship, but that was about to change. He didn't think what he had to say should be said over the phone, nor did he think he should let it wait. And the truth was that he liked the arrangement he had with Tamara Elkin. It kind of reminded him of his relationship with Marcy, but that was a friendship with perks and it had run its course years ago. Not that the perks hadn't been great. They had been. Marcy certainly seemed to enjoy their intimacy as much or more than he did. It was just that sometimes Jesse got the sense that there was an element of revenge in it for her, a kind of middle finger to her ex-husband and the men who'd done her wrong. Maybe there was an element of revenge in it for him, too. In any case, things had changed since then. He had changed.

Tamara was just coming out of the autopsy

room when he ran into her. At first she smiled at him, then the smile evaporated as she remembered what had happened between them the previous evening.

"You didn't exactly catch me at my best," she said, gesturing at blood on her scrubs.

"That's okay. About last night, I wanted to apolo—"

She waved her hand at him. "Don't. Please, don't. I've got to get cleaned up. Why don't you go wait in my office for me? I'll be in as soon as I can. Here." She handed him a file. "You can save me the trip by putting that on my desk for me."

"Rough one?" he asked, pointing at the autopsy room behind her.

"Yes and no. An old woman with late-stage Alzheimer's. She fell at the care facility, so they needed an official COD. The autopsy was pretty routine, but these cases . . . I don't know. I've seen death in all its various forms, probably some that not even an ex–homicide detective has seen, and there's just something about Alzheimer's that scares the hell out of me."

"Me, not so much," Jesse said.

"You die of almost anything else and at least you have something to hold on to on the way out. But with Alzheimer's you're just lost and confused."

344

He thought she might cry and, without thinking, reached out and stroked her cheek. She let him.

"You don't know who you are coming into the world," he said. "Why worry about it as you leave it?"

She smiled a weak smile at him. "I'll see you in my office in a few."

Jesse sat in Tamara's office and did what people do alone in offices. He looked around. Looked at the photos on her walls, the diplomas, the knickknacks on her desk. Funny, but Jesse often found a person's workplace as or more revealing than his or her bedroom. During homicide investigations, he had always made it a point of visiting the victim's and/or the suspect's workplace. People who were meticulous and guarded at home could sometimes betray themselves at the office, at their desk, or in their school locker. He didn't expect to come to any great revelations about Tamara Elkin. She had come to him, armed only with a bottle of Black Label and the truth.

Jesse smiled at the photos of her in her track outfits, the shots of her leaning forward as she came across the finish line ahead of the other runners. He liked seeing her with the ribbons and medals around her neck. There was one photo of Tamara — in high school, he guessed — holding a bouquet of roses and standing in between a man and a woman Jesse thought must be her parents. The pride on her parents' faces was remarkable to see. And for some reason, at that precise moment, he thought of Suit. Jesse laughed at himself. He decided he needed either to start drinking more heavily again or to begin seeing Dix as often as he could.

"What's so funny?" Tamara asked, catching Jesse in the act.

"Me." He pointed at the photo. "These your folks?"

"That's them. Dad's a gastroenterologist. Mom's an English professor."

"Any smart people in your family?"

She laughed and then saddened. "They're both from New York and moved us down to Dallas when Dad went to work at Baylor University Medical Center. They were both so proud of me when I got that ME position back home in New York. Wasn't really my home. I was little when we moved."

She sat behind her desk and Jesse sat across from her.

"I know you don't want to hear this," he said, "but I'm sorry about last night. Jenn and I . . . we can't ever seem to totally let go even after we've let go."

"Don't beat yourself up over it. I acted like a jealous little girl."

He nodded.

"What I said about us being friends, I meant it, every word, and so far I think we're really good for each other. But that doesn't mean that when I'm with you that I don't want your full attention. No one wants to be treated like a disposable razor."

"Okay. I hear you."

"Good."

He asked, "Are we allowed to go to dinner together?"

"A date?"

"Friends don't go on dates. They just go eat together and split the check."

She smiled.

He smiled back.

"Where?" she said.

"Not the Gull."

She reached for a pen and a pad, wrote something down, and handed him the sheet of paper. "My place. Friends cook for each other sometimes, too. Eight?"

He stood. "See you then."

65

John Millner had gotten out of the taxi two blocks away from the marina, paid the cabbie, and, just like he'd been told, walked away from the harbor for a few blocks before doubling back. He thought all the James Bond stuff was a bunch of crap and he was still confused about why them two houses had to get torched. The last thing on earth he wanted to do was to call attention to himself and what they had done all those years ago. He just didn't see the upside. Still, he had to admit that he liked sticking it to Jesse Stone and that jerk Luther Simpson. He enjoyed the hell out of it.

But the way he figured it, they got away with what they done to them girls for twenty-five years, and that with Zevon out of the picture, all they had to do was wait it out. They all had bad moments before when the guilt got really intense, but those moments passed. Sure, he felt sick about how that had come down. He always felt crappy about that, they all did, but he couldn't undo what they done. None of it. None of them could. It wasn't like in the street games he played as a kid in the Swap. No do-overs in murder, whether you meant it to happen or not. Nobody meant for them to get hurt like that. And Zevon? Well, screw him, he brought that trouble down on his own head. He as much as signed his own execution papers the minute he walked back into town. He had to know that, the stupid bastard.

The marina was a ghost town this time of year and it was creepier than a freakin' cell block a few hours after lights-out. You just knew some bad stuff was going down in the dark, but no one dared cry out or call for help. That was the worst part of being inside: the dark. And Millner didn't like knowing there was water under his feet. He didn't like the slickness of the planks or the way they swayed to the will of the water. The thought of slipping off the dock and into the icy-cold water scared the hell out of him. He couldn't swim worth a damn and drowning scared him more than anything. Even now he panicked at the thought of water rushing into his mouth, choking him, his lungs seizing up. He didn't want to die cold and alone. That was the worst part of what they did to the girls, leaving them in that cold, dirty hole all them years. At least they was together.

He hoped this wasn't going to take long, because he had hated boats. Always had. If he hadn't been so drunk that night, he wouldn't've gotten into that damned rowboat and none of this stuff would be his worry. But he had gotten in that damned little rowboat, Ginny Connolly sitting next to him, taking big swigs of Southern Comfort and gagging, then taking some more in between tokes. Mary Kate sitting behind them, refusing the bottle, passing the joints every time they came her way, asking, like, a million times if Warren was going to be there. *You're sure he's gonna meet us there? He's gonna be there, right?* If that idiot Alexio hadn't stabbed her when things got crazy, Millner thought, he would have stabbed her himself just to shut her the hell up about Zevon.

Millner saw the *Rainha* dead ahead of him in the dark, its cabin lights lit. Of all the boats he hated, he had a special hatred for the *Rainha* because it smelled like rancid old fish guts. He laughed to himself, thinking that most of the time Alexio didn't smell too much better. He tried thinking back to

350

high school, when they played ball together. *Did he stink so bad then?* He couldn't remember. It was stupid to look back. That's all he did when he was inside, look back. There was some stuff he liked remembering, like about the other girls he'd been with and about when they all played ball together.

That's what Millner was thinking when he stepped up to the *Rainha* and a hand came out of the dark to help him aboard.

"Where's Alexio?" he asked.

"He's below, drunk as a skunk. You know how he gets. Looks like I'll be skippering our little excursion tonight."

Millner shook his head. "Stupid Alexio and his drinking."

"You bring the gun?"

"Yeah, here," Millner said, handing the revolver over. "I don't want no part of that thing no more."

"I don't blame you. When we get out a little ways we'll toss it and the knife into the water. Wash our hands of it all, finally."

Millner liked the sound of that. "Good thinking. Be rid of that stuff forever. What's Dragoa drinking? I could maybe use something, too."

"We all could. Do me a favor and untie her. Then go keep Alexio company below while I get us out of here."

Millner shrugged. "Whatever, but let's move it, huh." Then he carefully climbed back onto the dock, untied the *Rainha,* and climbed even more carefully back aboard.

When the *Rainha* had moved several miles out of the harbor into the Atlantic, Alexio Dragoa and John Millner felt the engines cut back.

"I got to use the head, man," Millner said. "Then we can get this stupid nonsense over with and I can get back on land."

Dragoa nodded, so drunk he could barely speak.

While he steadied himself in the bathroom, Millner heard footsteps on the short staircase that led to the cabin. There was a brief moment of strange quiet, then he heard Alexio slur, "What the fuck?" Less than a second later, the world flipped over. Two shots roared through the *Rainha*'s cabin and something banged to the deck with a hollow thud. Millner zipped up, flung the door open, and stepped out of the head.

He opened his mouth to ask what the hell was going on, but the only sound that came out of him was a gasp. He looked down, not understanding the jolt of pain in his guts — the likes of which he had never felt — nor the sudden weakness sucking the strength

352

out of his limbs. And looking down, he saw Bill Marchand's hand pulling the knife out of his liver and shoving it back in again and again. Millner looked up at his old teammate and instantly understood that he and Alexio had been set up to take the fall for what the three of them had done.

Millner tried to clamp his big hand around his old pal's throat and squeeze, but it was useless. Any strength left to him, his body was using to keep upright. Marchand laughed at him, swatting the maintenance man's hand away as if it was a mosquito.

"I hear it really hurts, getting stabbed in the liver," Marchand said. "I hope it does, you dumb son of a bitch. Before you got here, Alexio told me what you did to Zevon before you killed him. You shouldn't have beat him with a pipe that way, Johnny. You shouldn't have done that. He was the best friend I ever had."

In his head, Millner's last word sounded like a scream. It came out a whisper. "Alexio?"

"Look behind you, moron. You shot him while he was stabbing you. That's how Jesse Stone will see it, anyway. Really too bad, the way that worked out for you guys. You shouldn't have turned on each other when you thought the cops were getting close. At least I'm almost out from under. Jesse's going to find nearly everything he needs to tie up the case with a pretty red bow. Goodbye, Johnny."

With that, Marchand stuck the knife into his old friend one last time and pushed Millner to the floor. But Millner wasn't dead. As Marchand went back up to bring the boat closer to shore, Millner crawled behind him.

Marchand looked down at him from the top deck. "Good boy, Johnny, keep coming. You always were a dumb bastard, but a stubborn one. Your blood on the stairs will make it look like even less of a setup. When I'm done with you and Alexio, there'll be just one last detail to take care of."

Millner looked up at Marchand, shock taking control of him, his mind failing. He was gripped with fear like he had never felt before, not even after what had happened with the girls on Stiles Island that night. It wasn't fear of dying. He knew that was coming, soon. It was the fear that Bill Marchand might throw his body overboard or, worse, throw him overboard while he still had some life in him. He couldn't let that happen, so he gave in to gravity, sliding back down the stairs greased with his dark, almost black

blood, and surrendered to the long-overdue
bill waiting for him on the other side.

66

Tamara Elkin's condo was in a new development built to look old. It was in Swan Harbor, the village just to the north of Paradise. Swan Harbor was a lovely place with its own rocky beaches and bluffs. It was a little more upscale and a bit snobbier than Paradise, owing to the fact that it was founded when burning witches and handing out scarlet letters were the favorite local pastimes. Tamara's development was close to the center of town, near enough to the beach to get great views of the ocean. Problem was that most of her unit's windows faced due west.

"Too bad the Rockies block your views of the Pacific," Jesse said, looking out her living room window at the Swan Harbor firehouse.

"Who says police chiefs don't have a sense of humor? Wine or scotch?" she asked, holding a bottle of each.

Jesse pointed at the wine. As he watched the wine pour into the glasses he thought that he should consider moving back into the heart of Paradise. It wasn't that he didn't enjoy his house. He did. It was awfully pretty out where he lived — peaceful, too — but it had never quite suited him. He wasn't lonely, not exactly. While not a total disaster, his experiment with cat ownership hadn't done the trick. His house was the kind of place to share with a woman and he was less sure now than ever that he would get married again.

He supposed that if Sunny Randall had been able to extricate herself from her marriage, they might've worked together. But she was equally inept at distancing herself from Richie as he from Jenn. Though they still kept in touch, that ship had sailed. He thought about Diana again. They could definitely work. He would be willing to try. The thing was, he didn't know if she was willing. She made the right noises about it and when they were together that one weekend none of the magic between them had gone away. He wondered if Diana was too independent and too much about the action to be tied to a small-town police chief. Her physical beauty notwithstanding, the things that attracted Jesse to Diana probably made her an unlikely bride. Maybe that's why he had never fully let go of Jenn.

Jesse shook his head at himself. All this wondering, all these what-ifs, were new to him. He had never been the type of man to go round and round with himself like this. He'd never been a man to second-guess or to waste too much energy on regret. Then he laughed silently to himself. Jesse had a sneaking suspicion that Dix's views on these matters would likely differ greatly from his own. He would probably never know, as Dix seemed to delight in not sharing his own feelings about Jesse with Jesse. He could hear Dix's voice in his head. *It's not important how I feel about it. How do you feel about it, Jesse?* Suddenly, Jesse got out of his own head, stopped looking at the wine being poured, and readjusted his eyes to the woman doing the pouring. He just felt very lucky that Tamara Elkin had come to the door.

"You seem deep in thought," Tamara said. She handed him his wine and sat down on the sofa next to him. They clinked glasses and sipped. "What were you thinking about?"

"Luck."

"What about it?"

He shrugged. Tamara moved farther away

from Jesse so she could study his expression.

"What?" he said.

"You're an interesting fella, Jesse Stone."

"Better than being a dull one, I guess."

"*Interesting*'s not the right word." She tilted her head as she continued staring. "No, definitely not."

He took a long sip of wine and played along. "Then what is?"

"You're what my daddy calls a Chinese box."

"A Chinese box?"

"Beautiful on the outside, full of secrets, and impossible to open."

"Not impossible," he said.

"Certainly not easy."

"What fun is easy?"

She laughed. "I don't know. Sometimes easy ain't too shabby."

He nodded. "Point taken. Then let's go back to the beautiful-on-the-outside part."

"After dinner," she said. "Dinner was promised and dinner you shall have."

"We can skip a meal if you're not up for it."

"Not this one, Jesse. I'm hungry. Get in the dining room."

"Sure, Doc."

Jesse stood, wine in hand, and walked to

the table. As he walked past Tamara she shook her head at him.

"A Chinese box, all right," she said. "A Chinese box."

67

Suit had been happy to once again escape the front desk and didn't much care how or why. Getting to go into Boston was just an added benefit, and he liked that Jesse had let him take a Paradise cruiser to collect their "guest." Suit knew he should have been long past the stage where strutting around in his uniform or driving a marked car mattered, but it did. He didn't think he would ever get over his love of being a cop, though the bullet scars across his abdomen and the last month inside the station house had surely put a strain on that romance. So, too, had the drive from Boston back to Paradise.

Suit was no Sigmund Freud, but it was easy to see that this Jameson guy he'd collected at the bus station had a few pieces missing from his jigsaw puzzle. His hard blue eyes were very far away and staring at something no one else could see. And it was pretty clear, too, that he was either home-less or most of the way to the street. He smelled of old sweat and smoke, and a razor hadn't touched his face in months. His beard was ragged, long, and black. His jeans were filthy and the cuffs were frayed to the point of disintegration. His once-beige desert boots were now blackened, scuffed, and held together with layers of duct tape. He wore an equally tattered fatigue jacket that bore the bald eagle sleeve patch of the 101st Airborne and the name JAMESON written across the left side of the chest. Most of the snaps and buttons were missing or broken and the zipper pull was gone. Beneath the jacket he was wearing a Bubba Gump Shrimp Company T-shirt that had to be as old as the movie.

Although Jameson had saluted when Suit introduced himself, it had taken all of Suit's *golly-gee* and *aw, shucks* charm to get the guy's rank — corporal — and that was all he got. He wasn't about to offer up a first name or much of anything else. Getting him into the cruiser wasn't easy, and even then Suit wasn't sure that his passenger would stay planted in the backseat. At every traffic light and stop sign, Suit steeled himself, preparing to deal with Jameson if he tried to jump ship. Suit knew that with the cage between the front and back seats and with the back-door security locks in place, it was nearly impossible for a prisoner — or, in this case, a passenger — to escape. But none of that meant Jameson wouldn't attempt it. Prisoners, the drunk and drugged-up ones, the crazies, sometimes did. They'd try to kick out a window or claw through the cage. It was never pretty and it could be dangerous for everyone involved. Suit finally relaxed a little when they hit the highway.

He tried to make conversation with Jameson, but had no luck with that. All Jameson did was keep his head on a swivel during the whole ride up to Paradise. Out of frustration, Suit asked Jameson if he'd like something to eat or drink. That usually worked to break the ice with everyone. Jameson was the exception. But when they passed the road sign that welcomed visitors to Paradise, Jameson stopped swiveling his head. He leaned forward in his seat as far as his shoulder belt would allow.

"Do you know Molly Burke?" he asked.

It was all Suit could do to keep his concentration on the road. Maybe this guy really was legit, Suit thought, but he wasn't sure he should answer. When he didn't say anything, Jameson spoke again.

"She was very pretty."

Suit figured he better say something. "I know a Molly."

"Is she very pretty?"

Suit ignored the question. "How do you know your Molly?"

It was Jameson's turn to ignore Suit's question. "He said Molly was very pretty. The prettiest girl he ever knew."

"He? Who's *he*?" Suit asked.

All that did was get Jameson to withdraw. He sat back in his seat and once again began scanning the road from side to side.

Suit tried to rescue the conversation. "Yeah, the Molly I know is very pretty."

But it was no good. Jameson had gone back to that faraway place in his head. When he pulled up to the station, the reporters all rushed the cruiser. Suit called in to get some help, to clear the way, but it was too late. Jameson was in full-fledged freak-out mode, kicking at the street-side back-door window. Suit hopped out of the car, yanked open the roadside passenger door, and grabbed Jameson. The guy may have been a mess, probably twenty pounds too skinny for his frame, but even Suit had a tough time handling him.

"Listen, buddy, I know this is some crazy stuff going on here," Suit said in his calmest cop voice, one that let his earnestness and sweetness show through. "But let's you and me get this over with. Ten, fifteen steps with me leading the way and we'll be inside. We can do it, man. Just me and you. Let me help you."

Suit felt Jameson stop fighting him. He let Suit help him out of the back of the cruiser. Suit closed the cruiser's door.

"Ready, Corporal?" Suit asked.

Jameson nodded, but that was when things went cockeyed. An engine revved, a loose tailpipe rattled, tires screeched. Although it would all take less than a second or two, Suit sensed what was going on, but thought he'd be powerless to stop it. The pickup truck was a blur from out of the corner of his eye. Jameson sensed it, too, and was in the first step of his retreat when Suit threw himself between Jameson and the pickup. The pickup's front bumper clipped Suit and literally sent him flying into Jameson. Jameson's head bounced off the cruiser's front door. Both men crumpled to the pavement, motionless.

68

Jesse and Healy paced in opposite directions along the floor in the waiting room, anxious for the doctors to give them something to hang their hats on. At least Suit had pretty quickly regained consciousness, though he wasn't making any sense. He kept talking about Molly when Jesse asked him if Jameson had said anything of value on the ride up from Boston. Things weren't looking as bright for Jameson. He was still unconscious when they wheeled him into the ER.

Healy said, "I'm sorry, Jesse. If I had left my man on the fisherman, this might —"

"Forget it. All your man would have done is follow him. He wouldn't have known what Dragoa was going to do and he couldn't have stopped it. How's that thing in Framingham?"

Healy shook his head and made a sour face. "People are such idiots."

"Really?"

"Sarcasm's not usually your style, Jesse."

"Sorry. Okay, I'll bite. How are people idiots?"

"The wife put two high school kids up to it. They left a trail a blind man could have followed."

"She sleeping with them?"

Healy nodded. "Of course. Here's the sickest part. They were friends of her daughter."

"It's been done before," Jesse said. "Old story."

"Yeah, they made a movie about it with Cruise's ex. You see it?"

"I like Westerns."

"Don't make many of those anymore."

"There's your answer, then."

Healy changed subject. "You're sure it was Dragoa?"

"It had to be Dragoa," Jesse said, a bit of hesitation in his voice. "He did it in front of reporters, cameramen, and photographers. We've already got pictures of the truck, tag center of the frame. Trust me, that rusty old piece of crap he drives is unmistakable."

"Then why do you sound like you're trying to convince yourself instead of me?"

"Doesn't figure, him doing it like that. It's as good as a confession that he murdered the girls."

Healy shrugged. "Maybe it doesn't figure, but he did try to run your man and this Jameson guy over. No denying that. He probably fell for all the crap you've been feeding the press. You say this Dragoa guy's a real hothead and drinker, right?"

"Uh-huh. Major-league."

"Okay, so he feels the walls closing in on him. He ties a big one on and loses it. Desperate people do desperately stupid things, Jesse. You know that. I've heard you say it."

Jesse wasn't convinced. The phone buzzed in his pocket before he could say so to Healy. It was Molly on the phone.

"We found Dragoa's pickup in back of the Lobster Claw, but his boat's gone."

"I guess that seals it," Jesse said, still sounding less than positive about it.

Molly heard it in his voice. "Come on, Jesse. How many people saw him do it? Anyway, how's Suit?"

"We don't know yet."

"The other guy, Jameson?"

"Same. We don't know. Listen, Molly, alert the Coast Guard and the staties' marine unit."

"Little boat, big ocean," she said. "And Dragoa probably knows every cove and inlet from Maine to New Jersey."

"He hasn't had much lead time."

"True. Okay, Jesse."

"Molly."

"Yeah."

"Do you know why Suit would be muttering your name after Dragoa ran him down?"

She laughed. "Secret long-term crush?"

"No, that would be me, not Suit."

"You'll make me blush," Molly said, her voice thick with sarcasm.

"So you have no clue about why Suit would be talking about you?"

"Sorry, Jesse."

"One more thing. After you call the Coast Guard and the staties, have someone get the names of John Millner's most recent cell mates. His alibi might be airtight, but I wonder if his old pals can account for their movements on the day of the fires. I think we need to have a talk with the ones that are on the outside."

"Should be easy enough to get that info."

"Thanks."

When Jesse put the phone back in his pocket, Healy tapped him on the shoulder and pointed at the doctor coming their way.

69

The doctor was in his mid-thirties, but he already had the you-can't-show-me-anything-new attitude that trauma specialists and veteran cops develop to insulate themselves from the tragedies that surround them. He wore his long brown hair in a rubber-banded ponytail like a biker, but sported a pair of eyeglasses that cost him more than a couple bucks. His blue scrubs were a size too big. What Jesse noticed most of all were his matching blue Crocs.

"Dr. Crier," he said, offering his hand to Jesse and Healy. It was a practiced gesture, neither sincere nor insincere. It was just what he did, a part of the ritual. "Your cop is going to be fine. He's got some pretty nasty bruises and some scrapes. Has he been a recent victim of gunshot trauma?"

"Uh-huh. About six months ago."

Crier was pleased with himself. "I knew it. Anyway, he just needs some rest. I gave him something for the pain and wrote him a prescription. Nothing too strong. Just something to take the edge off. He's going to be pretty sore for about a week, but he can go home tonight."

"No concussion?" Jesse asked.

"No. Why do you ask?"

"Forget it. What about Mr. Jameson?"

Dr. Crier frowned. "Still unconscious. No skull fractures. Some swelling, but nothing that appears too serious. We hope he comes around in the next several hours. Longer than that and we might have cause to worry."

"We've already got plenty of that," said Healy.

"Excuse me," the doctor asked, only half hearing Healy.

"Nothing."

"Well, I've admitted him. He's already up in ICU. Check on him in the morning. We should have a better idea of his prognosis by then."

Jesse noticed the doctor shaking his head as he spoke about Jameson.

"What is it, Doc? What aren't you saying?"

"Mr. Jameson's had a rough life. He's been an intravenous drug user. He's definitely been wounded in battle. He's had a lot of work done on his legs and there's pretty extensive burn scarring as well."

Healy asked, "But how do you know he was in the military?"

"The tattoos. And believe me, I've seen battle scars. Those are battle scars."

Jesse remembered his own words in describing his John Doe to the press. The tattoo, the intravenous drug use.

"Doc, does Jameson have tan lines?"

Both Crier and Healy looked at Jesse like he had suddenly sprouted antlers.

"That's a bizarre question," the doctor said.

"Humor me."

Dr. Crier shrugged. "As a matter of fact, he does. Pretty intense ones."

Jesse asked, "Can we see him?"

"He's unconscious."

"Then he won't mind, will he?"

Three minutes later, Crier, Healy, and Jesse were standing around Jameson's bed in the ICU.

Jesse asked for the doctor to show him Jameson's wounds and the proof of his drug use.

"I'm sorry, Chief Stone, but I'm afraid I can't —"

"Listen, Doc, I've got three unsolved homicides that the man in that bed might have the answers to. Can you guarantee me he's going to wake up?"

"Guarantee? No."

"Then show me what I asked for, please. I don't have time to run around getting court orders."

The doctor took hold of Jameson's left arm and gently turned it over to expose ugly track-mark scars. "It's the same on his other arm," Crier said, pulling up the sleeve of Jameson's gown to point out the sharp lines of demarcation between the sun-browned skin of his arm below his triceps and the sickly pale skin above it. There were the tattoos: military and prison tats, just as the motel clerk from Diablito had described them to Jesse. Jameson had to be the man who had spoken to Suit over the phone. Then Crier pulled down the blanket that covered Jameson from his waist. The scars on his legs were just as the doctor had described them. They were painful to look at.

"Thanks, Doc," Jesse said.

"You surprise me, Chief."

"How so?"

"You haven't asked to see the other tattoo. The one on his left side, under his arm," Crier said. "Pretty creepy. It's of a cross and a —"

"Two-headed rattlesnake," Jesse finished

373

his sentence.

Crier's eyes got big. "How could you know that?"

"Not now, Doc. Where are Jameson's clothes? I need to see his clothes."

70

Healy left Jesse at the hospital, saying he had to wrap some things up in Framingham and that he would give the state marine unit a call to help motivate them to look for the *Dragoa Rainha.* Jesse didn't doubt there were loose ends that needed tying up in Framingham and he appreciated any help Healy could give him tracking down Dragoa. But the real reason Healy left had much more to do with what Jesse found stuffed in Jameson's jacket pocket than the search for Dragoa. Over the course of his career, Healy had delivered all kinds of horrific news to people. People who'd done nothing to deserve the tragedies that he brought to doorsteps. Even so, hardened as he was, he didn't want to be anywhere near Paradise that night when it was Jesse's turn to bring tragedy to someone's door.

First Jesse had to drive Suit home. But before he could do that, Bill Marchand showed up at the ER. Maybe he'd judged Marchand too harshly the other day, Jesse thought. No one else from the town government had showed up to check on Suit. In most municipalities, it was tradition for the mayor to pay a visit to the hospital when a cop is hurt on the job. Not in Paradise, apparently, and not when the town had gotten so much bad press. Jesse had to give Marchand credit for coming.

"How is Suit?" Marchand asked, shaking Jesse's hand.

"He'll live. If the gunshot didn't kill him, that rusty old pickup wasn't going to do it."

"And the other gentleman?"

"Jameson," Jesse said.

"Who is he, exactly?"

"He'd come to town to help us identify our John Doe. Unfortunately, he didn't get the chance."

"What's his condition?"

"He's still unconscious. The doctor thinks the next few hours are critical."

"What do you think about what happened, Jesse?"

"I think what Alexio Dragoa did is a strong indication that he had something to do with the deaths of Ginny Connolly and Mary Kate O'Hara."

"But you don't think he acted alone?"

"I don't have any real evidence even he was involved," Jesse said. "But I think the mayor can exhale and relax a little. We're close. I just need to find Dragoa."

"Good luck, Jesse. Let me know if I can help. If you can give the mayor something soon, I'm pretty sure you'll keep your job."

"You just like winning at softball."

Marchand smiled. "There is that. Now I'd like to go talk to Suit for a minute, if I could. I'd like to express my appreciation."

Jesse pointed to his left. "Suit's in there. Tell him to hurry up, that getting hit by a truck is no excuse for making me wait."

For a brief second, he considered calling out to Marchand and telling him what he'd found in Jameson's pockets. He decided against it. When he was this close to finally putting the murders behind him, he thought he'd better make sure of his facts. A misstep at this point by raising expectations too high might lose him the job he thought he had just saved.

71

He caught Molly at the station as she was about to leave for home. Jesse was inscrutable by nature. He didn't wear his heart on his sleeve. His face wasn't an open book. So for him to look at her the way he was looking at her meant something was wrong, terribly wrong. Molly could feel her heart pounding. Her mouth was cotton, her palms wet. She was light-headed. Her vision blurred at the edges in stark contrast to the painfully sharp image of Jesse's face.

"Is it Suit? Did something happen to Suit?"

"He's fine, Molly. I just dropped him at home."

"My kids! Did something —"

Jesse grabbed her shoulders and shook her just enough to get her attention. "It's not like that. Come on into my office."

He let go of her arms, but somehow she couldn't move. She felt glued to the floor.

Her legs leaden, numb. When she realized Peter Perkins and the other cops coming on shift were staring at her, and she remembered losing it outside the collapsed building where she had discovered the bodies of her long-missing friends, she talked herself into putting one foot before the other. She wouldn't let the others see her be weak. She had had to fight that fight to be accepted as an equal for years and wasn't up to doing battle on that front again.

Inside the office they sat on opposite sides of Jesse's desk. They were quiet together. It was an intimate thing sometimes for two people to be silent together, and this was an intimate moment between them. Jesse broke the silence.

"We think we've finally IDed our blue tarp John Doe."

Molly was confused. If Suit was all right and her family was fine and this was just about a body in the morgue, why, she wondered, had Jesse's expression been so grave? She couldn't make sense of it.

Jesse understood her confusion and handed a plastic evidence bag to Molly.

"We found that in Jameson's jacket pocket."

In the bag was a small, white-bordered, color-faded photo, what used to be called a wallet-size print. It was the type of print you used to get when cameras had film inside them instead of memory cards and folks carried photos in their wallets instead of in their phones. These prints were usually offered as bonuses by photo booths as an incentive to have the developing done by them. *Print two or more thirty-six-exposure rolls with us and we'll throw in small prints for friends and family.* As Molly stared at the image of a pretty teenage girl in the arms of a tall, brown-haired boy, Jesse thought back to a time when every strip mall and parking lot in the country had a little photo hut.

"I don't understand," Molly said, her eyes locked on the evidence bag. "I don't understand."

It was clear to Jesse that Molly understood perfectly well, but that she needed his help to let her heart catch up to her head.

"That's you in the photo, isn't it, Molly?"

She nodded.

"You were really pretty even back then," he said.

She smiled a heartbreaking smile as sad as a June day is long. "Not until that spring." Her voice was choked and barely a whisper. "I was always so plain until then."

"That's Warren Zebriski holding you."

She nodded again and then repeated, "I

don't understand."

"The guy in the hospital, Jameson, he called the station and spoke to Suit right after we released the description of our John Doe and the photos of his tattoo. But he wouldn't tell Suit anything. When I called back to talk to him, he had gone. To come here, I guess."

"But what's he got to do with Warren?" she asked.

"He's got that same tattoo in the same spot. The two-headed rattlesnake around the horizontal crossbeam. Come on, Molly. I think you can stop pretending now."

She nodded. This time, it looked painful.

"Can you give me a minute alone in here, Jesse?"

He came around the desk. "Sure," he said.

"Please don't let anyone come in here."

"No one will come in here until you tell me. Take all the time you want," Jesse said. "As long as you need."

72

They sat across the booth from each other at Daisy Dyke's, Molly barely touching her food. When Daisy noticed that most of the meat loaf and mashed potatoes she had served Molly was still on her plate, she made a face, and not a happy one. Daisy was a character and Paradise's favorite lesbian crusader, but diplomacy wasn't one of Daisy's strengths. In fact, Jesse used to think that if we ever wanted to incite a third world war, Daisy could probably do the trick.

"Not good enough for you?" Daisy said.

"It's fine, Daisy. It's good."

"Look at Jesse's plate. It's so damned clean, I don't think I'll need to wash it."

"Sorry," Molly said, "I'm not that hungry."

Jesse shook his head at Daisy and she got the message.

"Okay, hon, I'll wrap that up for you,

then. Let me get you two some coffee," she said, scooping the plate off the table. "Maybe something in the coffee from my private stock?"

Jesse gave Daisy the thumbs-up. Molly opened her mouth to protest, then closed it.

"Be right back with those special coffees."

Daisy was gone.

"Molly," Jesse said, leaning forward, "do you think Warren had anything to do with the homicides?"

"No, Jesse. No. He was gentle, not only with me. He could never have hurt Mary Kate or Ginny. He told me once that his coach was after him all the time, yelling at him to toughen up, that he was too much of a pussy to make it in college."

Jesse didn't bother protesting that he had heard the same sorts of defenses from friends, families, and lovers of some of the most cruel and cold-blooded killers to walk the earth. He didn't see the point in arguing with Molly.

"You mentioned Warren's coach. Was it Coach Feller?"

Molly shrugged. "I don't know. Maybe, I guess. I didn't follow basketball. I liked Warren because he was nice and he was handsome."

"And because Mary Kate thought so, too."

Molly bowed her head and said, "Yes, and because of that."

Daisy brought the coffees and, before she left, told them there would be as many refills as they needed. They thanked her and sipped their coffees. The ratio between the scotch and coffee was about fifty/fifty.

"Okay, Molly, if Warren wasn't involved in killing the girls, why did he disappear? And why would the real killers feel the need to kill him?"

"I don't know, Jesse. All I know is he wouldn't have hurt Mary Kate or Ginny. He couldn't have."

"Stop thinking with your heart now, Molly. I need you to be a cop. Why couldn't he —"

"He didn't do it!" She was loud enough that some heads turned.

Jesse pressed her. "But how can you know that?"

"Because I was with him."

"What do you mean you were with him?"

"Do I have to draw you a diagram, Jesse?"

"It's like that."

"We spent all night together. His folks were away with his little brother. I just got back into my bedroom and into bed in time for my mom to come wake me up to tell me that Tess O'Hara was on the phone in a panic. It went from being the best, most exciting night of my life to the worst."

"But something doesn't fit, Molly."

"If he didn't do it, why would they need to kill him?"

Jesse said, "There's only one answer to that."

And Molly supplied it. "He knew who killed the girls and kept it to himself all these years."

Jesse nodded.

"But why would he do that?" she asked herself as much as she was asking Jesse. "And why would he come back after all these years?"

"I think we'll have those answers if Jameson ever wakes up. But one thing's for sure."

"What's that?"

"He never forgot you, Molly. He carried that picture of the two of you around with him his whole life. He must have given it to Jameson for safekeeping when he left Arizona to come east."

She smiled that sad smile.

"I have that same picture. It's buried at the bottom of a box in the attic of my mom's house. I haven't looked at those old pictures for a long time. I couldn't deal with them. You know the weirdest part, Jesse?"

"What?"

"Mary Kate took that picture of Warren and me. There's one just like it that I took that day of Warren and her. That was the day I guess we both realized . . ."

"Does Warren have any family left in town?" Jesse asked, finishing his coffee. "You mentioned a little brother."

"I don't think so. Maybe. Why?" Then it dawned on her. "Oh, for DNA analysis."

"Finish your coffee and go home to your family. With Suit out of commission for a few days, I need you back in the station with me."

Daisy came by the table, dropped off the bill and the wrapped-up meat loaf, and delivered a warning. "I spotted some vultures out front."

Jesse peeked to see a bunch of reporters and camera crews by the front of the eatery.

"We'll use that back door," Jesse said, handing cash to Daisy.

73

Molly got clear, but Jesse didn't make it to the back door. Healy was calling him on his cell phone. Daisy's wasn't crowded, but it wasn't empty, either, and he didn't want to have a conversation with Healy in public, even if listeners could overhear only one side of it.

"Hold on a minute," he said, then locked himself in the men's room. "You found the boat?"

"Nope. Sorry, Jesse. No word on the boat yet. I made the call and our people are out there looking for it."

"Then what?"

"The panties."

For the last few days, Jesse had been so focused on other things — the funerals, the arson, Millner, Jameson, Dragoa — that he had to remind himself about Maxie Connolly and the missing cabbie.

"What about the panties?" Jesse asked.

"Lab found soil traces consistent with the soil from the Bluffs. Also found two DNA hits on them."

"Let me guess: Maxie Connolly and Wiethop."

Healy laughed. "One out of two. You got Maxie Connolly."

"And the other one?"

"Unknown contributor."

"Not Wiethop?"

"Definitely not Wiethop," Healy said.

"Doesn't make sense. Did the unknown contributor leave semen?"

"No semen. Skin cells. Lots of 'em. Some gray facial hairs, too."

"Gray facial hairs and skin cells," Jesse said to himself out loud.

"Wait, it gets even stranger. Wiethop did leave prints and DNA on the other things you guys found in his apartment, but the unknown contributor left nothing on those items. Only on the panties. What do you think?"

Jesse said, "I think someone's jerking us around."

"Wiethop?"

"Maybe, but I doubt it. He's an ex-con cabdriver living over a deli, not a rocket scientist. For now, I'm more focused on Dragoa."

"Like I said, Jesse, the marine unit's out there searching. Between them and the Coast Guard, they'll find the boat."

"Do me a favor, Healy. Fax me the report."

"Already done. Jameson still unconscious?"

"Uh-huh."

"You have that talk with Molly Crane yet?"

"Just got done."

"How'd she take it?"

"About as well as you'd expect," Jesse said, "but she alibied Zebriski for the entire night of that July fourth. She wouldn't lie to me about that."

"You sure about that, Jesse? You remember being young and in love. Women are kinda peculiar about their first loves."

"I'm sure."

"But why kill this Zebriski guy if he had no part in it? And what was he doing back in Paradise?"

"Those are two of the million-dollar questions."

There was a knock at the bathroom door. "C'mon, man, sometime this week, huh?"

"Okay, Healy. Talk to you tomorrow."

When Jesse stepped out of the men's room, one of the news crews' cameramen was on the other side of the door.

"Sorry about that, Chief. I didn't know it was you in there."

"If you knew it was me, would you have had to go any less?"

"I guess not. And speaking of that . . ."

Jesse stepped out of his way.

74

Stu Cromwell was in his office, a nearly empty bottle of rye and a pretty tall glass of it on the desk in front of him. Although he had told Jesse to come in, he looked lost in thought and time. Maybe it was Martha. Maybe not. Maybe, Jesse thought, Cromwell was just drunk.

"Bad time?"

"The last few years have been a bad time," Cromwell said, eyes still looking into the middle distance. "Since Al Gore invented the fucking Internet, it's been a bad time for newspapers. Why should today be an exception?"

"Fair question. How's Martha doing?"

"Just a matter of time for her."

"Matter of time for all of us, Stu."

"She's got less of it than most," the newspaperman said, finishing the rye in his glass and pouring some more. He didn't offer any to Jesse. "If she wasn't in so much pain, I'd say she was the lucky one. But there I go again, feeling sorry for myself."

"Sorry it's been rough."

"Sorry. Yeah, me, too, for a lot of things. You know Edith Piaf, Jesse?"

"The singer?"

Cromwell nodded, taking another drink. "She has this song, *'Non, Je Ne Regrette Rien.'* I have no regrets. I wonder if she meant it. Do you think she meant it? You think it's possible to have no regrets? I wonder sometimes what that would be like, having no regrets."

"Everybody's got regrets."

Cromwell laughed, but it was unclear exactly why. "I had a roommate in college, Jeff Rosen. His dad was a rabbi. He told me once that his dad used to say that to live was to have regrets. Do you think that's true? I guess you do."

"What's going on, Stu?"

Cromwell ignored the question.

"Regrets. We all have 'em. Some of us more than others."

Jesse asked the question he had asked before. "What's going on?"

Cromwell went silent and looked at Jesse as if just realizing Jesse was really there with him. "Why are you here, Jesse?"

"To keep my word. I've got something for you."

Cromwell laughed that odd laugh again and tossed some legal-looking papers at Jesse. "The bank's foreclosing on me."

"Sorry to hear it. Isn't there anything you can do? Can you stall them?"

Cromwell finished his drink and poured the remainder of the bottle into his glass. "We've depleted most of Martha's inheritance propping the paper up and they've already restructured the loans three times. This is the end, *das Ende.*"

"What will you do?"

He laughed. It was a hollow laugh. "I don't know. Maybe I'll open up a self-defense dojo for broken old men. Oh, don't look at me like that, Chief," Cromwell said, an unfamiliar nasty edge to his voice. "I've got black belts in jiujitsu and aikido, though I haven't trained in years. I'm the world's most dangerous newspaperman . . . ex-newspaperman. Maybe you can use me on the Paradise PD. I hear you're another man short. Suit okay?"

"Banged up."

"And the other man?" Cromwell asked, unable to turn off his newspaper instincts.

"Not great. Still unconscious. When are you closing shop?"

Cromwell looked at his watch. "As of two hours ago."

Jesse stood and offered his hand to Cromwell, but Cromwell was off in his head somewhere again.

"Old men do very foolish things, Jesse. Desperately foolish things. They do things to hold on to the crumbs they've accumulated, only to find out the crows have already eaten the crumbs. But you can't take things back, can you? You can't undo things once they're done."

"If we could undo things," Jesse said, "Piaf would be right and Rabbi Rosen would be wrong."

"So even though I have no paper to print the story in, let me feel like a newspaperman one last time. Tell me what you came to tell me. Please."

"It's about Maxie Connolly. Doesn't matter now."

Cromwell finished the rye in his glass and with tears in his eyes began singing in French, " *'Non, rien de rien . . .'* "

Jesse closed the door behind him. Even halfway down the stairs, he could still hear Cromwell singing.

75

Jesse had a long talk with Ozzie Smith over a few Black Labels. The thing with Suit hadn't hit him until he was on the way home that evening. He'd taken his usual drive around town, but added a slow cruise along Trench Alley past what was now a cracked concrete slab where the bodies had been found, and a drive up into the Bluffs. With the exception of the detour down Trench Alley, it was the same route he'd taken the night of the nor'easter. That storm had brought more with it than wind and snow. It brought with it the past.

As he sat in his Explorer on the grounds of the old Rutherford mansion, the place where he'd confronted John Millner the night of the storm, Jesse remembered something he'd once read in a magazine on a long bus trip from Vero Beach to Fort Myers. That's what you did in spring training, you rode buses to away games. And on those long, boring bus rides, you read or played cards or listened to music. That was a special spring, the spring he'd been anointed, the spring when the GM of the Dodgers told him that if he hit at all in Triple-A, he'd be a September call-up to the big club.

The article he'd read on that long-ago bus ride was about an almost perfectly preserved P-38 Lightning discovered in the North African desert. It had disappeared in late August 1944 and the military had given up all hope of ever finding it. The article said that this sort of thing wasn't that unusual. That in the scheme of things, given the enormous scale of Allied air force operations during the war, dozens of planes had gone missing in every theater of battle, the most famous being a B-24D Liberator called *Lady Be Good*, lost in Libya in 1943 and discovered in 1958. The remains of the crew were discovered miles away from the wreckage in 1960. He remembered that he'd heard about the *Lady Be Good* even before reading about it. You grow up in Arizona, the home of the airplane graveyard, you hear stories. And the *Lady Be Good* incident had inspired one of his favorite *Twilight Zone* episodes.

The thing about the P-38 that made it different was that it had been buried in a sand dune for forty years and it had been uncovered, finally, by a historically violent sandstorm. Another thing that made it different was that the remains of the pilot, who'd apparently been killed on impact, had been found in the plane. Not only had the plane been preserved, if somewhat flattened by the weight of the dune, but so, too, had the remains of the pilot. He had been sort of mummified by the sands. It was no wonder to Jesse why he should be thinking about that long-ago bus ride and the article he'd read. The parallels were obvious enough. But there was something eating at him. Something about the article that he'd forgotten, that he wanted to remember yet just couldn't.

By the time he'd made it home, his mind had turned back to Paradise's own case of history delayed and his complicated feelings about Suitcase Simpson. Suit had acted with incredible valor, shielding Jameson from Dragoa with his own body. Jesse wasn't sure he would have reacted as quickly as Suit had. So why had he been unable to bring himself to pat Suit on the shoulder for a job well done? Ozzie Smith was of no help.

"I don't know, Wiz," Jesse said, shaking

his head at Smith's poster. "At least I can get a reaction from Dix. I may have to pinch-hit for you next inning."

76

When he walked into the station, he was surprised to see Molly Crane at the desk.

"What are you still doing here?"

"We're short cops and I could use the overtime," she said.

"That's if I can get any overtime authorized."

"You'll figure something out. I have faith in you."

"Don't you Catholic girls believe faith is only really rewarded in the next life?"

"I can wait," she said. "Besides, I would be climbing the walls at home, thinking about . . . you know."

"Warren?"

She nodded. "About that. I think I might be able to track down his brother. I made a few calls to old friends. One thinks he might've moved to New York and one says at least one of Warren's parents might be alive and down in Florida."

"Good. Where's Millner?"

"Not here," Molly said.

"What do you mean he's not here? Did a judge kick him loose?"

"He wasn't at home. And he hasn't been to work for two days. Hasn't called in. He just never showed up."

Jesse clenched. "Damn! He ran."

"Maybe."

"Okay. Let everyone know," he said.

"Already done."

"Healy know?" Jesse asked.

"First call was to him."

"I knew there was a reason I kept you around."

She folded her arms and made a face. "Just one reason?"

"One or two."

Molly said, "Al Franzen called a little while ago. He's checking out of the hotel tonight and heading home."

"Any news on Dragoa or his boat?"

"Still nothing."

"I'm going to go over to the hotel."

"I thought you might."

Ten minutes later, Jesse was at the Whaler Lounge in the hotel with Al Franzen. Franzen ordered a frozen strawberry margarita and Jesse a Black Label neat. Franzen raised his drink to Jesse. They clinked glasses.

"To Maxie," Jesse said.

"To my Maxie."

When he sipped the margarita, Franzen made a sour face.

"Feh!" he said. "I hate these froufrou drinks, but my Maxie loved them. She loved drinking. She loved anything with alcohol in it."

Jesse smiled. "Yeah, I didn't figure you for a frozen-margarita man."

Franzen seemed not to hear. "My Maxie . . . who am I kidding? She was never mine. She wasn't the type of woman who could ever really belong to any one person. Sometimes I don't even think she belonged to herself. I hated that about her, but I also loved her for it, too. I'm not making much sense, am I?"

"You're making perfect sense."

"She was such a restless woman. It's funny, Jesse, but I can't imagine even death could tame her."

"I only met her once and I know exactly what you mean."

"But now she has her girl back and the pain is over with." He gulped the pink drink. "It is a terrible kind of pain, a grinding, gnawing pain that leaves you empty. Maxie tried to fill it up with . . . I'm repeating myself, aren't I?"

"It's okay, Al. It's okay."

A slender African American man in his early twenties came into the lounge and called out Al Franzen's name. Franzen waved to him. "Over here."

"Mr. Franzen," he said, "your car to the airport is here. I'll load your luggage into the trunk, if I may?"

Franzen slipped him a ten-dollar bill and told him to go ahead. When he'd gone, Franzen got off the bar stool and shook Jesse's hand.

"Thank you, Jesse. You've been very good through all of this."

"I'm sorry for your loss. Maxie was something else."

Franzen took a step, then stopped. "I hope you find out who killed Maxie's girl and the other girl, too. But if you don't, I'll understand. Maxie would understand. She knew what I told you the last time we talked. Sometimes the devil wins. It has always been so, I think."

Jesse watched Al Franzen make his way through the lobby and vanish behind the night-colored glass of the lobby doors.

77

When Jesse stepped out of the shower the following morning it was to a chorus of ringing phones. He chose the landline because it was closest.

"Jesse Stone."

"Morning, Jesse."

"What's up, Molly?"

"Two things."

Jesse asked, "Good, bad, or mixed?"

"Good. Jameson is coming out of it, but the doctor says he's not up for visitors yet."

"Not even the cops?"

"Especially not with cops. He's agitated and confused."

"What's the other thing?"

"I got a line on Millner," she said.

"Did you get any sleep last night?"

"A little. Then I came in early. Don't you want to hear what I've got?"

"Sorry, Molly. You were saying you got a line on Millner."

"Two nights ago he took a cab from the Swap to over by the marina."

"You thinking what I'm thinking?"

"That Millner hid out on Dragoa's boat and then they both split after Dragoa tried to run Jameson down."

"That's what I was thinking."

"It's them, Jesse. It's got to be them who killed Mary Kate, Ginny, and Warren. It's got to be."

"Evidence, Molly. Evidence. They look guilty, but looking isn't being. Wake Peter Perkins up and tell him to get down to the station. Call the DA and get warrants for Dragoa's house and property, and for Millner's apartment and for the maintenance shed at Sacred Heart," Jesse said, walking over to his dresser to retrieve his cell phone. He looked at the message and saw it was from Healy.

"Anything else, Jesse?"

"You believe in prayer?"

"I guess."

"Then start praying."

He put the phone back in its cradle, toweled off, and got dressed. He went downstairs and put up some coffee before calling Healy.

"About time you called back," Healy said.

"Good morning to you, too."

"Our guys found it," Healy said. "About an hour ago."

"The boat?"

"Yep, the *Dragoa Rainha.* They found her just a little ways up the coast from you, north of Swan Harbor in a little rocky inlet called Shelter Cove. Blood everywhere, but no bodies."

"No bodies?"

"I was getting to that. Swan Harbor cops found two bodies washed up onshore about two miles north. Male Caucasians tentatively identified as —"

"Alexio Dragoa and John Millner," Jesse said before Healy could finish.

"How'd you know?"

"I didn't know, exactly. Molly tracked down a cabbie who took Millner to the marina area two nights ago."

"One of my guys has seen the bodies. They still had their wallets in their pockets. He says Dragoa's got two holes in him and that Millner's guts look like Swiss cheese. I think your case is finally closed, Jesse."

"How's that?"

"There's a confession. Come on up. I'll meet you there."

78

An hour later, Jesse, Captain Healy, and assorted cops — state and Swan Harbor — stood on the rocks at Shelter Cove, a small wedge-shaped cut-in two miles north of the Swan Harbor town line. If the boat had drifted into the cove at night, it was easy to understand how she'd been missed. In the dark, she'd be nearly impossible to see. Now, ten feet below them, the *Dragoa Rainha,* secured to some makeshift moorings, bobbled gently in the water. Jesse had never been to Shelter Cove before, but he'd seen a photo of it. He just couldn't remember where he'd seen it.

"My guys are almost done in there," Healy said. "Then you can have a look before the marine unit tows her back to wherever the hell they tow boats to. Jeez, that boat smells of fish."

"Fishing boats are like that."

"Funny man, Jesse. Funny man."

Jesse asked, "Where are the bodies?"

"On the way to the morgue."

"You said something about a confession."

Healy smiled. "I thought you'd never ask."

Jesse scowled.

"What bug crawled up your nose this morning?"

"It's too neat."

"You won't be saying that when you've had a gander belowdecks. Looks like the floor of a butcher shop without the sawdust."

"That's not what I mean," Jesse said.

"Then what?"

"These two guys, Dragoa and Millner, they weren't the confessing types."

"I don't know," Healy said. "A man, any man, carries a burden long enough, the weight will begin to drag him under. Maybe that's what happened here."

Jesse shook his head.

Healy kept at him. "Look, aren't you the one who's always saying to follow the evidence?"

"I am."

"Then follow it. You haven't even seen the damned confession or the shape of the boat."

Jesse asked, "Which one of them wrote it?"

"Millner."

"Okay, that's better. If you said it was Dragoa, I would have called bullshit on that."

"Why, the fisherman a man of few words?"

"Few words that weren't swearwords," Jesse said. "Let me see it."

"Tommy," Healy called to one of his men. "Tommy, get me the confession letter."

A few minutes later, Tommy handed him an evidence bag. Jesse could read the typed note through the clear plastic. The letter was addressed to him. He read it aloud.

Cheif Stone

I guess I shoud start by saying that me and Alexio killed Mary Kate and Ginny all them years ago. Not that it means nothing now, but we didn't mean to do it. I swear. It just started out as some fun that went bad. Me and Alexio and Ginny was high and shitfaced. That bitch Mary Kate woudnt get high or drink or nothing. If she hadn't gone all psycho on us, none of this woud of happened. We was all just supposed to go out to Stiles to Humpback Point and have some fun. Ginny Connolly and me kind of had a thing for each other and I asked her to meet me at the park that night and then to go out to Humpback Point with me but she said she woudn't go out to Stiles without Mary Kate with her. And the only way I could get that bitch Mary Kate to come was to tell her Zevon woud meet us there because she was all hot for him. I figured if Mary Kate had to come along, I woud bring Alexio with me because we was pals. You wasn't around then, Stone. Zevon is what we used to call Warren Zebriski. We was all on the Sacred Heart hoops team together. Anyways, we get out to Humpback and me and Ginny are getting naked and stuff and Alexio got carried away and started trying to kiss Mary Kate. She was screaming her head off and shit and Alexio ripped her clothes off and forced her. Ginny pushed me off her and went to help Mary Kate. When she tried pulling Alexio off Mary Kate, Mary Kate kneed him. That's when it got real bad. Alexio lost it and stabbed Mary Kate and kept stabbing her like a million times. Finally I get him to stop but Mary Kate is dead. Then Ginny is freaking out, Stone. Next thing I knew I had a big rock in my hand and Ginny was on the grass there naked and not moving or nothing. Alexio took the rock

out a my hand and hit her in the head
again. He said we wouda had to kill her
anyways. We waited until it was real late
and the harbor had gotten emptier. We
loaded the girl's bodies on the rowboat.
Alexio said he knew what to do. He
knew a place to ditch them that nobody
would find them. We rowed to a place
Alexios dad told him about. A secret
place where you could get into Pennacook Inlet. The rest was easy. That old
building on Trench Alley was easy to get
into. We scuttled the boat in the inlet.
It's still probably there. We was crazy
nervus for a few months then things
were cool. Then when Zevon came home
that next summer him and me got drunk
one night and I got all guilty and
confessed. Me and Zevon was tight and
he kinda freaked out. I was scared he
would go to the cops but he didn't. He
just went away and if he stayed away I
woldnt be writing this. But he came back
saying he found God and needed to tell
what he knew and that he hoped that
me and Alexio would go with him and
confess our sins. We coudnt do that, so
me an Alexio, we done the one thing we
had to. We killed Zevon the night of the
big storm in the shed. Alexio was ditch-

ing his body next to the girls when the building started to go down. He figured he'd come back and get Zevon next morning and dump him out in the ocean but it was too late. Killing Zevon brung it all back to me and I coudnt take it no more. Alexio told me I shud get somebody to burn down the two houses because of DNA stuff you was talking about and to throw you off me and his tails. So I paid a guy I knew a few hundred bucks to do that and get rid a my van. Im going to tell Alexio that I gotta confess. I hope I got the balls to do it. Tell Mrs. O'Hara I didn't mean it and I guess neither did Alexio. He was just crazy drunk. I think I'll be telling Maxie Connelly myself soon.

Jesse handed the letter back to Tommy. Somebody called up from the boat.

"Come on, Jesse," Healy said. "We can take a look now."

Healy hadn't exaggerated. The boat was slaughterhouse bloody. Healy's forensics guy walked Jesse through it.

Knife is standing here. Gun is standing in front of Knife, maybe two feet away. Knife lunges. Stabs Gun. Gun fires,

411

wings Knife in shoulder. See the hole in the wall and the blood spatter over my left shoulder? Jesse saw the hole and the spatter. We dug a slug out of there. Wounded, Knife stabs and keeps stabbing Gun. Gun fires again, this time wounding Knife in the abdomen. See the spatter and the hole behind me slightly to my right? Jesse saw the spatter and the hole. We dug a slug out of there also, but it wasn't in deep in the wall. So now both badly wounded, they collapse to the floor. See those two large pools of blood, there and there? Jesse noted them. Gun drops weapon and crawls up the steps. Knife follows sometime later, weapon still in hand. On deck, both having lost considerable amounts of blood and in shock, they struggle. The deck slick with blood and seawater, they both go overboard. When the boat was found, it was out of gas and indications are the engines had been running. The boat drifted into Shelter Cove under power. The bodies were washed north by the current and came to shore. We recovered the .38 in the cabin and a four-inch Buck hunting knife up top.

79

Jesse was about to do something he'd never done before, something that went against his nature to do, but he felt like he had nowhere else to go. There was no one else he could talk to about this situation who would understand. It'd eaten at him the whole ride back down to Paradise from North Swan Harbor. And when he approached the station and saw the mob of press outside, he turned his Explorer around and pulled into the Lobster Claw parking lot. He reached for his phone, pressed CONTACTS, and tapped his index finger to the letter *B.* He scrolled to the name he wanted and stared at the screen.

He had tried talking to Healy about it, but Healy didn't seem to want to understand what he was getting at. The object was to clear cases, so why look for trouble? He couldn't talk to Ed Barstow, the Swan Harbor police chief, about it. Ed was a good guy, but not much of a cop. He was the chief of a small police force in a town of rich folks. He had no ambition and no desire to make waves in a high-profile case. And this wasn't the kind of thing he could discuss with Molly or Suit or Peter Perkins. Finally, Jesse tapped the name on the screen and put the phone to his ear.

"Yeah, hello. What's up?" said the man who answered the phone on the first ring.

While not exactly a strange voice, it was no longer a familiar voice to Jesse, because he hadn't heard it for more than ten years. He recognized it as belonging to the man he'd called, but the voice was older — of course it was — and it was thinner than Jesse remembered it.

"Javy B.," Jesse said, finding it difficult to speak.

"No one calls me that no more. Who is this?"

"Jesse."

"Jesse?"

"Jesse Stone."

There were a few seconds of very uneasy silence.

"Stone," said Javier Baez, Jesse's first partner after he made detective.

"Javier."

"Why you calling?"

It had been many years since the LAPD had shown Jesse the exit door and many, many more since they had worked together, but the disappointment was thick in Baez's voice.

"I needed to talk to someone about a case," Jesse said.

"The dead girls and the John Doe?"

"Uh-huh."

"I've been reading about it. Watching the news reports. Sounds like a mess. But what you want from me? I'm just a retired detective with bad kidneys and alimony payments. You're a big-shot police chief, no?"

"You were the best detective I ever met, Javy. You taught me the ropes."

"You had a chance to be better than me, but you pissed it away. You still a drunk?"

That hurt Jesse more than he believed it could, but he wasn't sure which part of what his old partner said hurt worse. The part about Jesse's potential as a detective or about his alcoholism.

"I still drink, yeah. Not like I used to, not usually on the job. If that makes me a drunk, then I'm a drunk."

"One thing I'll give you, you're not a liar. Could never abide my partners lying to me. You called to talk about a case, okay, talk."

Jesse ran down the essentials of the case.

Described Dragoa's attempt on Jameson's life, told him the details about the scene on the boat, the confession letter, about how and where the bodies had washed up.

"Sounds like you're about to close some cases," Baez said, an edge to his voice that Jesse had hoped to hear. An edge that said he was thinking what Jesse was thinking. "It's all the evidence a detective could ever want and it's all wrapped up in a nice little package with a pretty red bow. So what's your problem?"

Jesse said, "You know what the problem is. There's too much evidence. You would have been suspicious as all hell, we ever turned up this much evidence. And I didn't even turn it up. It all landed in my lap. Pretty convenient the two killers turning up dead like that."

"What is it you gringos say? Don't look a gift horse in the mouth. Whatever the hell that means."

"Don't give me that poor dumb Mexican bullshit, Javy."

"And don't be calling me Javy. You lost that right when you disgraced the shield. You put your partners at risk. You didn't learn that from me. You called me for a favor. I owe you that much, but nothing more. We clear on that?"

"Clear."

"Why not wait for the forensics?" Baez asked.

"Because I bet they're going to come back consistent with what I told you."

"Maybe there's a reason for that. Maybe because they're right."

"Here's something I did learn from you. Forensics and statistics don't lie, but they can be massaged and manipulated."

"Work the case. Go find the masseuse."

"Be nice if I had an idea where to look."

"Right now you're three thousand miles off the mark. Whatever you're looking for isn't in L.A."

"You always were a comedian, Javy — Javier."

"You know where to look, Stone. I taught you that on day one. Look right in front of you."

"Thanks, Javier."

"Stone."

"What?"

"Watch yourself out there."

Javier Baez clicked off. And once again Jesse found himself staring at his cell phone. He hadn't even noticed that it was snowing. He drove out of the parking lot and headed for the hospital.

80

Jameson had been moved out of ICU and was in a private room on the second floor. Jesse got the room number easily enough. He didn't bother getting the doctor's permission. When Jesse knocked and walked into the room, Jameson was in bed, his head turned to the right, eyes transfixed by the big, lazy snowflakes falling outside the window.

"Haven't seen snowfall since Afghanistan," Jameson said, not turning to look at Jesse. "I've seen snow. Seen a lot of it up in the mountains and a lot of snow on my way here, but none of it falling."

"That where you got wounded, Afghanistan?"

"Yes, sir. IED exploded right under our vehicle. Blew Bobby G's legs clean off. I was the lucky one. Only sometimes I guess I don't feel so lucky, sir."

Jesse walked to the bed and pulled up a

chair. He didn't want to loom over Jameson.
Jameson turned finally to look at his visitor.

Jesse offered his hand. "I'm Jesse Stone,
the police chief. I'd like it if you could call
me Jesse."

Jameson reached across his body and
shook Jesse's hand. "Corporal Drew Allen
Jameson, sir."

Jesse didn't correct him. "How you feeling, Corporal?"

"Headache that won't quit, but otherwise
intact, sir. How is that fella that drove me
here? I don't recall what happened but the
doctor told me he saved my life. Will you
thank him for me, sir?"

"Officer Simpson is fine. Just a little
banged up. And you can thank him in
person in a day or two."

Jameson had already moved on. "Is this
really Warren Z's hometown?"

"It is. Paradise, Mass."

"Warren was real torn up about this place.
Said he left his heart and soul here. Said he
wanted to come back to get a piece of both
of them back if he could."

"Do you know what he meant by that,
Drew?"

"Been a long time since someone called
me by my first name, sir." Jameson turned
back to watch the snowflakes. "Warren said

he wanted to come home to see Molly again, not to talk to her or nothing like that. He just wanted to see her again. He left her picture with me for safekeeping. I could understand why he would want to come back to see her. Warren used to talk about her all the time. Said she was pretty, but that wasn't it. She was special. She was his heart."

"Yes, she is special," Jesse said involuntarily. "What about his soul?"

"Said that he lost it at nineteen and didn't find it again till God found him in the desert."

Jesse didn't want to push Jameson, so he just let him talk.

"We met back in Arizona, Warren and me. We was both working for an adobe brick and clay tile company outside of Tucson. You know what adobe is, sir?"

"I grew up in Tucson."

Jameson smiled at hearing that.

"It's hard work out in the sun for not much money. Warren and me, though, we liked it. We weren't neither of us much for other people's company, but we had things that held us together."

"Like heroin?"

"Yes, sir," Jameson said in a whisper. "That and pain. That's what the two-headed rattler is for on our tats, sir, our two demons: drugs and pain. But when God found Warren and when Warren helped me find God, we fought those demons off together. That's what the cross is for, for Our Savior's grace. Warren drew the design out on a piece of paper and we went down to this Mexican gal in Nogales and she did them up perfectly on Warren and me. Cost us each three days' pay, but we didn't care."

"You said Warren came back to reclaim a part of his soul. How was he going to do that?"

"By introducing his friend to Our Savior and by confession of their sins."

"Did Warren say who that friend was or why his friend needed saving?"

"Wouldn't never tell me who, sir. Not that I didn't ask. I did, but Warren said that would be another betrayal and that too many folks had already been betrayed and too much blood spilled."

"But he did tell you why?"

Jameson nodded. "He did. Said this friend had done a terrible thing and confessed it to him one summer when they was drunk. Keeping that confidence had ruined Warren's life. It was a cross too heavy for him to bear, tore him all up inside. I know how that is, sir, getting all torn up inside

421

and out."

"Did he ever get more specific than that?"

"Said this friend told him that he and two other friends had done murder and —"

Jesse kept his voice and demeanor calm, but his mind was racing. "Drew, are you sure that this guy told Warren that there were three of them?"

"I may be half the man I once was, sir, but I recollect that perfectly. This friend had told Warren that it was him and two friends."

"There were three of them, but he never used names."

"No, sir. No names. Warren always said his sin of omission, that's what he called it, was his alone to suffer. Warren didn't talk much, but when he did his words said a lot. He said that sharing details would infect me with the sin and he wouldn't do that."

"Did he ever give you any details of the murders? Maybe who the victims were?"

"No, sir. Warren said it was for my own protection, but after we talked about it we would always pray on it."

"And when you saw the pictures of the tattoo on TV, you came east?"

"It was the least I could do, sir."

Jesse was about to reach out his hand to say good-bye to Jameson, when it struck him that Javier Baez had never been more right. The answer was right in front of him. "You up for getting out of here, Drew?"

Jameson's face lit up. "You bet."

"Your head ache?"

"I've handled worse, sir. Much worse."

"I don't doubt it, Corporal," Jesse said, handing Jameson his ratty clothes. "I've got some calls to make."

81

An hour later, Jesse was in the library of Sacred Heart Boys Catholic with Tommy Deutsch. Deutsch was the skipper of the varsity baseball team at Sacred Heart Boys and the second baseman on the Paradise PD's slo-pitch softball team. Tommy was a spry sixty and still had that competitive fire in his belly that was the difference between mediocre players and coaches and great players and coaches. Jesse and Tommy recognized the fire in each other the first time they met at a charity pancake breakfast the year Jesse moved to Paradise.

"What's this about, Jesse?" Deutsch asked, turning his key in the library door. "Usually when you want a favor, it's to take grounders and to test out that bum arm of yours. Never thought we'd meet here."

"Got something against books, Skip?"

"Nothing at all. I'm just curious why you called me out in the snow to open up the library for you."

"I'm curious, too."

"About?" Deutsch asked, clicking on the lights.

"Were you around during Coach Feller's time as the basketball coach?"

Deutsch frowned. "Our paths crossed during my first few years here. Can't say as I cared much for the man."

"Why's that?"

"Feller was a Neanderthal. Cruel to his boys, you know. The type of coach who thought Leo Durocher was too soft on his players. But he got results. Won a lot of games without much talent. His teams were always tough and smart. Pressed from the opening tip. Slowed it down when they had the advantage. Pushed the ball up court when they were behind." Deutsch tilted his head. "What's this about, Jesse? Deke Feller's been dead for fourteen or fifteen years."

"They keep copies of the yearbooks in here?"

"Of course they do," Deutsch said.

"Where?"

"Okay, Jesse, I've played along up to this point, but if you want me to keep playing, you've got to give me a little bit more than this."

"That's fair, Skip."

Deutsch walked Jesse to a dark, windowless corner of the library. There was a faint musty odor in this part of the library. "Far as I know, they're all on these shelves right here. If any are missing, I can't help you."

"Thanks."

"So what is it you think you're going to find in these yearbooks, Jesse?"

"Three murderers."

Tommy Deutsch blanched. "I'll leave you to it, then. Just click off the lights and close the door behind you when you leave. It'll lock itself."

"Skip," Jesse said. "This is between us. Just us."

The baseball coach nodded, then left.

When Deutsch was gone, Jesse counted back twenty-five years, pulled a yearbook off the shelf, and carried it over to the librarian's desk. The spine was clean, but the top of it was covered in a downy layer of dust. He brushed off the dust and ran his hand across the textured crimson-and-white cover. The spine crackled with age and resisted as he pulled open the cover, and the pages, unwilling to surrender their secrets, stuck stubbornly together. One page at a time, Jesse went through the yearbook, looking at the photos, reading some of the captions. He recognized some of the names, some of the faces. Even had a laugh or two. *So that's what he looked like when he had hair!* Then he came to the page he was looking for, the sports team photos.

The basketball team photo wasn't perfectly in focus, but it didn't need to be. Coach Feller looked exactly like Jesse expected him to look. He was a hulking, sourpussed man with his gray hair in a military brush cut. He was dressed in an unfashionable brown suit, a white shirt, a tie that didn't match, and mean shoes. There were many more familiar faces in the shot. In the back row were two faces he immediately recognized. There were three familiar faces in the front row as well. Two he expected to see and one he had hoped not to. In his years as a street cop, homicide detective, and police chief, Jesse thought he had learned his lesson about hope. He knew better than most just how little purchase hope ever really has.

82

It didn't take long for Bill Marchand to show up in Jesse's office after the news hit the street that Drew Jameson had escaped from the hospital while under police guard.

"Jesse, what the hell is going on with you guys?" Marchand was red in the face, and his voice was strained and loud enough to be heard beyond the office door. "The ice you're on is already thin enough."

But Jesse just gave him a crooked smile and gestured for the selectman to sit. "Relax, Bill."

"Relax! How can I relax? You guys look like the Keystone Kops. Isn't it bad enough that —"

Jesse held up his palms. "Bill, we know who killed the girls. We have two out of three of them."

"What are you talking about? Why haven't I heard any of this?" Marchand asked, finally taking a seat.

"Because two of them are dead. The bodies of Alexio Dragoa and John Millner washed up on the beach in North Swan Harbor early this morning. Millner shot Dragoa and Dragoa stabbed Millner. They struggled and both fell overboard. Dragoa's boat drifted into Shelter Cover. Do you know it?"

Marchand shook his head.

"Blood everywhere on the boat. We haven't announced anything yet because we wanted to confirm the identities of the deceased and get the autopsy results. Captain Healy is busy rounding up next of kin of both dead men in order to make the identifications."

Marchand asked, "But how do you know they were connected to the murders?"

"Millner wrote a confession the state forensic guys found on the boat."

"John Millner wrote a confession?" Marchand asked.

"Typed one, yeah. We found the typewriter at the maintenance shed at Sacred Heart. Why, you know Millner?"

"We played ball together at Sacred Heart. Alexio, too." Marchand shook his head. "They were both jerks, but I never thought they were capable of this."

"Nobody knows anybody, Bill. Not really.

When was the last time you saw those guys?"

"Years ago. Maybe at Coach Feller's funeral. I mean, we pass each other in town. So about this confession . . ."

"Pretty detailed. At least we now know for sure who the third body was Molly found the night of the nor'easter. Guy grew up in Paradise. Warren Zebriski. Seems that Zebriski knew about the murders all these years and came back to Paradise to ask the killers to confess. They chose to kill him instead."

Marchand bowed his head. "The body was Warren Zebriski's? Zevon's?"

"You and Zebriski close?"

"I liked him better than those other two morons, but he was closer to Millner."

"Bill," Jesse said, "we're almost there."

"About that, Jesse. You said you had two of the three killers. What am I missing here?"

Jesse smiled that crooked smile again.

"I've got no doubt that Dragoa and Millner had a hand in killing the girls and that they killed Zebriski, too, but there's a third hand in all of this. I sensed it from the beginning," Jesse said, tapping his nose. "And our one witness to any part of it, Lance Szarbo, says there were five people on the rowboat he saw going out to Stiles that Fourth of July. Three guys and two girls. He was drunk, but I think he's right."

"Your nose and a drunken witness. Not much to go on. Did the confession mention someone else?"

"No."

"Well, there you go," Marchand said. "Why go looking for trouble? You saved your job. You got your killers."

"You're right, and if that was all I had, I'd take the confession at face value, close the cases, and never look back."

"But . . ."

"But I've got more," Jesse said. "I went to visit Jameson in the hospital this afternoon when I got back from Swan Harbor. We had a pretty interesting conversation. It seems he and Zebriski had gotten to be pretty close friends in Arizona. Worked together, used to do drugs together, and pretty much found God together. They even got the same tattoo as a show of solidarity. You've seen it. The two-headed rattlesnake around the cross. He explained what it meant. But none of that was half as interesting as the other part of what he had to say."

"And that was what?"

"That he knows who the third killer is."

Marchand leaned forward. "Come on, Jesse, I'm on pins and needles here."

431

"Sorry to disappoint you, Bill, but Jameson wouldn't tell me. Said he didn't trust me or my department. And given that he got run down thirty seconds after getting into town, I couldn't really blame him."

"I guess I can see his point. But now you're screwed. He's gone with the wind."

Jesse shook his head. "No he's not, but it's what I want the killer to think. I'm going to let him know where Jameson is. Then all I have to do is sit around and wait for him to show. He'll have to come after Jameson. Jameson is the only thing standing between him and never having to worry about the murders again. Not in this life, anyway. He's risked this much. What's one last risk?"

"Pretty dangerous to use a witness as bait, Jesse. The liability of the town would be —"

"I'm not using Jameson as bait, Bill. Give me a little more credit than that. I would never risk a witness's life that way. I'm going to tell my suspect that I've got Jameson stashed at the Helton Motor Inn with one guard on him, but he's nowhere near there."

"So you have an idea who the third killer is?"

"No, not an idea. I know who he is. I just can't prove it yet."

Marchand had just opened his mouth to

speak when there was a knock on the office door.

"Just one second, Bill. Come."

It was Molly.

"Sorry, Jesse. Sorry, Mr. Selectman."

"What is it?" Jesse asked.

"Our guest is hungry and he says there's not much in the fridge."

Jesse slowly rubbed his palms together as he thought. "Who's on the desk tonight?"

"Ed."

"No problem." Jesse looked at his watch. "Ed will be here in a half hour. When he comes on shift, go to the sandwich shop, pick up a few sandwiches, and deliver them to our guest. If you're feeling generous, pick him up some groceries, too. Keep the receipts. I'll put you in for two hours of OT."

"Thanks, Jesse." Molly closed the door.

"Sorry, Bill. What were you saying?"

"I wasn't saying anything. You were telling me that you knew who the third killer was, but that you couldn't prove it."

"That's right."

"Well, who is it, for crissakes?"

"Robbie Wilson. It has to be him. He showed up at the scene of the building collapse almost before Molly had a chance to find the bodies. He was there five minutes before his men. How is that possible? I'll tell you how. He never left. He was disposing of Zebriski's body when the building went. Then, when Molly showed, he dragged her out of the building and did everything he could to delay us from getting to the bodies. When I checked around I found out that he was old friends with both Dragoa and Millner. He's been totally uncooperative with the entire investigation. Then when I mentioned DNA evidence to the press, bang! Two convenient fires so sloppily set that we never thought to look at the fire chief. Oh, it's him, all right. I'm going to enjoy nailing his Napoleonic little ass to the wall. We've got a major-league trap set at the motel." Jesse checked his watch again. "And speaking of that, it's about time for me to buy Robbie a drink and to let some information slip. After that, I'm heading over to Helton to spring the trap."

"I've got work to do as well." Marchand stood, shook Jesse's hand. "I hope you know what the hell you're doing."

"Me, too, Bill. Me, too."

83

Jesse had always been the wild card, the one person in this mess whom he had worried about from the start. Now, as he worked his way through the woods that covered the northern approach to Jesse's property, he knew he had been right to worry. Everything he'd done since Zevon had shown back up in Paradise was to throw suspicion away from himself and aim it squarely at Alexio and John. Yet in spite of the hoops he'd jumped through and the incredible risks he'd taken to throw Jesse off his scent, Jesse had almost gotten it right. Almost. He'd just picked the wrong suspect.

Kneeling at the edge of the woods to collect himself before he had to cross the little clearing between the woods and the footbridge that led to Jesse's house, he laughed to himself. To think that idiot Hasty Hathaway had hired Jesse because he thought Jesse was an easily manipulated, incompetent drunk. As he took deep, slow breaths to calm himself, he went back over the steps he'd taken since he'd left the station house. He wanted to make sure he hadn't done anything to give himself away, because once he crossed the footbridge and killed Jameson, there would be no going back.

No, he thought, he had been careful, even more careful than usual. He had hurried back to the office and borrowed one of his junior agents' cars so that Molly wouldn't spot his big white Infiniti in her rearview mirror. The agent was only too happy to swap her ten-year-old Chevy Malibu for the boss's SUV for the night. He had hung far back, following Molly as she went from the sandwich shop to the market. And then when she left the market, he kept so far behind her that he nearly lost her a few times in the falling darkness. Then, when it was obvious to him Molly was headed to Jesse's house, he turned himself around. He'd gone back to the office and made noises about having a late appointment with a client in Boston. After that, he'd gone home, told his family the same story about a late appointment in Boston, and sent them out for dinner.

When he was sure they were gone, he went

down to the basement and got his classic Mauser K98 bolt-action with scope from the gun safe. If he got lucky, he'd be able to get a clean shot at Jameson through one of Jesse's windows at a reasonable distance. But because of how Jesse's house was situated with all the woods and water, he couldn't count on it. So he took out his cheap Cobra 32 that he'd picked up in the parking lot of a gun show in Tennessee years back. It was basically untraceable. He ejected the clip and thumbed the ammo out of the clip. He put on a pair of latex gloves, reloaded the clip with fresh ammo, wiped down the clip, and wiped down the gun. He loaded the Malibu with the rifle, the pistol, a knife, his hunting camo, and boots. When he was sure he had everything he might need, he took off.

He hadn't headed directly over to Jesse's place. That would have been careless, even reckless. No, first he rode back into town, past the police station, to make sure Jesse's Explorer was gone. He'd dropped by the firehouse to see if Robbie Wilson was around. Wilson's silly red Jeep was nowhere in sight, but that didn't mean he was headed to Helton.

"Sorry, Mr. Marchand," said the young volunteer on duty. "Chief said he wouldn't

437

be available at all tonight."

It was only then that the selectman headed out to Jesse's place.

Just as he anticipated, he couldn't get a clear rifle shot at Jameson. Although he could see lights on in two rooms in the house, all the shades and blinds were drawn. *Fucking Jesse!* He'd made Jameson take precautions, just in case. He could make out flickering from the TV and Jameson's shadow in the living room, but not clearly enough to risk a shot. If he missed, Jameson would be on the phone and the cops would be there before he could get back to the Malibu, which was hidden in some brush about a quarter-mile back up the road where he'd changed into his camo and boots. Unfortunately, he was going to have to get in close for this. Maybe as close as he had been all those years ago on Stiles Island.

He checked his watch. Laid the Mauser up against a tree. No sense lugging the rifle around with him. It would only slow him down and get in the way. He'd just pick it up on his way back to the car. One thing was working in his favor. Jameson liked the TV volume turned up high. It was so loud that Marchand could almost make out what show Jameson was watching. Still, Marchand was careful as he crossed the little footbridge across the pond. There were no cars in the driveway. *Good.* He went to the opposite side of the house, away from the living room, away from where Jameson was watching TV, and moved along the gravel path so as not to leave boot prints. There were no cars around back. *Better.*

Marchand was sweating pretty intensely and his mouth was dry. It seemed his heart was nearly as loud as the TV, but he didn't mind this feeling. He was at his best when stressed to the max. It was that way on the basketball court, in business, in politics, and in murder. He had killed three times now and, though he didn't like admitting it, it got easier each time. If it were only Alexio and John who had killed the girls, Marchand thought, they would have been caught before they got off the island. Without him they would have been lost. It was his quick thinking that had saved their asses. Now the time had come to finish saving his own.

He had decided to do it quickly. To break the back door's glass, open the lock, and charge into the living room before Jameson could react. He'd empty his clip into Jameson, ransack the place, steal something of value, and get out. *Poor Jameson. Wrong place, wrong time. If only the thief had known this was the police chief's house . . .*

439

Marchand removed his boots, slipped on his shooting gloves, and racked the Cobra's slide. He put in his ear protection and took one last deep breath before elbowing through the little glass pane nearest the door handle. Then it all came in a rush. The glass was broken. His hand was undoing the lock. He was through the door, out of the kitchen, past the dining room, and into the living room.

Perfect. The TV was blaring and Jameson was buried under covers, asleep on the couch.

Marchand aimed and fired. He kept firing until the clip was empty and the Cobra's slide locked. The room stank of hot metal and gunpowder. Smoke hung in the air like Jameson's ghost. With his work done, Marchand removed his earplugs and yanked the TV's plug out of the socket. The room was deadly quiet. Marchand turned to go upstairs to see what valuables of Jesse's he could take, but he got the sense that something wasn't right. He stood dead still and listened. When he heard the hammer click back, he knew what it was.

84

Jesse stepped out of the shadows, his .38 coming into the light before him.

"You shouldn't have emptied the clip," Jesse said, his voice steady and cool.

"With you there holding your gun on me, yeah, in retrospect, that was pretty dumb. If I left myself some ammo, I might've had a fighting chance. But there are a lot of things I wish I could take back."

"I'm sure that's true, Bill. We'll have time to discuss that later. For now, drop your weapon and kick it over to me. Slowly. Any sudden movement at all and I'll shoot."

Marchand did as he was told.

Jesse asked, "Do you have any other weapons on you?"

"A knife." Marchand tilted his head at his left hip.

"Same drill," Jesse said. "On the floor. Kick it over. I would hate to have to kill you, Bill, but if you force my hand, I won't think twice about it."

"I don't doubt it." Marchand noticed his voice was brittle.

Jesse asked, "Anything else?"

"There's a rifle out across the footbridge, but no, nothing else on me."

"You wouldn't lie to me, Bill, would you?"

"Never have before."

Jesse laughed. "Is that your nose I see growing?"

"Never before all this, I mean," Marchand said, feeling weak, the adrenaline draining out of him.

"Now, do exactly what I tell you to do the way I tell you to do it. Hands on your head. Turn around. Get on your knees as slowly as possible. I've had to kill men before and I won't hesitate to kill you."

As Jesse was cuffing him, Marchand said, "So you know what it's like to kill."

"Kill, not murder."

"Not so different," Marchand said.

"There aren't any two things more different in the world."

Jesse sat Marchand down in a chair as he called in to the station.

"How did you know it was me, Jesse?"

"I wasn't one hundred percent sure, not until today. After all the elaborate stuff you went through to cover yourself, it was the little things."

"Always is."

"Not always."

"What was it, then?" Marchand asked.

"Why, Bill, you want to make sure you don't make the same mistakes next time? There isn't going to be a next time."

"Humor me."

"I knew it was you for sure when you lied about not knowing Shelter Cove. The whole time I was hoping it wasn't you, but when you lied about that . . . When I was at Shelter Cove, it looked familiar, but I couldn't remember why. Then on the ride back to town, it hit me."

Marchand nodded. "The photo on the wall behind my desk. The one my wife took of me and my kids on the deck of my boat. It's been there so long, I forgot about it."

"You can erase your present, but you can't erase your past."

"Don't get cryptic on me, Jesse. It's not like you."

"How would you know what I'm like? It's pretty clear that we didn't know each other at all."

"Fair point, but I still want to know what that thing about the past and present means."

"Once we identified Warren Zebriski, you

were finished. Even with killing Dragoa and Millner, even with that tidy little confession, which, planted typewriter or not, I didn't buy for a second, you were done. Though I've got to say it took some nerve for you to risk running down Jameson in broad daylight with Alexio's truck."

"What choice did I have?" Marchand shrugged. "Besides, the attempt on Jameson's life gave me cover. As long as no one got a good look at me, I figured it was worth the risk. I almost got away with it."

Jesse shook his head. "I spoke to Robbie Wilson and Zebriski's brother in New York. I looked at the Sacred Heart yearbook. You and Zebriski were friends and you were forever connected to Dragoa and Millner, you were all teammates. I know something about old teammates. Once I was suspicious of you, I did some checking. Found out that your dad was big in commercial real estate around here. Seems that twenty-five years ago he owned the building where the girls were buried. You couldn't erase any of that."

Marchand laughed.

"Something funny?"

"The confession," Marchand said. "It's almost all there. Most of it happened just like I wrote that it did. Only it was me who had a thing for Ginny, not John, and if we'd

only ditched Alexio at the park, we probably would've been fine. John was a lowlife,
but he wouldn't have forced himself on
Mary Kate like Alexio did. Once Alexio got
alcohol in him . . . You know how it is with
him. How many times have you had to arrest him? John was fine, smoking a joint and
drinking, staring out at the ocean, but when
Ginny and me were getting it on, Alexio lost
it. It happened so fast. He just kept stabbing her. It was John that hit Ginny with
the rock the first time. I think she was
already dead, but I hit her again to make
sure. I mean, we couldn't leave her alive,
not after what Alexio did. I didn't have a
choice, Jesse. All we meant to do was to go
out to Stiles and celebrate the Fourth, I
swear."

Marchand went silent, slumped in the
chair, and hung his head.

Jesse said, "What's going on with you?"

"Zevon," Marchand said, as if that
explained it.

"Zebriski? What about him? Was he part
of what happened on the island?"

"No, no way. Warren was a great guy."
Marchand was offended. "I asked him what
he was doing that night, but he said he
already had plans that he wasn't going to
change for anything or anybody."

"I take it that it was you who confessed to him, not Millner," Jesse said, hearing sirens in the distance.

Marchand nodded. "When Zevon got back from college the next summer, we got really hammered one night and he asked me if the cops had made any progress finding the girls. I blew up at him. I told him that Mary Kate and Ginny Connolly were dead. I told him everything, every fucking detail. I begged him not to go to the cops. I kept saying how it was his fault, that if he had been there to make Mary Kate happy, none of it would have happened the way it did. That they were dead and that all of us spending our lives in jail wasn't going to bring them back. If only I hadn't confessed to him, it wouldn't have come back on me. But I guess it always comes back, right? You always have to pay in the end."

Jesse didn't answer, because the truth was that not nearly enough people paid in the end.

85

Molly and Healy were pacing around Jesse's office. Suit was firmly planted in Jesse's chair.

"Get up and do some pacing," Molly said.

"I'm pacing in spirit."

"Lazy."

"I just got hit by a truck."

"Whiner. Next thing you know, you'll be bringing up the gunshot wounds."

They all three laughed at that.

Then Molly turned to Healy. "What's taking so long?"

Healy said, "The man in there has twenty-five years' worth of confessing to do."

"But he's got a lawyer in there with him. Maybe he's changed his mind and —"

Jesse walked in before she could finish. Suit made to stand up, but Jesse waved him back down.

"So?" Healy said.

"Relax. He copped to everything. It's all

447

on videotape. Bill Marchand is never going to see another day on the outside."

Molly asked, "Did he kill Warren?"

"Millner," Jesse said.

"So who was driving the truck that hit me?" Suit asked.

"Marchand. Both Millner and Dragoa were already dead by then."

Healy shook his head. "How did he think he was going to get away with that?"

"He almost did. Everyone in town knows Dragoa's truck and that's what he was counting on, that people would focus on the truck and not the guy driving it. But he took precautions. Remember, he had access to Dragoa's spare clothes on the boat and he was about the same size as Alexio. With a watch cap pulled down low and the truck streaking by, he figured to get away with it."

"But what about the timing, Jesse?" Suit asked. "If Dragoa and Millner were already dead —"

"That's why he placed their bodies on the beach and didn't just dump them in the ocean," Jesse said. "It was cold but not freezing the last few days. He figured to confuse us with the time of death."

"Like that Lutz guy did with the bodies of Walton Weeks and his girlfriend a few years back."

"That's right, Suit, but Marchand only needed to buy himself about a twenty-four-hour window where Dragoa and Millner could have still been alive."

Molly said, "Why'd he try to run Jameson over."

"Two reasons: to fool us that Dragoa was still alive, and he couldn't risk Jameson talking to us if he really did know something. It's why my trap worked. After all the killing he'd done to cover his tracks, the only possible loose end was Jameson. He had to risk killing him, too."

"Speaking of Jameson, where is he?" Suit wanted to know.

"He's safe and with a friend."

Healy asked, "Who set the fires?"

"Marchand. He was at the wake for Maxie and Ginny, but made it a point to tell me he couldn't be at the church service because of business. Millner left the truck for him in Commonwealth Woods, and after he was done torching the houses, he drove back there and burned the van. Both Dragoa and Millner trusted Marchand implicitly. They always had, from the days they played ball together. Marchand was the point guard, the leader. He was the smart one, the successful one, and he was the one who had saved their asses the night they killed the girls. Up until the bodies were found, they had a common agenda. Once the bodies were discovered and Dragoa started acting guilty and unstable, Marchand decided it was too dangerous to let Dragoa and Millner keep breathing. After he made up his mind, everything he did was to make Dragoa and Millner look guilty and to draw our attention to them. Oh, yeah, the gun he used to kill Dragoa will match the gun used to kill Zebriski, and the knife your guys found on the boat will match the knife that killed Mary Kate O'Hara. He was thorough. I'll give him that."

Molly looked shaken. "If Jameson hadn't turned up, he would have gotten away with it."

"Maybe," Jesse said. "But like I told him, he could erase his present, but not his past. I would have looked at him eventually. Now, if you guys don't mind, I'd like a word with Suit."

Molly gave Jesse a wary look as she held the door open for Healy, but she didn't say anything. Suit was visibly worried and got up from Jesse's chair in pieces. It was painful to watch. Jesse sat in his chair and gestured for Suit to sit across from him. The pain forced him to sit, though it seemed to Jesse that Suit would rather have run.

"What'd I do now, Jesse?"

"Take it easy, Suit. I just want to say some stuff to you I should have said before this."

"Stuff like what?"

"Like thank you for having my back last spring. I should have thanked you then."

"Didn't turn out so good."

"I guess it didn't, but you didn't know you were going to get shot. It was a brave thing to do, Suit, following me like that even though you knew it might be dangerous and that I'd get mad at you. Easy to do things when you know you'll get rewarded for it. Hard to do them when you know you're going to catch hell."

Suit reddened. "That all, Jesse?"

"Almost. You know you saved Jameson's life, putting yourself between that truck and him?"

"I was only doing my job."

"Maybe. But you acted fast, without thinking of yourself. You saved a person's life. A lot of cops, good cops, go through a whole career without being able to make that claim. I thought about giving you a medal for what you did."

"No disrespect, Jesse, but I don't want a medal. I got lots of trophies and awards at my folks' house and they just collect dust."

"I know you don't, so I decided to give

451

you something that has meant a lot to me." Jesse stood, unholstered his .38, emptied the cylinder, and placed it in Suit's hand. "Luther, I would be honored if you would accept this from me as a measure of my respect for you."

Suit stared at the .38 as if he'd just been given a Super Bowl ring. "I don't know what to say."

" 'Thanks' will do."

"Thank you, Jesse. This means everything to me." Suit saluted his boss.

"You ever salute me again and I'll fire your ass."

"Stop calling me Luther and I'll stop saluting you."

"Deal."

They shook on it, their hands staying together a little longer than usual.

"One more thing, Suit," Jesse said when Suit had gotten to the office door. "When you come back on duty, you're on patrol. Now, get out of here and heal up."

86

When Tamara Elkin pulled back her front door, she looked exhausted and worried. He was exhausted himself, but the worries, at least for now, were gone. Jesse hugged her long and tightly.

When they broke their embrace, she asked, "Is everything all right? I was watching the news and fell asleep on the couch. Is it done?"

"It was him."

"Marchand?"

"Uh-huh."

"You arrested him?"

"After he broke into my house and killed the hell out of the dummy we use to teach CPR."

"But you're —"

"Fine. Marchand confessed to everything. There won't be a trial."

She smiled at him.

"He almost got away with it," Jesse said.

She shook her head. "You would have gotten him eventually."

"Maybe."

She smiled again, but this was a different smile.

"What's that smile about?"

"Water in the lungs," she said.

"What about it?"

"There wasn't any in either Dragoa or Millner. So unless they just happened to fall overboard the second after they both stopped breathing, someone would have had to push them overboard. You would have followed it back to Marchand."

"We'll never know. Tomorrow, compare the knife wounds in Millner to the wounds you found on Mary Kate's ribs. Marchand says it was the same knife."

"Will do."

He kissed her softly on the forehead. "Thank you for doing this for me. How's Jameson?"

"He's asleep in the spare bedroom. God, I was so nervous. Jesse Stone, do you know how long it's been since I've had a living patient? Don't you ever do this to me again."

Now it was his turn to smile. "Should I take him back to the hospital now?"

"He'll be fine until tomorrow. I gave him something for the headache, but he's not showing any other symptoms. That man's had a rough life. The story his body tells is very sad."

"That's a pretty unclinical analysis, Doc."

"There's a reason I'm more comfortable working with the dead, Jesse."

He didn't say anything to that. "Can I get a drink?"

"For a price," she said.

"Like?"

"I'll think about it."

"In the meantime, how about that drink?"

She hugged him. When she let go, she said, "This could be the beginning of a beautiful friendship."

"Depends."

"On?"

"If I ever get that drink."

"You are a persistent SOB, Jesse Stone."

"My most charming feature."

Without another word, she walked to her cabinet and twisted off the cap of a new bottle of Black Label.

87

There was a false spring that late February. Temperatures hovered in the fifties and southern New England hadn't seen snow since mid-January. Jesse had the softball team out for an early practice at the park. Mostly he wanted to see what he had with this year's team. Things had changed since last season. They had new uniforms, just not the ones Bill Marchand had ordered. Their new sponsor, the Paradise Credit Union, had supplied them. Suit, who, owing to the gunshot wounds, had missed the bulk of last season, was back at first base. Jesse liked having him there even though Suit's footwork around the bag wasn't quite what it used to be. Jesse had been forced to shift Tommy Deutsch to shortstop to take Marchand's place. Connor Cavanaugh had taken Deutsch's spot at second. Cavanaugh was all hit and no field, but on a softball team full of aging jocks, wannabes, and never-will-bes, there were only so many places to hide weak links.

After practice, when they were at the Lobster Claw drinking beers and moaning about all the things that ached and speculating about how much worse they would ache tomorrow, Molly came into the Claw to join them. A few months back, Jesse thought, he would have dreaded Molly showing up unexpectedly. But after a few rough weeks of grief and regret, she had returned to her old self. And he was glad of that. It wasn't only Molly who had returned to normal. Paradise itself had been quiet through the winter and now seemed to be the same little town it was before the trauma of the fall. It had put the murders and scandal behind it and resumed the natural rhythm of things. In L.A., he understood how that worked. Big cities are rife with tragedy so that one just swallowed up the next. Then he recalled Healy's words about small-town secrets and shame. And now Jesse guessed he understood about that, too.

Molly waved for Jesse to come over to the end of the bar to talk.

"Beer?"

"Sure," she said.

Jesse grabbed a pitcher and poured her a pint of Harpoon lager. "What's up?"

"I heard from Drew Jameson today."

Jesse asked, "How is he?"

"He says he's better and asked me to have you thank your friend Dix for getting him into the program."

"I'll do that. What did you guys talk about?"

Molly smiled that sad smile he hadn't seen on her face since the fall. "Warren. It feels good to be able to talk about him again. He was lost to me and Jameson brought him back."

Jesse was hesitant to say it but, in the end, didn't hold back. "Warren covered up a murder for twenty-four years."

"I know he did," she said, sipping her beer. "I'm not excusing that."

"I guess in the end he tried to do the right thing. He sure paid for it."

"A lot of people paid for it, Jesse. But what Jameson brought back to me was the Warren I knew for those few weeks before the world went upside down. Those were special days that are mine again."

"I'll drink to that."

They clinked glasses and finished their beers in silence. When he was done, Jesse said his good-byes. Molly caught up to him at the door.

"Jesse, I almost forgot."

458

"What?"

"Remember the missing cabdriver?"

"Wiethop? Sure. What about him?"

"The Connecticut State Police called. They found him dead in his car in a small lake that thawed early. They e-mailed over the full report as an attachment."

"Drowned?" Jesse asked.

"Broken neck."

"Broken neck, huh? Just like Maxie Connolly."

"Maxie Connolly threw herself off the Bluffs, Jesse."

"Or not."

"We back to that again?"

"It's suspicious. Thanks, Molly."

Jesse felt as achy as the rest of his team and his shoulder was killing him. Nothing like the combination of stabbing pain and burning to let you know you're alive. He didn't go home. Instead he walked back to the station and looked at the report from the Connecticut staties. It was all there: the written report of the troopers, the detective's report, the ME's report, autopsy photos, photos of the car, photos of the items found in the car with Wiethop's body. If he hadn't been a little buzzed from the beers, he would have spotted it the first time he looked at the photos. Then, when he scrolled through the photos a second time, he saw it. When he saw it, he knew. And the last unexplained bit of business from last fall fell cruelly into place.

88

The Parmenter House was one of the most beautiful houses in all of Paradise. People came from all over the States to see it. Unlike the muscular brick Victorians up on the Bluffs, the Parmenter House was a full-out painted lady. It had two turrets, a wraparound porch, a widow's walk, eyebrow windows, all manner of gingerbread turnings, and a gazebo. There were at least four different kinds of siding used to adorn the outside, everything from fish scales to clapboards. And the color scheme involved an equal number of colors. It had once been home to Wexford Parmenter, a railroad man who'd relocated from Boston in the 1890s. He'd left the house to his son Wexford Junior, who had left it in turn to his daughter Corrina, who had left it to her daughter Martha. Martha had willed it to her husband.

Jesse knocked on Stu Cromwell's door.

He supposed he could have bluffed his way through it and not waited for the lab results to come back. But to his way of thinking, Maxie Connolly's justice had already been months delayed and he wasn't willing to risk losing an arrest because of his impatience. So he'd gotten a comparison sample and sent it to the state forensics lab to make sure it matched the DNA from the unknown contributor's hair and skin evidence they found on Maxie Connolly's panties. As he waited on the porch, he noticed some hints of green on the confused hedges that lined the property. If the weather stayed this warm for another week, he wondered if confused bees would come out and join the party.

Stu Cromwell came to the door, and when he saw it was Jesse standing at his threshold, his body sagged, but he smiled.

"I suppose I've been waiting for you to knock since the day the weather turned warm. Come in," he said. "Go into the parlor."

Jesse didn't step in. Instead he pointed to the cruiser parked at the curb. "There's another car parked on Hemlock behind the house, so don't make this difficult." The nine-millimeter in Jesse's hand still felt odd to him, though he had owned one for many years and had occasion use it. He showed the semiautomatic to Cromwell. "And Stu, no martial-arts heroics. I've got a black belt in bullets."

"There won't be any trouble, Jesse. I give you my word. Please step in. I'll come out as soon as we're done talking."

Jesse went into the parlor and sat on a fussy brocade sofa with frills and tassels. The house looked a mess. Cromwell noticed Jesse notice.

"Since Martha passed, I haven't seen the point," he said. "Drink?"

"I'll pass."

"Then I'll drink alone."

Cromwell poured some rye into a cut-crystal tumbler. He didn't make any silly gestures or toasts. He just drank it. Quickly poured himself another and drank it, too. He sagged even more. "How did you know?"

"They found Wiethop's body in his car in a lake in Connecticut."

"I know that!" He slammed the glass down against the marble fireplace, smashing it to pieces. "I put him there, for heaven's sakes. I just needed to buy time until Martha died. How did you know it was me?"

"You left a bottle of rye behind in the car.

463

That was sloppy and it made me curious. Wiethop was a vodka drinker, and frankly, Stu, you're the only person I know who drinks rye. Once I got curious, it was easy for me to find out that you and Martha owned a cottage on another lake less than two miles from where they found Wiethop. Did you think you were going to get away with it?"

"The bastard was trying to blackmail me, Jesse. He had the letter."

"The letter?"

"The one I wrote to Maxie all those years ago. There were things in that letter I couldn't have come to light while Martha was still alive. After all she had done for me and with how she was suffering, I just couldn't have it. I *wouldn't* have it! I suppose if I had any money to pay that scummy little man, I would have paid for his silence, but the cupboard was bare."

"Did you kill Maxie Connolly?"

Cromwell ignored the question. "I loved her once. I don't know, maybe it wasn't love at all. But she had me under her spell. I lived and breathed her. When I had her I wanted her again while I was still inside her. She was magical that way. And the silly part is, she really, desperately loved me, too. Can you imagine a less likely pair?"

"But you were engaged to Martha."

"I was, but it didn't matter. I couldn't keep away from Maxie. I wrote these silly love letters to her. They were increasingly desperate. I was trying to explain to her how I couldn't give her up, nor could I break my promise to Martha. And in one letter, the one Wiethop found in his cab, I said some awful and foul things about Martha. I was just so lust-drunk and foolish. I had just never had a woman like Maxie. I was such an idiot. Once Maxie had the letter, she threatened me that if I didn't find a way to leave Martha on my own, she would show the letter to her and do it for me."

"You broke it off."

Cromwell nodded. "God, Jesse, you do understand. What else could I do? Maxie's threat was like a cold slap in the face, and I suddenly saw what I had done and with whom I'd gotten involved. I broke it off immediately after Maxie made the threat. I didn't care then if she showed the letter to Martha. It was better, I thought, than getting in any deeper with Maxie. But Maxie said she couldn't go through with it and that she was so sorry." He paused, drank directly from the bottle. "She said she was desperate, too. That she never thought she could have a smart man, a man with man-

465

ners and class." He laughed joylessly at himself.

"But it was too late," Jesse said.

"Exactly. I suppose I never stopped lusting after her. I always dreamed about sleeping with her again, but she disgusted me as a human being. She was so coarse. When I wouldn't have her back, she went wild, trying to hurt me and punish herself by sleeping around with almost anyone. She would call me and tell me about them and the things they would do. It was so low of her, but that sort of thing was all she knew. It was the only weapon she had and she used it. And even then, I . . ." Cromwell drifted off, lost in the memories of the woman he'd murdered.

"So when Maxie came back for Ginny's funeral, what? Did she try to blackmail you?"

Cromwell shook his head. "No, she offered to return the letters if I would only see her and be with her. She claimed that she had never stopped loving me. That she would do anything to make up for the mistake she had made twenty-five years before. So I agreed. We met at a spot up in the Bluffs that used to be our rendezvous. I made her believe we were going to have one last tryst and then I snapped her neck like a twig. I drove her farther down the Bluffs and tossed her over."

"But you took her panties. Why?"

Cromwell stared at Jesse as if he were speaking Arabic. "Haven't you heard a word I said?"

Jesse moved on. "Did she have the letters with her?"

"Yes. I thought so."

"Then why did you kill her?" Jesse said. "You didn't have to kill her."

"But I did."

"Why?"

"I couldn't chance Maxie talking, not after all that Martha had risked to buy the paper. She had risked everything for me. I couldn't let scandal and cancer eat up her last few months of life."

"Is that what you tell yourself, Stu? Does it help you sleep at night?"

Cromwell's face reddened, his voice strained. "What are you talking about? Of course that's why I killed Maxie. I had to."

"No you didn't. You had all the letters. At least you thought you did. Martha was in no state to care one way or the other. No, Stu, sorry," Jesse said. "I don't buy it."

The newspaperman bowed his head. "She hurt me, Jesse, in the most profound way I have ever been hurt. Maxie took from me the only obsession I ever had. She ruined that and for twenty-five years I bore what she did to me in my guts like a slow-leaking balloon full of acid. There were times that I thought it would eat me alive. I had to end the pain."

"How's that working for you, Stu?"

"I'm ready now."

Jesse cuffed Cromwell and walked him out. When Peter Perkins got to the porch, Jesse recited the Miranda warning and told Perkins to take Cromwell to the station and book him.

"You coming, Jesse?" Perkins asked.

"In a little while."

Jesse stood on the porch and watched Perkins load Cromwell into the backseat of the cruiser. The air, which earlier implied the scent of flowers, had turned a nasty shade of raw, smelling now only of chill and the sea. The late-day sun had disappeared behind a sickly gray veil of clouds, and the bare trees on the Parmenter property twisted in the gusts that had kicked up hard and mean. February had come back home to roost. Stepping down onto the granite path, Jesse wondered why victories were always short-lived and why the taste of a win was never quite as sweet as the bitter-

ness of losing. Someday, he would have to
ask the devil.

ACKNOWLEDGMENTS

I owe a huge debt of gratitude to Chris Pepe, Ivan Held, David Hale Smith, Helen Brann, and the Estate of Robert B. Parker. Of course none of this would have been possible without Mr. Parker's creation of the Jesse Stone novels. A big thanks to Michael Barson.

Thanks to Tom Schreck and Ace Atkins.

As always, my deepest love and appreciation goes to my wife and children. Without Rosanne, Kaitlin, and Dylan, none of this would have happened nor would it have meant a thing.

ABOUT THE AUTHOR

Robert B. Parker was the author of seventy books, including the legendary Spenser detective series, the novels featuring Chief Jesse Stone, and the acclaimed Virgil Cole/Everett Hitch Westerns, as well as the Sunny Randall novels. Winner of the Mystery Writers of America Grand Master Award and long considered the undisputed dean of American crime fiction, he died in January 2010.

Reed Farrel Coleman, author of the *New York Times*'s bestselling *Robert B. Parker's Blind Spot*, has been called a "hard-boiled poet" by NPR's Maureen Corrigan and the "noir poet laureate" in *The Huffington Post*. He has published twenty-one novels, including nine books in the critically acclaimed Moe Prager series. He is a three-time recipient of the Shamus Award for Best Detective Novel of the Year, a winner of the Barry and

Anthony Awards, and is a three-time Edgar Award nominee. An adjunct instructor at Hofstra University and an instructor for MWA U, he lives with his family on Long Island.